THE COUNTDOWN HAD BEGUN

Myrick's eyes bolted open. His trance state had changed. He stared, unseeing, suddenly out of Hart's control and doing something entirely unexpected and unexplainable.

"Plus seven days?" he rasped, his voice metallic and driven. "Crew. Unforeseen. Program in. Program in. Program in. One hundred. Sixty-eight. Sixty-eight. Are you silver? Are you silver?"

"What do you mean?" Hart asked, surprised and baffled.

"The mission will fail. My role is critical."

"No, Dave. The mission will succeed."

"You don't understand! It will fail! Sixty-eight! Sixty-eight! Are you silver?"

Other Tor Books by Jack M. Bickham

ARIEL
DROPSHOT
MIRACLEWORKER
THE REGENSBURG LEGACY
TIEBREAKER

JACK M. BICKHAM

DAY SEVEN

A TOM DOHERTY ASSOCIATES BOOK
NEW YORK

Copyright © 1988 by Jack M. Bickham

A TOR Book

Published by Tom Doherty Associates, Inc.
49 West 24 Street
New York, NY 10010

Cover photo courtesy of NASA

ISBN: 0-812-50581-6   Can. ISBN: 0-812-50582-4

Library of Congress Catalog Card Number: 87-51403

First edition: July 1988
First mass market edition: March 1990

Printed in the United States of America

0 9 8 7 6 5 4 3 2 1

DISCLAIMER

The Space Shuttle disaster of 1986, the later resumption of flights, and approval of the MarsProbe project in 1990 are of course historical fact. This book, however, is fiction. Superficial resemblances may exist between certain events narrated here and actual happenings connected with the MarsProbe catastrophe of 1994. But no one should suppose that this is a "true" explanation of the Mars debacle. As NASA has pointed out, we may never understand all that really happened.

—J.M.B.
Houston, October, 1995

one

Davidson Myrick was a man in disintegration.

Facing Myrick across the small office coffee table, psychologist Richard Hart maintained his relaxed posture. But he was worried. *I have to do this just right,* Hart thought, *or this man is going to crack wide open.*

And that simply couldn't be allowed. For one thing, Hart liked Myrick too much to allow it. For another, Myrick was too important in NASA's MarsProbe project, now in the last days before its crew launch.

"Slow down," Hart told Myrick. "Just take your time. Take a few deep breaths."

"Slow down?" Myrick repeated, his voice cracking. "Take my time? What do you think I've been trying to do?"

"Just take a few deep breaths, slowly," Hart gently insisted.

The tall, gray-haired space scientist tried to comply. His wide-set eyes closed by dint of sheer willpower. He spread large, capable hands on the arms of his blue upholstered chair, relaxing his fingers. Hart saw his broad chest heave, then slow as the man practiced the relaxation techniques Hart had taught him.

The office fell quiet. Somewhere on the busy Houston expressway nearby, a diesel horn sounded.

Hart observed Myrick with total intensity.

The chief of crew training for NASA's ambitious journey to Mars had himself been an astronaut in the early days of the shuttle program. Now fifty, the same age as Hart, he had gained a few pounds, but was still handsomely slim, tallish, with a powerful physique that would have been the envy of many younger men. His sandy hair might have turned gray, but it was still thick, closely cropped. A high forehead and thin nose and mouth lent him an almost priestly asceticism. His summer suit was pale tan, immaculate, his tie a splotch of confident blue against his off-white shirt. A film of sickly nervous sweat glistened on his forehead, and a nervous tic leaped under his left eye.

He had come to Hart complaining of bizarre dreams, extreme nervousness, uncharacteristic outbursts of anger, and pervasive dread that the United States Mars expedition would meet with disaster—somehow of his making.

Hart had known him casually for more than three years, and had considered him a model of stability before his call for his first appointment two weeks earlier.

Myrick had come secretly for treatment because "If I went to talk to NASA shrinks about this, they'd pull me off the project instantly—and I want to help make this flight go."

His visits to Hart's office were cloak-and-dagger operations in which he entered the professional building by the back door, wearing a scruffy London Fog and battered felt hat to conceal his identity not only from his employers, but from anyone who might recognize his familiar features. "You know what the press would make of it if they heard the astronaut training chief was seeing a shrink?" he asked, wringing his big hands. "Can you see the headline? *Mars Team Headed by Lunatic.*"

Hart had seen him three times before today, and had thought they were making progress toward calming some of the fears. But today Myrick had come in far more upset—frightened and desperate—than during any earlier visit. All Hart had managed to do so far was to slow Myrick's breathing.

He needed to do far more than that.

As Myrick tried to calm himself, his facial tic softened and his posture unbent slightly.

"That's better," Hart encouraged him.

Myrick's eyes shot open and the tic leaped again. "I've got to stop doing this. I've got to get hold of myself, stop having these damned dreams, get rid of this terror. What's wrong with me? Jesus, what if we send that crew up and I'm in the control room and I blow sky high—make some crew management error. I feel the mission simply *must* fail—"

"Take your time," Hart said easily. "Take plenty of time. That's better. Now to start off with, you're doing considerably better than you may think you are."

"I am? How?"

"You're here. Seeking treatment. Taking good care of yourself."

"For all the good it's doing me!"

"I read a report just the other night, and it was about someone with many of the same symptoms you've talked about. I want to tell you about it and see what you think. Listen very carefully."

Myrick stared intensely, hanging on every word, as Hart began telling him about an astronomer whose mountain retreat had become a seeming trap for him. In truth, Hart was ad-libbing the story as he went along, engaging every iota of energy in his patient's conscious mind so that he could slip up through the unconscious and induce a hypnotic trance.

Minutes passed and Myrick continued to listen intently. Hart slipped in a few logical fallacies to numb rational thought processes, and bored him silly with details. Myrick's eyes began to become fixed and glazed.

"Are your eyes tired?" Hart interjected. "Close your eyes."

Myrick's eyelids slid closed at once.

"So that *three* stars actually seemed to be only *two*," Hart said, resuming the tale he had been spinning, "and then the *two* became *one*."

He waited.

The office was tomblike.

Myrick slumped in the chair, head down, totally relaxed: entranced.

"So you see," Hart resumed in the same tone, which would have sounded to an outsider oddly singsong and too evenly cadenced, "how that story ended. Now I want to talk about some other things with you. I want to ask you to consider Pattern X, the pattern of feelings and ideas that lead to the dreams and feelings of dread. You want to change that pattern."

Myrick sat stone-still, totally relaxed but in an altered state of consciousness where he could receive the suggestions Hart wanted to anchor in him. Hart took several minutes, soothingly telling him how change was possible, how he could use relaxation techniques whenever the bad feelings seemed about to sweep over him.

"Remember that you can change," Hart went on. "You can—and will—find the dreams becoming less frightening, and in the days ahead you will find the daytime fears also becoming easier to handle. In a short time—a day or two, perhaps, from this hour plus seven days at the most—"

Myrick's eyes bolted open. His trance state had changed. He stared, unseeing, suddenly out of Hart's control and doing something entirely unexpected and unexplainable.

"Plus seven days?" he rasped, his voice metallic and driven. "Crew. Unforeseen. Program in. Program in. Program in. One hundred. Sixty-eight. Sixty-eight. Are you silver? Are you silver?"

"Explain what you mean," Hart said, surprised and baffled.

"The mission will fail. My role is crucial."

"No, Dave. The mission will succeed."

"You don't understand!" Myrick was staring into some remote emotional hell. "It will fail! Sixty-eight! Sixty-eight. Are you silver?"

"Dave!" Hart insisted sharply. "It's all right! Close your eyes. Relax again."

Myrick hesitated, staring, his chest rising and falling heavily.

"It's all right," Hart repeated. "Close your eyes." Slowly Myrick obeyed.

As Hart watched, his breathing began to slow, his hands to relax.

"In the days ahead," Hart told him, "you'll feel better. The dreams, no longer necessary, can fade. You know, Dave, that you will not die, you will not cooperate in your dying, you will not kill anyone else, you will not go crazy. You understand these things?"

There was a pause. Then Myrick said very softly, "Yes."

"You can relax now," Hart told him. "And when you want to open your eyes and rejoin me now, you can do so. Take all the time you wish."

Five minutes passed, and an onlooker might have thought Houston's most prominent and successful psychologist was sitting idle, watching a man sleep.

Then Myrick's eyelids fluttered. His hands moved, then his long legs stretched. He opened his eyes and looked around slowly, as if awakening. He stretched.

"How do you feel?" Hart asked.

"Fine," Myrick said, smiling.

"We have a few more minutes. What shall we talk about now?"

Myrick glanced at his watch. He seemed detached, eerily calm. "I think I should be going. I feel fine now. It's odd. I remember everything that happened. I felt like I was sleeping, but I wasn't sleeping. Is that hypnosis?"

Hart smiled. "More or less."

Myrick made a movement as if to rise.

"No hurry," Hart suggested. He wanted badly to explore what had just happened during the trance. But he could not insist; his patient did seem calmer, and this incident might be something that would make better sense on reflection. "If you want to visit—"

"No, I really ought to go."

Hart gave in, standing. "What does 'sixty-eight' refer to?" he asked casually.

Myrick stared at him. "I don't know what you're talking about."

"Really?"

"Really. But I know one thing. I feel better. —So that's hypnosis! Maybe my problems have all been just a matter of overwork—all the tension."

They talked on until near the end of the hour. Myrick seemed truly calm. Try as he might, Hart could not get the man to recall the strange words he had spoken during his trance; that part was not in his conscious memory.

At the end of the hour Hart walked him to the door, a hand on his shoulder. "Want to come in tomorrow?"

"Tomorrow is Saturday," Myrick reminded him.

"Forgot." It was a little trick to make sure the post-hypnotic patient was tracking accurately before letting him go to a car and Houston's insane afternoon traffic.

"But I want to keep the Tuesday appointment," Myrick told him.

"Good. I'll see you Tuesday at 1 P.M., then."

"Yes. And thanks. I really do feel a lot better."

Davidson Myrick exited the office via the mall-type corridor as always, and cut across the parking lot in the brilliant noonday sunshine to reach his automobile. The interior of the grayflake Z-car was furnacelike, and he adjusted air-conditioning controls as he backed out of the spot and drove toward the exit ramp.

Perhaps, if he had not been preoccupied, he would have seen the man in the nearby white Oldsmobile, observing and taking a series of rapid motor-assisted telephoto pictures of him as he drove away.

Or perhaps he would not have noticed anyway.

After Myrick was gone, Hart went to the cabinet beside the couch, opened the sliding door, and turned off his recorder. Removing the cassette tape, he penciled in the name and date.

He had never experienced anything quite like what had just taken place. He was puzzled and worried.

Going down the interior hallway to the front desk, he leaned over it to confront his receptionist, Charlene. Her pretty blonde head was bent over the keyboard of the word processor, and for a moment she didn't see him. Then she sensed his presence and raised startled, remarkable wide blue eyes. "Oh! Yes, sir?"

"Mrs. Johnson isn't here yet?"

"Not yet. But it's a few minutes early, and she always rushes in at the last minute."

Hart put the cassette on the counter. "Charlene, I need to have this tape of my session with Dr. Myrick transcribed. Please put it ahead of everything else."

"Sure!" the girl said cheerfully. "I've got a little billing to finish, but then I'll get right on it."

"No, start it right *now*," Hart snapped.

"Well, gosh! Okay!"

"I'm jumpy, Charlene. Sorry. But I need this done right away. I want to replay the cassette at home this weekend and study the transcript."

Charlene's eyes betrayed a moment's dismay, but then she hid it. "Sure," she said gamely, sunny again. "Want me to bring it by your apartment whenever I finish it?"

"I'll have some other work to do in here after lunchtime tomorrow. Why not just leave it on the table in my office?"

"Okay!" Cheerfully she began hitting keys to exit the computer file she had been in.

Hart returned to his office. For a few minutes he continued to ponder the bizarre thing that had just happened with Myrick. *What had happened when Myrick opened his eyes?*

He had no idea.

But it had been bizarre. Myrick had seemed to lapse into a trance-within-a-trance, saying those things about numbers and silver and the mission.

What did all that mean?

Hart couldn't guess. He thought Myrick was all right in the sense that he had agreed not to harm himself or anyone else. That had been genuine. But what did the rest mean?

Why did memory of it fill Hart with foreboding about the MarsProbe expedition? Had Myrick been saying he feared the mission might fail—or that it *must* fail?

It was a frightening conjecture.

The intercom beeped, signaling an end to time for speculation at the moment. It was time for Mrs. Johnson, and endless talk of her crumbling marriage.

With effort, Hart turned his mind to that.

* * *

"Charlene, dammit, we made our plans!"

Charlene sighed ruefully and tried her prettiest pout, teasing crimson fingertips along her boyfriend's neckline. "We can still go to Galveston, silly. I'll just go back to the office and finish that little tape this evening."

Boyfriend Jakie Donaldson grimaced, turning his back to clomp in his cowboy boots over to the drawn draperies of the apartment's balcony window. He hauled on a cord and made the curtains retract. A partial view of Houston's distant downtown skyline gleamed in the twilight distance, late sun burnishing the huge Republic Bank tower and reflecting off the stacked glass of Allied Bank.

"It's almost dark," he pointed out with impeccable logic. "We were going to go dancing."

Oh, he was just such a *hunk*, she just adored him! She swung her hips as she sidled over to him and pressed against him, her arms going around his neck. "I've done a lot of it already, and Dr. Hart was really a crab about finishing it. I'll only need an hour or so more."

"Yes, but Rick and Carolyn were going to meet us—"

"Now look, you," Charlene interrupted, silencing him with a piquant kiss. "You go meet Rick and Carolyn. I'll zip by the office, finish that tape for Dr. Hart in a flash, leave it for him, and meet you at the Zanzibar by eleven o'clock. Then we'll still have time to dance a little, and we can get an early start for Galveston in the morning, just like we planned. Okay?"

"Dr. Hart is unfair. He shouldn't expect an employee to use her own time."

"Dr. Hart," Charlene reminded her beloved, "pays twice as much as most professionals in that building. And when he gets mad, he gets *mad*. I don't want him mad at me. So you just run along and I'll join you soon."

Still grumbling, Jakie obeyed. They went downstairs together and he got into his Camaro and she into her RXZ. Waving, she zipped away fast.

Traffic on the expressway was dense as usual, but it was only three miles from Charlene's apartment to the center where she worked as Dr. Hart's receptionist. The parking lot behind the building was all but empty at this hour on a Friday night: a handful of vehicles for the deli nearby, a white Oldsmobile parked near the Dempster Dumpster trash bins, and an aged pickup she recognized as belonging to one of the building custodians. She parked close to the Oldsmobile, but not so close some ninny could bang his door into her sportscar, then got out and hurried into the hulking building with her purse tucked tightly under her arm.

The building was brightly lighted, but when it was empty it always felt a little spooky. Charlene hurried.

Silently unlocking the outer door of Dr. Hart's suite, she entered the reception area, flicked on the lights, locked the door behind her, found the cassette in her top drawer, and tossed it onto the desk beside the blackened word processor. Humming, she turned on the machine.

That was when she heard the slight *scraping sound* in the inner office.

Turning sharply, she inadvertently knocked the cassette off the desk. It went skittering under the big reception counter somewhere. *Oh, damn.* The last time she had had to crawl under there for something, she had wrecked a pair of pantyhose.

But the sound in the other office had her attention at the moment.

"Dr. Hart?" she called. "Is that you?"

Silence.

Feeling little chills down her spine and along her pretty bare arms, she walked to the seldom-used, direct-connecting door into Dr. Hart's office and turned the knob. The door swung open.

The instant Charlene saw the man standing there under the blaze of full lights, she knew she had made a very, very serious mistake.

"Who are you?" she gasped in fright. "What do you *want*?"

And then she saw the movement toward her, and turned to flee. But an arm snaked around her throat, cutting off her scream at the first hissing exhalation. Stark terror engulfed her. She tried to fight. There was a terrible little hot stabbing sensation in her back, and going deep into her body, and then the pain started to fill her. It was quite the most extraordinary pain she had ever experienced, beyond anything she could have imagined.

She wanted to protest, *"But I have to go to Galveston tomorrow!"* But when she opened her mouth, a huge gout of arterial blood gushed out. The lights dimmed and her hearing faded and she fell.

two

Joe Retvig dropped his wrench and it fell up over his head toward the Earth, more than 200 miles below.

"Shit," he grunted.

Inside the helmet of his EVA suit, the headphone crackled: *"Say again, Four?"*

Retvig released his white-gloved grip on the tower extending ninety feet into space from the Central Lab Module and drifted on the end of his dacron tether. Farther out on the girder network, the three other members of his construction shift turned helmeted faces, golden with reflected sunlight, to stare at him. Below his inverted head swam the aquamarine and white sphere of Earth; beyond his booted feet lay the infinite vastness of deep space, and countless icy stars; the other members of his shift were to his left, working nearer the end of the spiderweb geometry of interlocking tower sections forming the S&LC (Service and Launch Cradle) for the modified shuttle already locked in place after its rendezvous two weeks ago. The Central Lab Module, around which everything else had been built, was to Retvig's right. The sun blazed past the cylindrical outlines of the CLM, half blinding him.

His helmet hissed with radio traffic from inside the CLM once more: *"Say again, Four?"*

"I lost my spanner," Retvig reported.

There was a moment's silence. *They think I'm an idiot*, Retvig thought. *And I am.*

He had been tightening fuel-transfer hoses and prelaunch Comm cables along the side of the prefabricated tower, and adjusting the booster valves, when the wrench slipped away. Two of the three guys farther out on the tower network couldn't run their tests or make their adjustments until he was finished. And he had screwed up.

The CLM communicator came on again. *"Ah, Four . . . can you use your number six lug wrench for that?"*

"Negative," Retvig said bitterly. "It won't reach."

Another pause, then: *"One, do you have an extra FTH spanner in your chest kit?"*

"Negative," Bill Burlingame radioed back from his position at the far end of the tower, near the shuttle.

"Two?"

"Negative."

"Three?"

"Negative. Our packs don't have that item on the standard tool list."

"Ah, roger. Stand by."

Retvig drifted. His wrench was out of sight. His feeling of idiocy compounded itself. He was tired, that was why it had happened. But they were almost an entire shift time line behind already, and he had just added the latest in a seemingly endless sequence of errors, accidents, and fuckups.

He hated fuckups.

"Comm," he said, "I could come back in and get a spare out of the emergency cabinet just inside the EVA airlock."

Silence extended for what seemed a long time,

then the communicator replied, her voice toneless with controlled irritation: *"Negative on that, Four. We, ah, have less than forty minutes left on this shift time line, and, ah, by the time you got in and back out again, you wouldn't have any time left to accomplish anything. The, ah, judgment here is that we terminate the shift at this point in time. All crew members on EVA Team Two, begin securing your rigs and prepare to come back on board."*

Retvig exhaled deeply in disgust and began moving through the weightless environment of space along the narrow tower sections toward the airlock entry chamber of the CLM. He could hear the other guys on the shift team breathing heavier as they moved in from their stations farther out. One of them was muttering obscenities almost too low to be picked up by his helmet mike.

They had every reason to be pissed, Retvig thought bitterly. Crew capture and final launch were less than a week away. MarsProbe, a finely tuned, multistep operation involving more than 10,000 experts and millions of discrete components that had never been meshed before, was coming together at last in an atmosphere of crushing time pressure. There just couldn't be any extra screwups. But he had just committed one.

As he reached the airlock and grasped the reboarding assist bars on both sides of the circular port, Retvig paused to look around. Lightweight triangular tower sections extended out from the massive CLM in three spiderweb networks, forming a giant cradle for the modified shuttle that had flown up to dock so recently. At the end of an auxiliary arm far to his right, the two solid fuel boosters remained lashed in place, scheduled for attachment to the modified shuttle within seventy-two hours. Tangled jungles of cable, hosing, and power-transfer lines looked very much like real webbing draped from one tower section to another, and into and around the CLM. For a moment Retvig was struck again by a sense of awe that he was really a part of this fantastic venture.

Then, however, he happened to look beyond the broadly sloping deck of the CLM itself, past the extended golden wings of the solar array and UHF antennas, into dark space beyond the rear engine nozzle package.

There the sun glinted blindingly on another object in space perhaps a thousand miles away, moving in slightly higher Earth orbit: the Soviet space-docking station *Lenin*, larger than this United States configuration, and according to daily reports sent up from Earth-Comm at Cape Canaveral, evidently still running ahead of its time line and likely to rendezvous with crew—and blast out of orbit for Mars—any day now.

Taking his eyes away from the twinkle of the damned distant Russian station, Retvig opened the hatch and slid carefully, feetfirst, into the airlock. In any case he would have hated being second to the Russians. In this competition, second simply was not going to count.

There was only one prize.

He was still in the crew suit-handling chamber next to the airlock when the other guys from his shift came in. As he helped a technician unscrew his helmet linkage, Ingersoll gave Retvig a look like one might give an insect. Retvig didn't flare. He was still thoroughly pissed at himself, and whatever anybody said, he figured he had it coming. *Damn!*

The July heatwave cloaking downtown Houston had penetrated the television studio, despite its heavy-duty air-conditioning. Seated on the left of her two NASA colleagues at the table, astronaut Christie Hart felt perspiration soaking her pale lemon summer dress and wrecking her studio makeup. All she needed, she thought, was to look harried and uncertain when the commercial break ended.

Their interviewer, Larry Amaker, would love it if viewers thought she was cracking under his trademark nasty questioning.

The Bounce commercial on the nearby color monitor concluded. A red light came on on one of the three hulking studio cameras, and Amaker's thin, sardonic face filled the screen.

Folding his hands on the small table facing the one for the three NASA spokespersons, Amaker grinned at the camera. "Back in Houston for CNN, and our exclusive interview with NASA MarsProbe Crew Training Chief Dr. Davidson Myrick, Support Systems Analyst T. Pickett Fowler, and astronaut Christie Hart."

He turned slightly to make eye contact with Christie. "We have only a few minutes left. Briefly, Christie, how do you feel about receiving so much attention as being, quote, our prettiest spacewoman, unquote, rather than being considered on your merits as an electronics expert and commercially rated private pilot?"

Watch it! Christie thought. *He's just trying to get you mad again.* She said sweetly, "I hadn't heard the quote about my appearance, Larry, and although I'm flattered, I consider our mission much too important to waste time dwelling on observations of a personal nature."

Amaker's grin widened and took on a leering quality. "Then you reject Congressional charges that you were selected more on the basis of your looks—for public relations reasons, to 'put a Miss America' in space—than for your abilities?"

Christie took a slow breath and broadened her sweet, innocent smile. "My goodness, Larry," she cooed. "I hadn't heard anything like that. *That* idea is as silly as someone saying people on TV, like yourself, are picked more for looks than intelligence."

The tiniest spot of anger splotched Amaker's cheeks. But he recovered smoothly, glancing at his notes. "Dr. Fowler," he resumed, jumping to the enormous bald man on the far right of the table, "a moment of philosophical soul-searching, if you will. Here we stand as a nation tonight, within days of the ultimate steps in our most ambitious, costly, and dangerous mission in space, a journey to the red planet of Mars.

"Halfway around the globe, space engineers of the Soviet Union race against their own clock to send up a Communist crew to dock with the *Lenin*, make final preparations to enter the Russian Mars vehicle, and blast out of orbit, intent on beating the free world to a prize of unknown value on that mysterious planet.

"And in West Germany, the Common Market consortium is preparing an unmanned spacecraft designed to soft-land a laboratory, examine the beacon site, and pick up anything its tracked collectors can locate."

Amaker paused, staring for a dramatic moment at Fowler, whose moon face glistened under a film of sweat. Then Amaker asked, "Isn't this duplication an enormous waste, doctor? Shouldn't Washington and Moscow have tried to get together? Isn't it tragic that financial aid to the NATO alliance has somehow found its way into the pirate Common Market effort? Isn't our mad competitive urge driving us toward a launch that may be unsafe, sent before there has been time for due scientific caution and testing? And all for a dubious prize—"

As Amaker had hoped, T. Pickett Fowler exploded. "Dubious prize? My God, man! There's *someone out there*. This expedition represents the most momentous step in the history of humankind! We can't afford *not* to go there, whatever the cost!"

"Ah," Amaker sighed with deep satisfaction. "'Whatever the cost,' you say? Even if the lives of three courageous crew members are placed at risk?"

"The risk is not that great," Fowler shot back.

"Ah! 'Not that great,' you say? Then you can assure all of us that beautiful Christie, here, and her two crewmates are *perfectly* safe?"

Fowler saw the trap too late. "No crew is ever 'perfectly' safe—"

"And we *know* there really will be something out there on Mars to justify the cost and risk?"

Fowler clenched fat hands on the tabletop, but they trembled anyhow. And the camera instantly focused on them and showed him his own distress on the nearby monitor. "Only a few religious fanatics are against this probe."

"I remember another public official from long ago who had blanket condemnations for all his critics," Amaker smiled. "He was a senator from Wisconsin—"

"Oh, come off it, Amaker!"

Things were about to explode, just as CNN's resident gadfly had hoped. Christie watched in dismay. It was the man between her and Fowler, Davidson Myrick, who intervened.

"We're all under pressure, Larry, that's true," he said coolly, with an unthreatened smile. "But every safety provision has been put into MarsProbe. And—"

"Are you saying—" Amaker tried to break in.

"Please," Myrick said with heavy sarcasm. "I know you want to hear my complete comment. If you'll recall, the president tried unsuccessfully for more than six months to get the Russians to join with us in this effort. They refused. As to the European unmanned effort, I think I would rather have Christie and her team members up there instead of a little electric lawnmower with an erector-set arm."

Amaker was twisting a little in the breeze. He tried to recoup: "And as to the unknown alleged benefits—"

"Larry," Myrick cut in again with a smile that

went out over the nation—a smile that masterfully managed to combine gentle sympathy with surprised superiority—"*surely* you don't contest the idea that our first contact with an alien race from some other planet or galaxy is *news*?"

For an instant Amaker was caught without a comeback. In that instant, a floor man signaled ten seconds remaining.

Amaker gave the camera a ghastly forced smile. "We have talked tonight with Dr. Davidson Myrick, Dr. T. Pickett Fowler, and America's loveliest astronaut, Christie Hart. Clearly there are many unanswered questions. We hope we have shed some light on a few of them. This is Larry Amaker reporting for CNN."

The moment the camera lights went out, he was on his feet and being charming, thanking them for a good show. When Christie was safely in the next room with Myrick and Fowler, and out of his hearing, she hugged Myrick. "You were wonderful!"

Fowler added, "He had me going there. You pulled it out for us. Good job!" He lumbered out of the room.

Myrick mopped his face with his handkerchief. "All we needed was some new controversy. With all the people already against the expense, saying we don't need to make contact—"

"But you did great."

"Thanks in part to your dad."

Christie tensed. She was the only one at NASA who knew he was seeing her father professionally, and she had come upon the information by the sheerest accident while visiting her father's office. It was a professional confidence on her father's part which she would honor, despite twinges of worry about this man she admired so much.

Aloud she said, "I'm glad he's helped."

"He's helped enormously. I think I'm back together. He hypnotized me today—got me entirely out of most of my tension syndrome."

"That's wonderful, Dave!"

Myrick winked and started for the door. "Late work at home tonight. See you Monday."

Christie went to the restroom and then also left the TV station headquarters. Climbing into her Celica, she got the air-conditioning on high power and drove into the traffic.

She was tired and tense. Assignments like tonight's, being ordered to appear on TV as part of NASA's public relations mania, drove her up the wall. She hated things like that—the hoopla, and NASA's constant need to sell itself, which bordered at times on paranoia. The pose was always the same—cheerfulness, confidence, poise—while underneath she might be tired, disgusted, unsure of success, and plagued by questions as to whether she really wanted any of this anyway. The questions were always the same, too. And her answers. —Oh, yes, she was *so* excited to be a part of MarsProbe. And of course she felt perfectly safe about the journey. And her husband, Don? Yes, he was all for it. Yatata yatata.

She wondered what they would say if she told the truth: that sometimes she was scared out of her mind, not only of the ten thousand things that she knew could go wrong on the trip, but of whether she was even doing the right thing personally, trying to find satisfaction in this way . . . whether she would ever entirely feel at peace with herself or with her father . . . whether she would come back from Mars and find that a place in history couldn't quite compensate for the continuing feeling of emptiness, and loss of a husband she loved.

She had always tried to excel. She had learned early from her father that that was what people named

Hart did, as an obligation of their name and genetics. So she had made A's in school, struggled to get her Ph.D. in engineering, entered the aircraft industry, pursued her flying with an intensity bordering on obsession. When the chance came to join NASA as a possible spaceflight crew member, she had had no hesitation.

Accepting challenges, after all, was what Harts *did.*

Sometimes she was so proud of being a Hart, and so filled with joy in her life. But other times she hated it and wished she could just be herself once in a while, and not have that little voice in the back of her mind whispering to her that her every action had to be judged against a yardstick: *What must I do to live up to my birthright?*

She sighed. The decision was made. What she had to do now was fight to make herself enjoy it, and never look back on what might have been in a simpler world . . . with a simpler family.

Thirty minutes later she walked into her apartment.

"Here she is, 'America's loveliest astronaut,'" Don said mildly, looking up from the easy chair that faced a color TV set.

"Keep talking," Christie grinned, "and get a knuckle sandwich."

Don Dillingham uncoiled from the chair, a tall, tanned, thinly muscular man of her own age, and sauntered over in his faded Levi's—nothing else. He looked like the kind of uncomplicated man who loved life, and could accept almost any blow, and that was exactly the kind of man he was. But even Don's radiant outlook on life had been shaken by this damned adventure. He hadn't wanted her to volunteer, had been crushed when she became a member of the first

crew. He was scared for her, and scared of what the
months of separation would do to their relationship.

"If our relationship is strong, we'll be fine," Christie had told him.

"I hope so," he had said, somber.

He was giving it his best shot now, however. He
looked determinedly cheerful as he gave her a hug.
"You were great."

Christie pressed her face gratefully against his
chest. He felt warm and strong and wonderful, and
she felt little and weak. "That Amaker is such a shit."

"He worked you over."

"Yes. With nothing but lies."

She felt him stiffen. He stepped back from her.
Part of his cheerful facade had fallen. "Right."

"They *are* lies," Christie said defensively.

"Not the part about the danger."

"Don! We've been over this a hundred times, and
I'm tired—"

"Fine! Then go on to bed, and the househusband
will sit up with the goddam cat!"

"Don—!"

He stormed across the living room and flopped
onto a chair. Christie felt miserable. She followed him,
and draped herself across his lap. "Oh, honey, I know
you worry, but everything has been tested and re-
tested. The equipment is proven stuff."

"But none of this has ever been *done* before," he
retorted bitterly.

"Well, a lot of it, no. But the simulations—"

"Fuck the simulations! It's your body they're putting on the line up there!"

"I'll be fine! I wouldn't be going if I wasn't confident."

"Yeah. You be confident. You blast off and have
your adventure, and eighteen or nineteen months
from now—if you don't lose your pressurization, or

have a major equipment malfunction, or get hit by a meteorite, or land on Mars and then find you can't get the engine to fire to get you back off of there, or blow up—you can come back and we can see if we can get reacquainted—see if we still love each other."

"I'm going to be *fine*," Christie insisted with more certainty than she secretly felt. "And we'll still love each other. —At least I know I'll still love you."

He met her eyes. His were almost glazed with fear and anger. "You don't know that."

"That I'll still love you? Oh, for gosh sake—!"

"It's eighteen months," he insisted. *"Eighteen months!* You'll change. You'll come back a celebrity. Who says you'll still want anything to do with an ass-hole like me?"

"Goose," Christie murmured, pressing her face against his. "I'll love you more." She realized she had tears on her face, and laughed through them. "What's that they say about absence making the heart grow fonder? You spell that H-A-R-T."

Her husband groaned, clung to her. "Is there any way you can get out of this mission?"

Astonished, she pulled back. "I don't want to get out of it!"

"You're not scared?"

"Honey, at times when I allow myself to think of all of it, I'm petrified. But—my God—the *honor* of being selected . . . the excitement and adventure that's waiting out there—"

"And your marriage and I don't mean a shit," he cut in, the bitterness back.

"You mean *everything*."

"Second to MarsProbe, that is."

"We've talked all this out," she said with dismay. "You agreed. I thought we were past this point."

"I don't want to lose you, Christie. I don't want you to go."

"But I've *got* to go, darling. It's my job! This is what all the training was about!"

The look he leveled on her was filled with the bleakness of a private hell, and her insides sank. She thought, *If I go when he's feeling like this, he's right: I will lose him.*

But she had committed long ago, and nothing was going to hold her back from this adventure.

Even the multilevel fear inside.

Richard Hart stood at the garden windows of his tower apartment, looking down at the Houston traffic far below, and the lights playing over Christ Church Cathedral. The tower building sometimes gave him the feeling of a fortress, as it was supposed to do, basing its high lease rates on impregnable security.

Hart wondered why he didn't feel invulnerable at all.

Behind him, a soft sound came. He turned to see Kecia Epperly uncoiling sinuously from her batwing chair.

"Can I get you something?" he asked.

She smiled and shook her head. "You're somewhere else tonight. I'm going home."

He went to her. "I'll do better."

"Gotta go."

"No. Really. Stay, Kecia."

"You know better, doc. My first student is due at eight in the morning."

"How many teachers at the university have Saturday conferences with their kids?"

Kecia smiled. "All of us who don't have tenure."

"Marry me and let me take you away from all that."

The smile faded. "Sure."

"You know I mean it, Kecia."

She stood straight, suddenly a little stiff, defensive. "I'll think about it, okay?"

He ached. "You know I love you."

Her temper flared. "I told you a long time ago. I adore you. We have fun together. Isn't that enough? I warned you: I'm not ready for anything more than that, and I may never be."

He struggled to refrain from striking back. "Just so you're thinking about it."

"Sure." She started to turn away, cool, remote suddenly.

"Kecia," he said in exasperation, "you've been thinking about it for a year."

"Six months."

He grinned, trying to relax, play it her way. "Damn you pedants anyhow."

"Yep." She started across the living room.

The best way to deal with the tension and uncertainty between them was to joke about it, he thought. "Don't wait too long," he called after her.

She turned back, the light of the open kitchen area behind her making a halo of her golden hair, gleaming off long, bare, athletic legs. "I've told you. Maybe I'll always feel just the way I do now. I *had* a committed relationship once, and what did it get me? I may never want one again."

"Ouch."

"I warned you a long time ago, doc: I don't always play fair." She walked on across the vast living room, with its vaulted beam ceiling and walls of rock looking down on contemporary furniture. She went into the kitchen, where he could still see her through the divided partition. Hart watched her all the way, thinking how astonishingly she affected him.

She was beautiful, he thought, and terrifyingly bright, and her sense of humor was wonderful. She touched all the right chords inside the childlike part of him, and there was just no question that he was crazy about her. None of which was a problem.

She was also thirty-five, a full fifteen years younger than he. Which was a problem for him sometimes, although he had managed to get past most of the bad feelings he had started out with over it—worry that he couldn't keep up with her, that she would learn to hate him as he aged further and she was still young.

Worse, however, was her fear of ever trying again, of committing. Her marriage had been one of the worst and cruelest he had ever heard of during his extensive practice. Her husband had been a genius at manipulation, and more than a little crazy. She might never have broken free, Hart thought from hearing her talk about it, if her husband hadn't finally made one of his affairs so blatant, almost destroying her in the process of taunting her with things he had done.

Experiences like that, obviously, went deep. With Kecia the healing process—learning to trust again—was even harder because she had so loved the man and tried so long and hard. As a clinician Hart wondered often whether she would ever be able to risk trying again.

He could have told any of his patients how to deal with these problems in less than an hour's therapy time. He was incredibly good at helping others, if they would listen. Kecia was like a gentle, wild creature; whenever he so much as approached the topic, she ran. So he had decided to wait and hope and risk it. And love her.

Sometimes, like tonight, it was not very easy.

Watching her now across the expanse of the living room, he was struck again by how great-looking she was. A shade too tall to be a classic beauty, perhaps, too long-legged, perhaps, too casual about her hair and makeup. But his breath had caught the first time he met her, and their year-long relationship had only made him love looking at her more.

She stood now in the kitchen under the overhead light, her face partially averted. A wisp of tangled blonde hair decorated her forehead, which was wide with intelligence and uncluttered by extraneous worries. She was wearing pink shorts that did nice things for those long legs, sandals, and a Gatorade T-shirt that the bounty of her breasts gently strained. In repose, her face was smooth and unlined, betraying none of the traumas of her earlier years, and her big hazel eyes and wide, curving mouth bespoke love of life and quickness to laughter.

He was struck again by how lucky he was.

Even if they never quite worked it out and he eventually lost her, times like this made any risk of future pain acceptable.

She came back in from the kitchen, hips gently swaying. "So good night, doc."

"Sure you won't stay?"

"We've both got work to do tomorrow. You said you're going to need several hours, maybe, with that tape of Dave Myrick."

"I'm not sure I'm quite so concerned after watching him on that CNN talk show tonight. He looked great, not at all like the man I had in my office today."

"Oh, by morning you'll have worked up some worries again. I trust you there."

"Bless you, my child."

"Thank you, father time."

They laughed. He moved to embrace her. Everything nice and loose and easy. Then they touched. The joking stopped instantly. Their emotions reached a flashpoint. Her tongue darted into his mouth, her pelvis rotated against his hips, his fingers probed hard into the curvatures of her back. When they stepped back and stared at each other, both were shaken.

"Wow," she whispered. "Hey, what's up, doc?"

"Wow yourself. And I think you know."

"Save it. I have to be fresh at 8 A.M. to discuss the wonders of comma splices and sentence fragments."

He walked her to the private elevator and rode
down with her to the parking garage, where they
kissed good night under the polite scrutiny of a security guard. Kecia waved as she drove out. Hart rode
back upstairs alone, wishing she hadn't gone and
thinking again about Dave Myrick and the day's bizarre events in the office. When he reentered the
apartment, his telephone was ringing.

Thinking it could be Christie, he picked it up.

"Dr. Hart?" The voice was male, reedy, a little
tired, familiar. "This is Detective Bud Slagerfeldt. Remember me?"

"How could I forget, Bud?" They had met when
Hart was an expert witness in a homicide case, and
had discovered a mutual interest in horse racing.
Hart's interest was casual, however, compared with
Slagerfeldt's. The detective's consuming passion preoccupied him through bits of every day and guaranteed a
good living for a local bookie who, day in and day out,
took his unbelievably bad bets.

Before making a trip to Louisiana Downs with
Slagerfeldt the previous year, Hart would never have
believed that a man could study the ponies with such
religious fervor, yet never pick a winner. Slagerfeldt
had made a believer out of him.

It had been months since they had been in touch.

"What's going on?" Hart asked. "Did you finally
pick a winner?"

There was a sepulchral tone in the detective's
voice, and he did not rise to the joke. "I think you'd
better come down to your office right away."

"My office? What for?"

Slagerfeldt told him. He felt sick.

three

Chilly fog shrouded the giant gantry tower and nearby fire emergency equipment flanking the modified Vostok rocket. But the layer of fog was thin, the wind still, the forecast excellent here at the Soviet Union's Baykonur Cosmodrome in remote Kazakhstan.

The two Soviet cosmonauts had been strapped inside their Soyuz III spacecraft atop the Vostok for more than four hours, and all had proceeded normally.

Radio signals crackled between automatic equipment on board the spacecraft and monitors in the hulking control complex. Final words were exchanged between mission control and cosmonauts Valeriy Zubakov and Alexi Picaran.

The countdown moved inexorably to its climax. Fire gushed from the inverted conical engine configurations at the base of the tall, slender rocket, the gantry towers retracted, and the Vostok rose majestically into the fog, its rising fire making a crimson-yellow glow that could be seen for many miles.

The earth shook, and then the rocket became a fast-diminishing eye of blinding brilliance, and the Soviet scientists in their control room solemnly shook hands, holding their elation in check.

Certainly a successful launch was only the first step in a thousand most critical maneuvers over the next seventeen months. But the start seemed auspicious. Mother Russia was ahead in a race that could mark an epochal turning point in the course of humankind.

Richard Hart, wearing Levi's and a sweatshirt, stood in the waiting room of his office suite. Shock chilled him. He hadn't had time, in the few minutes since the telephone call, to grasp this, get some kind of handle on it.

But everything in the room spoke the ghastly truth: a lank policewoman in dungarees, wielding a motor-driven Nikon and strobe as she methodically took pictures of everything, from every angle; the three uniformed patrolmen moving with cumbersome caution around Hart's furniture in the next room; the older detective dusting flat surfaces for fingerprints with pinkish powder and a little paintbrush; the wizened man from the coroner's office sitting on the plastic couch, diligently filling in a long form held by a clipboard on his knee; the two ambulance attendants standing solemn in the doorway; Detective Bud Slagerfeldt kneeling on the carpet to smooth back the plastic sheet over the sprawled dead body of Charlene Lewis.

"Her boyfriend found her?" Hart asked numbly. "I don't understand. If she was in here—"

"We took him to the hospital already," Slagerfeldt replied. He was a tall man, mid-thirties, with a beaky face, very little remaining hair, and a million pale freckles. His summer suit looked slept-in and his blue eyes looked like he had never had any sleep. "He was pretty crazy when we got here, throwing himself around, yelling—shock. You know."

Hart nodded. He knew, all right. He was not tracking quite right himself at the moment.

He forced himself to concentrate on meaningless details, looking for a familiar mooring: "But did he come with her, or what?"

Slagerfeldt shook his head. "She said she had some notes to transcribe or something. She came alone, was to meet him later at a party. When she didn't show up, the boyfriend—Jakie Donaldson is his name, you know him?"

"We've met here at the office. Go on."

"Yeah. Well, he got concerned. Called here. No answer. Came over, found a janitor and persuaded him to come check. That's how they got in, master key. —And there she was."

"And nobody saw or heard anything?" Hart insisted in disbelief.

"The building is virtually deserted at night, doc. You know that."

Hart thought of the rush job on the transcription of the Myrick session. If it hadn't been for that, Charlene would still be alive, at a party with her boyfriend. It was crazy.

Slagerfeldt went over and spoke with the crime lab photographer for a moment, then signaled to the ambulance attendants. They brought a gurney in from the hall and with surprising gentleness and care bundled the form under its plastic covering onto the stretcher. As they went out, they left an outline of the body marked on the carpeting with duct tape: tangled legs, outsprawled arms. And a viscous puddle of black and red.

Slagerfeldt came back to Hart. "It looks like someone broke in, seeing the 'Doctor' title on the door, probably looking for drugs. Didn't know what kind of doctor you were. You saw how the cabinets in your inner office were all jerked open, the drawers pulled out. Maybe kids. The file drawers were broken open, as you saw, but you can't see that any files were taken?"

"No," Hart said. "But that doesn't mean someone couldn't have pulled some pages from one or more files—or photographed some of them. Everything in there is confidential. That's why I rent in this building. The security is supposed to be exceptional; they make a big point about that. It's the same at the towers, where I live. An ant couldn't get in there."

"You keep stuff at your apartment, too?"

"Not regularly, but I work on records there sometimes. This couldn't have happened there, believe me!"

Slagerfeldt nodded. "I know the towers are like Fort Knox. Obviously, this place isn't. Of course a good thief can get in almost anywhere."

"Then you're saying it *wasn't* kids, after all?"

Slagerfeldt's lips turned down. "A lot of kids are real good thieves, doc."

Hart took a few deep breaths. Jesus Christ, he thought, kids looking for dope. Or maybe not . . . maybe someone wanting information out of a psychological file to hurt a divorcing partner, or blackmail someone into a better court settlement, or to set up revenge. He could never screen all the files and hope to discover any missing documents from memory. Charlene's death had hit him hard.

He was trying to teach sanity in an insane universe.

"Also," Slagerfeldt went on with inexorable boredom, the kind sensitive cops sometimes donned as an apron against corrosive realities, "the things taken certainly support the kid theory. As I understand what you've told us, all you can find missing are a table radio, a twin-cassette recording machine, a handful of tapes, a digital clock, and a plastic cupful of change for the Coke machine down the hall?"

"That's all I see right now."

"Okay, doc. Thank you. And I'm sorry we had to drag you down here for something like this. You know how much I think of you and the work you did with the department recently. I guess you can clear out. We'll stay awhile. Then I'll lock up."

Hart hesitated. "What about the . . ." He pointed at the mess on the carpet, the overturned chairs.

"I'll tell maintenance to get in here tomorrow if you like. We'll have finished up. Oh, I'm afraid we'll be cutting out most of that spot in the rug and taking it with us. I guess you can toss a throw rug over it for now, and your insurance probably covers it."

Hart nodded, shook hands, and left. They were still loading the body into the ambulance downstairs, and the flashing red-and-blue lights had drawn a small crowd. Somebody turned on blinding TV news flood-lights, and Hart had to stifle an impulse to go for the lights and dismantle him. Instead, he hurried to the car, got in, drove away with sunbursts still dancing in his vision.

"God damned ghoulish bastards," he said aloud.

He drove along the expressway, feeling the first sense of shock starting to give way to grief and con-fusion. Charlene—of all people, *Charlene*. As inno-cent—in every true sense—a person as he had ever known. And for a random burglary. . . .

Hart was fifty, had been in the private practice of psychology for fifteen years, knew people's bottomless capacities both for being amazingly good and for fuck-ing themselves up. He had learned a lot about the lat-ter from his own life.

Texas was adopted home for him after growing up and attending college as an undergraduate in Indiana. After the army—he had gone to school in the days when it was neither unusual nor weird to enroll in ROTC, and let the government help pay for the educa-

tion—he had married his high school sweetheart and
started back to school in Chicago. A few years passed,
he began practice in a county health clinic, he imagined everything was just fine with a wife he loved and
a daughter he adored and a son who was . . . if not
exactly *typical*, at least possibly okay.

But Chuck had been hyperactive, over-demand-
ing, from the start. Phyllis spoiled him, gave in to him,
stood between him and his father most times that Hart
tried to inject a little discipline. Hart had overreacted,
become harsh. Subtly their conflict over the child became an ignored wound, festering. Chuck, like all children, was quick to sense and exploit their differences.
The marriage went on, Hart and his wife told themselves it was all right, but it was not all right. Then,
after endless years of chipping-away pain that they
foolishly tried to ignore, came the call. Was their son
named Charles Hart, age sixteen, part-time employed
at Krogers on Center Street? Yes. Well, sir, they were
sorry to inform you, sir, that your son had tried to rob
a liquor store and had been shot. And he was dead.

It had taken another six months for the full devastation of their loss to finish wrecking the family. Phyllis said it was Hart's fault—his damned harsh
demands, refusal to bend, his lack of real compassion,
his clinical coolness. Hart, torn apart, had tried to convince himself that some of the fault—if fault had to be
assigned—must be hers, for allowing the boy to run
over and exploit her, so that he respected nothing and
no one, certainly not a father rendered impotent by the
mother's intense protectiveness.

But it was a long time before Hart could begin to
sort out where he had gone wrong, where Phyllis had
gone wrong, how their marriage had been destroyed
by pain and pretense that neither of them could have
avoided, being the people they were then. But by the
time he began to understand their tragedy, the mar-

riage was over, he had moved to Houston, daughter Christie was herself in college.

Now it was better, most of the time. Coincidence and her entry into the corps of astronauts had brought Christie to Houston, too. She had learned her dad's passion for excellence, something he had once bemusedly traced back through generations of his family that had included a United States senator, two physicians, a noted journalist, and an Olympic athlete. Christie would fly on MarsProbe. The idea scared hell out of Hart, but he was filled with pride, too, and knew she could be no different, whatever the risks. She had gotten that from him.

And there was Kecia. But he would not think about Kecia right now because he got so frustrated, wanting her with him all the time.

His office practice was good, his professional reputation superb, there were no money worries, and until tonight things had been going along with reassuring calm.

Perhaps things had been going almost too well. Charlene's violent death had shocked him deeply, and its senselessness filled him with a kind of bitterness that mixed with the grief. His emotions ran away sometimes. One thing led to another. Now, pained over Charlene, his thoughts took off: *It's too much risk; Christie shouldn't go. I could lose her. And Kecia is never going to be ready to commit. I'm living in a fool's paradise of optimism that none of the facts support.*

He shook himself mentally and stopped *that* line of unreason.

Reaching his apartment building tower, he parked in the garage and rode the express elevator to the top. Entered his penthouse apartment.

The night beyond the windows seemed less friendly now, alien. So did the space inside the apartment. *God damn it, Kecia—!* He mixed a drink and flipped on the TV again, knowing sleep would come only much later.

A local newscaster was doing a newsbreak. His words were caught in the middle as the volume came up and the sixty-inch screen cleared: "—and so another setback, but NASA does have backup personnel for every slot on the MarsProbe team."

Thinking instantly—fearfully—of Christie, Hart leaned forward sharply and pressed the remote control to bring up the volume so he could hear what had happened to affect MarsProbe. The bulletin was over, however, and the station reverted to a movie in progress.

Concerned, Hart started switching channels to find another newscast.

He found CNN's roundup that had started at 2 A.M. They had the story.

An hour or two earlier, Davidson Myrick had plunged seven floors to his death from the balcony of his apartment building.

four

When Christie Hart walked into Building 9-A at the Johnson Space Center Saturday morning, she had to fight her own feelings to walk confidently, without vivid memory of the problem with her husband. She got the depression in line when she found her two fellow MarsProbe I astronauts already on the scene.

Mission Commander Buck Colltrap and botanist/health systems specialist H. O. Townsend were already in their NASA blue coveralls and earnestly conversing with one of several white-jacketed technicians swarming busily all around the full-scale mockup of their shuttle ship, *Adventurer*.

The training room was like a hangar, with a high, girdered roof. Esoteric test, simulator, and computerized communications equipment stood everywhere in racks and wheeled cabinets, with thick connecting cables snaking this way and that. Heavy air-conditioning kept the vast chamber chilly despite banks of canted spotlights suspended from the roof area. The room was always serious and businesslike, except when Townsend's unpredictable horselaugh occasionally racketed through it without warning. Today, as a result of Myrick's death, the atmosphere was more grim.

Two-inch heels clicking on the spotless white tiles, she hurried toward the training mockup to join her fellow crew members. *Be cheerful, dammit!* "Hey, am I late?"

Townsend turned to greet her. He was not wearing his usual lazy grin. He was slender, like all the astronauts, twenty-nine but already balding, with soaring ears and close-set dark eyes that sometimes gave people the mistaken impression he was not a genius. "Hey, Chrissie, how ya doin'?"

"Under the circumstances, okay."

"Yeah. Know what you mean. Poor Dave."

Christie hesitated. Myrick's death had hit her hard. Any unexpected development affecting the mission would have threatened her right now, but she had liked Dave a lot, and his visits to her father's office had seemed to draw them closer.

She had tried to talk to her father about it this morning, but had gotten only messages on his recorders. Maybe that was better. If she had gotten through, she might have blurted out her gnawing fear that MarsProbe was destroying her marriage.

She said cautiously, "Anything new on how it happened?"

Buck Colltrap shook his head. He was forty-six, his face showing every year in weathered lines around keen eyes and tight-lipped mouth, and he had a full head of iron-gray hair. A lot of people thought he had iron in his nervous system, too, and his heart.

"Nothing new," he told her.

"I feel awful. I was just on TV with him last night."

Colltrap didn't blink. "Yes. It's sad. But any of us can be replaced. Technical staff and crew are just like the onboard computers: redundant backups on line. We'll fill the gap."

Townsend studied his commander with cool eyes. "You've got a heart of gold, Buck, God love you."

Colltrap stared at him, looking for all the world in that instant like Spock. "Say again?"

Townsend turned to Christie. "You heard about the Rooshians?"

"The Russians?" Christie echoed. "What have they—oh, God. Do I want to hear this?"

Townsend looked perversely pleased to be the breaker of bad news. "Yup. The devils went into Earth orbit early this morning. Telemetry intercepts and tracking show they're linking to the *Lenin* right now. They've stole the march on us, Chrissie m' luv."

"Shit," Christie said under her breath.

"Precisely," Colltrap said. "The brass are setting up a strategy meeting right now to talk about it. The tentative time is in two hours—at eleven hundred."

At about the same time Christie Hart was hearing the bad news about the Soviet orbital launch, some fifteen miles away Mona Reynolds was examining herself in her dressing room mirror.

It was one of the things Mona Reynolds did best.

And with the most self-satisfaction.

Bending slightly at the waist to see to the best advantage in the five-foot-square reflecting surface, which was encircled by small white lights not unlike those of a traditional star's dressing room, Mona looked closely and liked everything she saw: lustrous, dark hair, expertly tinted to hide the gray and coiffed to best frame her beautiful features; large gray eyes without a trace of deep age-lines around them, courtesy of Houston's best cosmetic surgeon who had also done the little tuck in her neck to keep it smooth and youthful; a wide and sensual mouth with even white teeth, straightened by Dr. Stode of Dallas and capped by Dr. Eppenheimer here in Houston; the palest and smoothest shoulders and arms, shielded always from the direct sun and treated monthly at the skin care clinic; lovely upright breasts, tightened and augmented in the same surgical procedure in New Orleans a year ago; a flat belly and generously curved hips, firm and perfect in response to the thrice-weekly workouts at the spa, and hidden in the deep socket of her navel, the little smiling scar that promised the lifelong sterility which assured her freedom to do whatever she wanted with whomever she wanted, with no bothersome preventive devices and no consequences to tip off her boring husband unless she got careless and selected a momentary partner with the bad taste to have herpes or something. Which she had no intention of doing.

Satisfied that she was wonderful as usual, Mona applied her makeup, consulted her closet, selected a summer dress of the latest fashion and matching heels, and, with a last approving glance in her favorite appliance, glided into the adjoining master bedroom.

Her husband, Boyd—Dr. Boyd Reynolds, NASA director of onboard computer systems for MarsProbe— sat on the side of the huge, rumpled bed. He was fully dressed in dark summer suit with white shirt and tie, holding a portable computer on his lap and punching code in through the ivory-colored keyboard. He didn't hear her enter.

He looked distinguished, Mona thought, with his lined face and white hair, and she knew some women thought him attractive. But he was oblivious to other women because, Mona thought, he was as dull sexually as he was intellectually away from his computers. Or possibly he was just old. He was forty-seven, the same age as Mona. She worked all the time at appearing to be about thirty-five. He didn't seem to care, and looked fifty. Mona hated him for that; someone might look at them together and guess *her* age, and stop considering her outrageous and glamorous. Then she could end up like Joan Collins, who had been her heroine in earlier years before Collins's face finally dropped so far the surgeons didn't have enough thread to pull it all back up again.

"I'm leaving now," Mona told her husband's back.

He turned quickly, startled out of his concentration. "I didn't hear you, honey. I was trying an instruction subset here on the NEC . . . I thought it might save some ferrite memory onboard the landing module. Best of all, if it runs, I can make the change onboard in less than an hour . . . not hold any part of the schedule up in any way."

"How exciting," Mona murmured.

Boyd Reynolds looked more carefully at her, taking intense pleasure in it and feeling the anxiety at the same time. She was so beautiful! He was crazy about her. He was painfully conscious of his fear of losing her—of not being man enough for her.

It was a fear he lived with every day.

He volunteered, "I was hurrying because I've got to head to the shop in a while. We've got an emergency meeting called for eleven." He waited for his wife to inquire, so he could share with her the few details he knew about Davidson Myrick's shocking death and the orbital linkup achieved by the competing Soviet space team.

Mona did not oblige him. Touching her perfect hairdo, she said, "I'll be leaving now." She patted him on the shoulder with a gesture that was supposed to be affectionate but somehow felt condescending, the way a mother would carelessly pat a fretful child.

Reynolds hesitated, then gave in to his worry. "Where to today?"

"Shopping. Carolyn and I are going to the mall, then to lunch."

The dull sludge of jealousy stirred. Mona couldn't

know that he had talked to David, Carolyn's husband, yesterday: Carolyn was in South Carolina for a week.

He wanted to blurt, *Who are you really seeing?* He didn't. He knew the accusations that would follow. He was trying to control her as if he owned her, Mona would say. He did not own her body and she had a right to do with it anything she wished, she would say. He was being selfish, chauvinistic, and weak, she would tell him.

And then the fear of displeasing her—losing her altogether—would combine with the quickly-ready guilt he had soaked in from two decades of feminist propaganda, and he would smile and play dumb. And die a little inside.

So he said nothing. What he didn't know couldn't hurt him . . . could it? And he had no real evidence that she had ever been unfaithful to him—suspicions of that kind were just his weakness showing—right?

She started for the hallway door.

Another anxiety made him speak. "Mona?"

She turned. "Yes?"

"Kind of take it easy on the credit cards the rest of this month, all right?"

"Are you," she asked icily, "suggesting I not go at all?"

"No—no, of course not. No. Certainly not. You have every right. . . . I just know we're a little overextended on VISA and American Express, and I need a few weeks to catch up. Just a few weeks, Mona," he added, hearing the wheedling tone in his own voice.

"Don't be silly, Boyd, darling. We have lots of money. I know the state of our accounts."

"Mona—!"

"Don't worry, sweet. I'll just look. I'll let you know before I sign any dotted lines."

She blew him a kiss and vanished into the hallway beyond the bedroom door.

Reynolds gritted his teeth in an agony of frustration. He bit so hard, a stab of sharp pain lanced down into his jaw. Muttering to himself, he backed out of the computer program he had been in, removed the minidisk and pocketed it, powered the little unit down, and stood with the feeling of a man about to face a firing squad.

He had felt this way for so long that he hardly could remember better times. *God damn her*, he thought wearily. *I'm not made of money. How can she do this to me? It's almost like she wanted to destroy me.*

Reynolds knew, however, that Mona loved him. The little shots and witticisms were just her way. She had stuck with him, hadn't she? When every man who ever saw her was bowled over, ready to fall in love with her on sight? God, she was wonderful. He was very, very lucky.

Lurking in the back of his mind, however, was the near-certainty that Mona would not put up with him very long if he failed to provide her the luxuries she insisted were her right. After all, as she liked to say, she was like so many other women who had sacrificed their own professional fulfillment to support a husband, raise a child. If it hadn't been for him, she might have been an actress, or even a writer.

And she was right. Men *were* selfish, grasping, over-controlling bastards, most of them. He certainly was. It was Mona's *right* to be cared for, loved, pampered, and given absolute freedom.

And besides, if he didn't see the wisdom of her assertions and act accordingly, she would leave him for someone else.

The money pressure, however, was extreme. Just Mona's spa and beauty bills exceeded $2,000 a month. She was known as one of Texas's most glamorous and stylish women, so naturally she had to have the most costly new clothes. Her trips to New York and Paris every few months cost a fortune. Her Mercedes 450 was only six months old, but all the wrong color for her, she had decided.

Reynolds owned proprietary rights to three enormously powerful—and profitable—software systems used in most of America's major corporations. He had developed those and copyrighted them before accepting NASA's flattering invitation to work on Mars-Probe. His income exceeded a quarter of a million dollars a year.

Mona was going through considerably more than that.

How had he gotten into his present financial disaster? How had he ever been crazy enough to take the outside "consult" job—when part of him knew at the moment of the offer that it was really an industrial spy job? And how—oh, Jesus!—how was he ever going to get out of it—live with himself again—if they kept bleeding him for reports on the mission planning, giving him those exorbitant cash payments to keep him in line, making him surer and surer that he was the worst kind of man—a traitor to his country?

The sense of entrapped guilt was extreme. Reynolds was soaked with nervous sweat even as he left his sprawling country house and set the nose of his Jaguar on the center line that aimed at the distant NASA complex.

He had no idea who wanted the progress reports . . . the intricate detail information on mission procedures . . . he kept supplying. He wanted to believe it was relatively harmless stuff. But who could say? If he could just be *sure* he was not doing any direct harm to MarsProbe, he might feel a little better about it.

He thought of Davidson Myrick. His death would complicate final mission preparations and put an additional strain on all the staff. Now, with the Russians in orbit with their Mars expedition crew ahead of ours. . . .

The meeting in an hour would be interesting. Phones were probably already ringing from the White House and a dozen prominent congressmen, demanding action on the American expedition *now*. Everyone on the team was working too hard already. . . . *And I'm selling out some of our technical secrets to parties unknown.*

It was a bad thought.

So Boyd Reynolds did with it what he did with anxieties about Mona. He blocked it out of his mind.

The medium conference room felt like a big thermos bottle: sealed tight and pressurized. Air Force security men had been stationed at the doors along with NASA security personnel, and nobody had gotten in without eyeball identification or all the credentials.

The press had no idea of the meeting, nor would they.

Christie and her two fellow mission astronauts sat in the third row of the theater-type room. The rows ahead were scatter-filled with the best scientists and experts in the effort, and several other backup crew members and high-ranking technicians sat in the six rows behind. More than forty people, and all of them looking grim.

Warner Klindeinst, chief of the agency, walked in from a door at the side of the stage. Wearing a dark suit and somber tie, he was a big man, heavy, with Teutonic features and a close-cropped white beard. He carried a clipboard under his arm.

Behind him came John Selmon, the project director, and LeRoy Ditwhiler, chief of operations. These two high-ranking officials were in rumpled summer slacks and shirtsleeves, and looked like they had been up through the night.

Klindeinst walked to a small podium. The room hushed.

"The Soviet team," Klindeinst announced in a slow, guttural tone, "has completed orbital linkup with the *Lenin*. As most of you know, their space station was operational weeks ago, and fuel and supply transfers evidently were finished about last Wednesday. So sending up the crew is hardly unexpected."

Klindeinst paused, looked at his notes on the podium. Then he raked the room with bleak eyes. "We have every reason to expect them to blast out of Earth orbit and start their journey to Mars within twenty-four hours."

There was a collective exhaling of breath and a few groans of dismay in the auditorium. Christie felt a sharp pang. After a year of training, she and the U.S. team were going to be *second*—totally out of the ballgame.

Klindeinst seemed to read her thoughts, and indeed stared at her as he resumed heavily, "We have just completed a mission evaluation session. The tragic accidental death of Dr. Myrick further complicates our planning, but it is our best judgment that we can move our own efforts forward by several days—without undue risk to crew—and still make a competitive launch."

Someone—a fuel utilization engineer named Slade—asked from the back of the room, "How many days' head start are they likely to have, and how can we make it up?"

Klindeinst gestured to Project Director John Selmon, who stepped to the podium. Over six feet, six inches tall, lean as a bone, Selmon bleakly surveyed the room for a moment, lantern jaw seeming to unhinge and wobble. When he spoke, however, it was with quiet discipline.

"Screen, please?" he said, looking toward someone in the rear projection booth. A screen lowered, whirring softly, from the ceiling. "Thank you. Lights?" The lights went very dim. "Slide, please."

Light lanced out of the rear booth and a geometric diagram appeared, white lines against a cobalt background. Christie saw that it was a diagram of the inner planets of the solar system, with a number of Earth–Mars routes represented by long, complex curved lines.

Selmon pointed at the screen with a light wand which highlighted a small, circular portion of one of the route lines. "If the Russians launch within thirty-six hours, this will be their trajectory, around the moon, using the slingshot effect, then out in this direction well beyond the sun to intercept Mars over on the far side . . . here . . . in a little more than eight months."

Selmon moved the light wand to highlight another track. "As all of you know, this was the route we have been planning, not so close to the moon *or* the sun, inasmuch as our larger spaceship configuration allows us more ample stores and fuel for in-course corrections. This window opens in two weeks and again in five weeks, for maximum efficiency."

A voice out of the dark said respectfully, "We can't win the race if we wait even the shorter interval."

"That's right," Selmon agreed at once. "That's why we're running a computer profile right now on *this* route."

The pointer moved.

Christie sensed her two astronaut companions tensing even as she did in recognizing the trajectory.

"This route," Selmon said calmly, "has an opening later this week and again the following week. It takes our ship much closer to the moon, and slingshotting on, considerably closer to the sun, too, as you can see."

Buck Colltrap spoke: "I thought that path was rejected in earlier modeling. The threat of intense heat—
bombardment by radiation—"

"Earlier modeling," Selmon cut in, "gave this
route a priority of four because some of the factors you
just mentioned have never been tested in a manned
vehicle."

"'Crewed,'" Christie chirped.

Selmon looked momentarily baffled in the light reflected from the screen, and a few people in the room
got it and chuckled.

"'Crewed,'" Christie prompted him. "Not
'manned.'"

Selmon grinned. "Okay. I stand corrected, Christie. —The point I was making, though, is that this trajectory was given low launch priority only because it
hasn't been tested in a—with people in a spacecraft.
Every bit of data we have says that it's well within the
design limitations of the spacecraft and poses no serious danger to a crew."

"If we go that way," Colltrap asked, "how much
time do we gain?"

"Because of the extra velocity gained from the
sun-approach, at least two weeks. That's one of the
things we're calculating now."

"You mean," someone said, "if we could launch
on that track, we could launch in a week or ten days,
and still beat the Russkies out there to the signal
source?"

"That's what we think," Selmon said. "And until
we get the rest of our data massaged, we're taking
steps to make it possible, anyway." He turned.
"LeRoy?"

LeRoy Ditwhiler stepped into the mottled light of
the projected image. He was chunky, balding, sunburned as always from his habitual fishing trips on
days off. Against all the regs, he had a cigar clenched
between his teeth.

"Jack Schaeffly is replacing Davidson Myrick in crew training operations," he announced. "Training is complete, and the job is now one of coordination with the crew in flight and other experts here on the ground and at the Cape. Jack is fully qualified and backup-trained, and no problem. —Right, Jack?"

Jack Schaeffly, tall, handsome, forty, waved from the side of the room and gave his best movie-star grin. Christie knew he was great-looking and awfully smart and awesomely ambitious. But she didn't know why the thought of his ascension gave her a touch of dismay. She had never liked him much and she had no idea why.

"Jack and the others on the launch team will be meeting again starting at one o'clock today," Ditwhiler went on. "Also, I can tell you that we have had a priority-basis update from the crews on the orbital platform, and they assure us that all work can be completed within forty-eight hours if the normal crew rest periods are waived." He paused. "Which they already have been."

Someone said incredulously, "*All* work on the platform?"

"All work," Ditwhiler repeated with heavy emphasis.

"How about at the Cape?"

"The launch vehicle is on the stand and can be ready by Tuesday."

Christie felt almost dizzy. She exchanged glances with her two crew members and saw that it was coming with shocking speed for them, too. They had been griping only days ago about the endless glitches and holds. Now, suddenly, they were looking right down the barrel.

It was the incorrigible H. O. Townsend who put her question into words. "LeRoy," Townsend drawled, standing so that his lank frame sent a long black shadow across the chart on the screen, "with all this hurry-up, how fast do you think we might be going up for the orbital linkup?"

Ditwhiler spoke without hesitation. "Wednesday. Or possibly even Tuesday."

The gasp in the room this time was general and heavy.

"*Next* Wednesday?" Townsend asked, forgetting to drawl.

"That's correct."

"Then when in hell would we be likely to launch out of orbit and git going for the big trip its own self?"

"The spacecraft is ready," Ditwhiler replied. His voice shook ever so slightly, denying the calm he was trying so hard to project. "Provisions are on board, the controllable solid-fuel boosters are Status Normal, everything checks out. Once the construction crews finish the launch rigging equipment, and as I said, they promised—"

"Hey," Townsend broke in with soft insistence. "*When* might we be headin' for Mars?"

"The window will be wide open"—Ditwhiler consulted his wrist chronograph for an instant—"between plus ninety and plus one hundred and forty hours. Next Wednesday earliest. Or Thursday."

London: a chill, cloudy day. In a small office reserved for just such purposes, two executives concluded their brief, clandestine meeting.

"Then evidently all the plans are still on track," said one.

"Yes," said the other. "You can assure your people of that. The incident in Houston is being taken care of. And of course it's already too late for the Russians."

"The Russians," the other conferee murmured sadly, "I don't care about. Arrogant bastards, they have it coming. But I just wish this didn't have to happen to the Yanks. Especially with a woman on board."

"Is there something sacred about a woman?" the first asked, eyes hard with sudden enmity. "Some kind of cheap sentimentality?"

"No," the other replied quickly, nervous. "I just—wish—it could be different, that's all. I've seen her on the telly, so youthful and vibrant. I *like* her, don't you know. Death—"

"Save it," snapped the more powerful of the two. "And if you're not strong enough to handle this, I'm sure we can find someone else, even at this late date. We can't have somebody going gaw-gaw because a skirt is involved."

The second speaker, a large man with bulky shoulders and a savage black beard, swallowed hard and nodded. "I'll—carry on."

"Good, then," snapped the one who had called the meeting. "Let's have no more telly gush, then, luv." She rummaged in her tan leather purse for her liptstick, touched it to her beautiful mouth with a deft, almost angry motion, and walked out of the room, heels tapping on the tile.

five

The wake for Davidson Myrick was Sunday afternoon in a contemporary-style funeral home not far from Houston's Galleria. Richard Hart, still shocked and angry, arrived about 2 P.M.

He still didn't understand what had happened. The Houston *Post* had said police thought the death was accidental, but were continuing to investigate. Myrick had gone over a chest-high railing on the balcony of his apartment, where he lived alone. There were no signs of drinking or of a struggle, and blood-work on the corpse had shown no alcohol or drugs. The only access door to the unit was locked and showed no signs of having been tampered with.

The possibility of a suicide had nagged at Hart. But Myrick had meant it when he pledged not to go crazy, not to kill someone else, not to take his own life. Whatever strange mental quirk had caused the unique episode in Hart's office during trance, Myrick had not left the office an unbalanced man.

Myrick left behind him a puzzle in the form of the words he had spoken which he hadn't remembered. But he had not left suicidal.

An accident seemed almost as unlikely. Myrick would have had to be wildly reckless to fall over that high railing. In Hart's experience, accidents which required gross negligence were seldom really accidental, but the unconscious taking over and making the worst happen.

But Myrick had been fighting for renewed self-confidence and *life*.

Two emergencies involving his patients at city hospitals had prevented Hart from returning to his office. But he planned to go later today. He wanted to hear that cassette tape of the session again, try to pry more sense out of it.

Myrick's two grown daughters, along with their husbands, were in the viewing room when Hart arrived. A number of NASA officials and scientists were there, too. Hart circulated, wishing he knew better how to help people like the young women, whose grief was intense.

Myrick looked puffy in the casket and Hart wondered what miracles the morticians had had to do in order to allow for an open casket at all.

After moving through the room, Hart retreated to a corner of the large, chilly room and wished for a cigarette.

A short, overweight man of about forty-five, red hair almost gone, shuffled into the room and made rounds of a number of the NASA people. He was wearing pale tan slacks that looked like they had been pegged in the old-fashioned way above heavy brogans. His shirt was yellow, wilted from heat, his tie a slash-bar brown and white, his sportcoat a rumpled tweed too heavy for Houston's summer weather. Hart saw him tug a narrow spiral notebook out of a coat pocket and jot swift notes as he spoke with one NASA scientist. A reporter, then.

Figuring he had stayed a polite length of time,

Hart started for the exit. He had just gone into the wide, dim hallway when a voice called softly but insistently after him: "Dr. Hart? Aren't you Dr. Hart?"

He turned. The reporter was hurrying to catch up with him. Closeup, the man was sweaty, with a million faded freckles on his face and bald pate.

"Dr. Hart?" he said, panting slightly. "Hi. I'm Joe Blyleven. Reporter for the *Post*. I wonder if we could have a few words?"

Hart shook his soft, damp hand. "I was just leaving, Joe."

Blyleven flipped his notebook open. There was a quick intelligence in his sky-colored eyes. "I help cover the space center, among other things, doctor, and I'm interested in poor Dave's death."

"I'm afraid I don't know anything about that, sir," Hart said. Some reporters he liked, and others he instinctively distrusted. He was unsure about this one. "I'm just a casual friend."

"Right, right," Blyleven murmured, scribbling something with a green ballpoint. "I was kind of a pal of Dave's, too. We played golf together every once in a while."

Hart had never heard Myrick speak of an interest in golf. "Is that so?"

"Sure. Yes. We never planned to play together, I guess, but sometimes we just happened to get out there about the same time and we paired up." Blyleven showed a great number of small teeth. The expression tried to be a smile, but became a nervous grimace. "He was a patient of yours, wasn't he?"

Hart felt a tingle of surprise. He went on guard. "Whatever gave you an idea like that?"

"I have sources, doctor, just like everybody else in the news business. Was Dave seeing you for serious psychological problems that might have included suicidal tendencies?"

"You son of a bitch, you ought to know I won't answer a question like that."

Blyleven's eyes widened. "Holy moley, doctor, I'm just doing my job here!"

"Nice to meet you, Mr. Blyleven." Hart walked out.

He was still stewing about the leak concerning Myrick's treatment with him when he reached his office later in the afternoon. Myrick had wanted his problem held in confidence, and Hart intended to continue honoring Myrick's wish. Saying anything about it to anyone at this point would accomplish nothing but a blot on Myrick's reputation among people who didn't understand, and that—unfortunately—still included the majority of the population, even in this last decade of the century.

He found the office cleaned up. The overturned chairs were straight again, a small, ugly occasional rug covered the place where police technicians had sliced out a piece of the carpet, and his inner office was again properly locked.

The files in his inner office had obviously been broken into and looked through, but except for a few folders out of alignment, he could not find any signs of real damage, and no indication that anything was missing. He took more than two hours checking his index directory against the names on the file folder tabs, and no files were missing.

Relocking the cabinets, he sank into his desk chair and allowed himself a cigarette, his first in a long time.

There was still the small mess of the cassettes tumbled out of the recording cabinet when the intruder ripped out the recording machine itself and took it with him. After smoking the cigarette, Hart put the tapes back into the cabinet, looking for the one labeled as Myrick's Friday session.

He was not too surprised when it was not there. It would be in the stenographic machine out under the reception desk, the one the burglar didn't take, or somewhere on the counter itself, he thought. He went out to look for it. It was nowhere to be found.

He looked again, carefully, and found nothing.

It was an added blow. If the burglar had taken the Myrick cassette, Hart was left only with his memory. And the intuitive fear inside him was starting to grow. What if Myrick's death connected directly with the Mars mission? Why had he said the mission must fail? Christ! Was Christie in danger here?

He didn't have long to find out.

Plus or minus seven days . . . program in . . . Are you silver. . . .

What the hell did it mean?

He called Bud Slagerfeldt and caught him at his desk.

"Detective Slagerfeldt."

"Bud, this is Richard Hart."

"Doc. What's going on?"

"When your people took in evidence, including Charlene's purse, did they pick up a cassette audio tape?"

"I don't think so." Papers rustled. "I got that list of stuff right here on my desk. "Let me see . . . no. No tape." Hart could almost hear Slagerfeldt's antennae go up. "Important tape, doc?"

"No," Hart replied easily. "Just one of many patient interview transcription tapes. No big deal. It was what she came in to transcribe for me, and it's certainly not here."

"Well, I guess the killer got that one, too."

They talked awhile longer. Slagerfeldt asked things about Charlene's personal life that irritated Hart, and he didn't cooperate. Slagerfeldt grew bristly. It was not a satisfactory conversation.

After hanging up, Hart smoked another cigarette and looked through the drawers in the reception counter area. No cassette. It was bad luck that the intruder had taken that particular tape.

—Unless, he thought quite suddenly, the Myrick tape was among the things the intruder had come specifically to get.

It was one of those crazy leaps of speculation that often led to discovery, the unconscious making connections to new possibilities that the conscious mind was nowhere near integrating. Sometimes such hunches were right, sometimes wrong. Hart had no way to evaluate this one. But it gave him a chill.

Suppose someone had learned Myrick was coming here. Suppose further that someone was threatened by Myrick's visits, wanted to make sure the NASA scientist did not leak certain information. Suppose—just for theory's sake—that the strange trance-within-a-trance somehow tied in. If all that were somehow true, then Myrick might have had to be killed. And all record of his office visits here expunged.

Hart was on his feet before the thought completely formed. Unlocking the files again, he burrowed for the Myrick file folders. There were two, one a personal and health history, the other visit notes. The first was complete and unharmed.

The second had visit notes in it as Hart had confirmed during his earlier cursory file examination. But the notes were for another patient entirely: the right number of handwritten notes, but not about Myrick at all.

When Hart checked the other patient's file against the off chance that Charlene had accidentally switched pages, he found it almost empty, only a few early-session pages still there.

He sat back staring at the folders, and a spooky sense of connection seeped through him. Charlene, he thought, had not died during an accidental burglary, and the office hadn't been broken into by kids or dopers. Somebody had been after the Myrick records.

Which meant *what*?

He did not call the police. He couldn't see what would be gained except publicity about Myrick's mental condition prior to his death. Maybe later he would call and suggest a possible connection between the two deaths. And maybe he wouldn't run the risk of seeing Slagerfeldt's lip curl as he asked how long the doctor had been reading Dick Tracy.

It was getting dark when he finally left the office, locking up carefully and going down alone in the big, chilly elevator. The security man at the front door ushered him out with a little salute, and relocked the building doors behind him.

Hart cut across the corner of the parking lot, the darkest part, heading for his Pontiac. Automatically he dug his keychain out of his pants pocket to unlock the car door. He was preoccupied with his suspicions, and turned too late when the sudden scuffling sounds at his back made his nervous system shriek with the certainty that somebody was attacking him.

The figure was tall and indistinct, wearing a nylon mask over his face, and Hart had no time to see more than that because the man was swinging a wrench or tire iron and it was already inches from Hart's face, and it exploded against his forehead before he could see anything else.

The pain was extraordinary, and the blow dropped him to his knees. Blood filled his eyes and consciousness waivered. He had enough presence of mind remaining to know that his last-second flinching had prevented the heavy metal object from connecting with the solid, lethal perfection with which it had been aimed. He tried to move—to protect himself from another blow—and managed to lurch sideways.

The second blow paralyzed his left shoulder.

The third one would finish him.

A wave of blackness swept over him and he slid to his side, losing control for a moment and feeling his face bounce off the hot asphalt pavement. *Need help.* But he couldn't seem to make a sound.

The blurry figure—red and black from the blood in his eyes—moved in. Hart realized distantly that he was lying unmoving, the pain in his skull and shoulder a faraway roar that could not galvanize his muscles to action. His attacker was bending over him, reaching into his coat pocket. Hart got a glimpse of the tire iron. If the man struck again, he would be finished.

Months before, he had watched a TV show about Houston's newest wave of petty crime and violence, and had gone out the next day and purchased three small, leather-encased gas tubes filled—the store owner assured him—with CS gas. The store owner had shown him a little promotional filmstrip that illustrated the way a shot from the tube could temporarily blind an attacker if shot in his face, or cause excruciating, burning pain and nausea if it touched any bare skin anywhere on his body.

Hart had bought three of the gadgets and had put one in his office desk drawer, one in his nightstand at home, and one on the end of his keychain . . . the keychain still in his hand.

He felt his wallet being torn out of his coat pocket. The man stood upright again, and Hart had a blurry glimpse of the tire iron being raised for a killing blow.

Hart found the gas gun in his hand, raised his arm a few inches with a supreme effort, and pressed the stud on top. *If this doesn't work—!*

It worked.

He heard the little hissing sound. His attacker let

out a hoarse scream of pain. The tire iron hit the pavement with a metallic clatter. Something—Hart's billfold—thumped lightly against Hart's chest as it was dropped. Feet scuffled, retreated. As Hart mopped at half-blinded eyes with his handkerchief, he heard a car engine start, tires squeal away. A minute or two later, someone else was bending over him, but this time it was a building guard.

Building security, always comfortingly paranoid, called Hart's apartment even though the guards knew Christie on sight. Bandaged head throbbing, Hart waited in his open doorway for her to come out of the elevator.

When she did, it was like a soft tornado, running to him in concern. "Daddy, dammit, you're *hurt.*"

"I think I'll survive, babe."

"Why didn't you call me *earlier?*"

"I had to go get a few stitches. And then the police wanted a report."

"You should have called me anyway!" Christie, pretty in pink sweats, looked around the big living room. "Where's Kecia?"

"When I talked to her at noon, she said she was going to stay in tonight at her place and get papers graded."

"You mean you haven't *told* her about this?" Christie stamped her foot. "Sometimes I think I could throttle you!"

"I'll call her later. Or tomorrow."

"I think I should call her now!"

"Christie, God damn it, I've been banged on the head and I've got a roaring headache. Do you want to just sit down and shut up, or get the hell out of here?"

Instantly contrite, she came to hug him again. "I'm sorry."

"Sit here on the couch by me and calm down."

She obeyed. "Tell me what happened."

He did, leaving out—as he had with the police—the distant and troubling suspicion that the attack somehow might have been more than a random mugging. He had been helpless on the ground for a moment. His wallet had already been pulled free. But if he had not had the gas gun, he would be dead now, his skull split open by another blow that was in no way necessary.

"That's awful," Christie told him solemnly when he finished the abbreviated version. "I still think you ought to call Kecia."

"Later. Where's Don?"

"He'll be here soon."

Christie held his hand and lapsed into troubled silence.

Hart let it extend. He sensed her pain. But he was preoccupied about Myrick and the events that all seemed related to the death. He was beginning to feel scared shitless about Christie's flight. If there was something that threatened her in all this, he had to find it. But how?

As if reading his mind, Christie said, "It's a secret, but it looks like I'm off to Mars this week."

Hart tingled throughout his system as he turned to stare at her. "Jesus Christ. Said as if you were planning a trip to the grocery?"

Her smile was sunny. "Hey, what do you want? Trumpets? This is confidential stuff, Pop."

He gathered himself from the surprise. So he had even less time than he had imagined.

He reverted to office form for a moment as he tried to regain his own equilibrium: "So how are you feeling about it?"

"A little excited. A little scared. A little worried I might screw up."

"And that's all?" He watched her closely, this girl he loved so.

She held her bright smile. "Sure." The smile cracked and she started to cry without making a sound.

"Aw, babe," he muttered, taking her into his arms.

She shook. "Damn Don anyway. He ought to know I'm weirded out by the whole thing. Does he think I'm a damned robot? Of course I'm scared! But all he can think about is being lonesome, and scared I'll change and he'll lose me—which makes it almost a sure thing he *will* lose me!"

The last was almost a wail. Her pretty eyes showed just how deeply scared and upset she was.

"Hey, I'll talk to him," Hart told her. "Maybe it will be just fine. I know you're scared and a little angry, babe. I am, too. I almost wish you weren't on this darn thing—"

"Oh, Daddy! Not you too!"

He pulled her close again. "No! I support you all the way, Christie. You know that. You're going to go and return just fine."

"The Russians," she said, muffled against his chest, "are in orbit already. We've got to get started too. Fast."

A few years earlier, the idea of a crewed journey to Mars would have seemed out of the question. Both the United States and Russia had quietly scaled down and militarized their space programs. Both also tried to recoup a fraction of their still-huge space budgets by selling to private industry or other nations such services as orbital satellite placement, oceanographic photo studies, chemistry and crystal formation experiments, etc. It seemed epochal voyages into deep space would remain the stuff of science fiction for a long time to come.

Another science fiction cliché became shocking reality, however, in October of 1989. And everything changed forever, nothing would ever be quite the same again.

Norwegian radio astronomers, using newly enhanced low-noise amplifying devices and computer massage techniques designed to screen out outwanted background hash ranging from the noise of catastrophic star system collisions to the malfunction of a doctor's X-ray machine, heard something quite unexpected at a wavelength close to six centimeters.

The Norwegians checked their equipment repeatedly, eliminated all the possible errors they could think of, and finally notified both Great Britain and the Soviet Union. Within hours—to the Norwegians' intense relief—the British, Russians, and Americans were all hearing the same super-faint signals, and not understanding how they could be there, either.

No one heard the periodic, repetitive signals quite as well as the Norwegians did at first. That was because other Earth radio antennae were not tuned to quite this portion of the radio frequency spectrum. The Norwegians had adjusted their dishes, amplifiers, and receivers to the frequency range as part of ongoing experiments with capture ratios and distant-object tracking error.

Within weeks, however, everyone was hearing the same thing at the same signal strength level, feeble, given to unpredictable fading due to the effects of space on polarization. Detection of the signals at their strongest would have been impossible only a year earlier, before the state of the art in low-noise amplification and computer enhancement took one of its periodic leaps forward.

The pulses were simple and always the same. On the screen of a monitoring device, they appeared like this:

•
••
•••
••••
•••••

Repeating monotonously, endlessly, with precision timing.

Someone somewhere was counting to five.

Tracking was not difficult. The signals were being generated from somewhere near the enormous abyss of Valles Marineris, in the southern hemisphere of the planet Mars.

Viking spacecraft, and the earlier Mariners, had carried no equipment to monitor systematically for such radio signals. Scientists agreed that there was some kind of radio beacon out there, and it was beeping away at us as it may have been doing for centuries . . . eons.

The technology to build such a virtually eternal beacon was beyond Earth's science. The existence of this bit of advanced technology suggested that there might be considerably more. A consensus quickly developed that the beacon must exist as more than a cosmic trick; whatever race had placed it there had done so for a reason—to signal other cultures and serve as a homing device. Would an alien race have gone so far (the thinking went) without burying or otherwise preserving its own history—and scientific secrets—somewhere nearby?

The radio beacon signaled the likely existence of a wealth of knowledge and practical technology that Earth scientists by themselves might require centuries to reach. That kind of knowledge and technology equated with power—perhaps limitless, unchallengeable power.

The president of the United States proposed a joint expedition to investigate, with the U.S. and Soviet Union pooling know-how and eventual crew. The Soviets rejected the proposal as a trick. India declared on the floor of the United Nations (just before it became finally defunct) that the superpowers had no right to toy with the future of mankind in any unilateral way, and then marched its armies into Pakistan on the pretext that this unsettled era was no time for allowing a hostile neighbor to continue border provocations. Iraq attacked Iran again. France signed a pact with West Germany to form a new consortium that would build an unmanned radio probe to send to the Mars-site beacon. Both the United States and Russia started independent crewed probe projects. And the race was on. . . .

Those decisions, however, were by now practically ancient history at the pace of the world of the '90s. The race was *now*. Everybody knew that the winner of the race to Mars might rule the world till the end of time. Everybody except the religious extremists knew that the trip had to be made. Everybody agreed on who should win, for the good of humankind. Of course there were several groups out there claiming to be "everybody."

Hart only knew that he wanted America to win. And that the thought of Christie going—within days—scared hell out of him.

She caught his stare and made a face at him, startling him. "What are you *thinking* about so hard?" she demanded.

"You," he admitted. "And being scared."

"I'm not really scared, exactly. I'm not."

"I am."

Christie made a little mewing sound and scrunched across the couch for another hug. He had to stifle a very strong impulse to just bawl. He felt desperate and helpless.

When Don arrived later, he found them holding hands and talking about a time when Christie had been a child and she caught a fish and fell out of a boat, and her father instantly reached over the side and rescued her. Both Hart and his daughter were laughing about it. Don manfully joined in, trying to hide the pressure he felt building around him and Christie.

For his part, Hart was feeling the thump of a ticking clock in his mind. MarsProbe was going up Wednesday or Thursday of *this week*. He could count in hours the amount of time he had to find out if Myrick's death meant peril for the mission. And all he had to go on was his memory.

Program in . . . Are you silver . . . plus or minus seven days. . . . What in hell did any of it mean—if it meant anything? How could he find out? What was he missing here? He felt like a vise was closing on his chest.

six

Space mechanic Joe Retvig gave a little final tug with the spanner, seeing the pressure gauge rise exactly to the pounds-pressure specified on the wrist card of his EVA suit for this clamp.

"Done over here," he said to his shift mates via the helmet radio.

"One more touch," radioed his buddy Ingersoll, farther out on the strut.

"Finished here," Simmons commented, floating free, a blinding silver reflection, on his tether cord.

Retvig heaved a little sigh of satisfaction, looking from the massive shadow of the Central Lab Module out through the gleaming geometry of girders and tower sections to the linked shuttle, astride its huge boosters and fuel tank. Inside the shuttle, technicians had finished final checkout of instrument systems and the Mars lander. Only a few routine communications checks remained undone.

Adventurer was ready for its crew.

Retvig had been working out of the CLM for almost two months. He was more than tired; he wondered if his slowly lowering calcium levels had anything to do with the general feeling of fatigue. He wondered how long it would take back on Earth for the daily monitoring to show his body returned to normal gravitational conditions once more.

He would be glad to get home. He thought of the MarsProbe crew, probably coming up within the next couple of days. After they entered the shuttle and began final checkouts, the same ship that had brought them up to orbit would take Retvig and the other construction workers back down. Retvig thought of the seventeen months that the trip crew would be in space, a zillion miles from home.

He didn't envy them. It was too far to travel, too dangerous, too filled with uncertainties. He just wasn't brave enough for that sort of thing, Retvig thought, releasing his grip on the aluminum strut and wafting gently out to the end of his tether 200 miles above the Earth.

Dr. Boyd Reynolds slowed his car as he approached the gate to the space center, being ultra-cautious about the forty-odd pickets straggled out in a line near the entrance. They were middle-aged, most of them, and mostly women, and they had signs with messages like GOD SAYS NO, PRIDE GOETH BEFORE THE FALL, FIRST FEED THE POOR, and PROVERBS 13:17. A brisk, humid Texas wind buffeted their signs and caked faces with gritty dirt.

Reynolds showed his laser photo pass at the heavily guarded gate and pulled through. The continuing presence of the pickets depressed him. The threat from terrorists was bad enough. But feeling among some of the fundamentalists was almost as extreme, and there had been violence near Huntsville on two occasions. As a scientist, Reynolds couldn't understand the bitterness of the religious opposition to MarsProbe.

He had even gone so far as to look up the persistent reference to Proverbs. He knew it read:

*A wicked messenger brings on
disaster,
But a trustworthy envoy is a
healing remedy.*

He didn't get it. If they wanted to attack the project, he thought, they would have been more rational to use another Proverb he had stumbled across in searching for theirs: *Boast not of tomorrow, for you know not what any day may bring forth.*

Parking in his assigned slot, he entered the main computer wing and walked directly, carrying his attaché case, through the security points and labs where a dozen or more of his colleagues were burning weekend oil at readout screens. He waved to a few people, but kept walking, entering the central computer section alone.

No one else was around. The massive mainframe computer sections loomed in the dimness of the frigid room like unmoving monsters out of a spook film.

His pulse rising, Reynolds walked directly into the D section, put his attaché case on a work table, extended a ribbon cable from the small NEC machine in the case to a twenty-five–pin socket on the control panel of the mainframe unit, plugged in, rapidly punched a few switches, set up his little NEC, and started high-speed data transfer out of the big computer's memory into the portable unit that belonged to him.

The transfer took less than three minutes at 9600 baud, but Reynolds was soaked in cold sweat by the time he powered down, latched his attaché case again, and left the section to hurry to his own primary work area.

Two hours later, he left the complex and drove back into Houston, parking at an all-day breakfast cafe not far from the Astrodome. He sat at a corner booth and ordered coffee, which tasted rancid when it came.

Ten minutes later, Smith and Jones walked in, walked over, sat down facing him across the table.

He knew their real names almost certainly were not Smith and Jones. Their bald use of obviously contrived names added to his sense of humiliation. But there was nothing he could do about that, either. It was all part of his entrapment.

The waitress came by and poured coffee for the newcomers. Jones stolidly stirred in some sugar and artificial creamer. Smith, younger and sandy-haired, an all-American boy type, exchanged jokes with the girl, who went away blushing a little with pleasure.

Then Smith eyed Reynolds. "You have what we asked for?"

Reynolds took the magazine off the seat beside him and slid it across the table. Smith took the magazine and put it under his arm, careful not to bend the compact diskette hidden among the pages. The silent Jones, meanwhile, fished a folded copy of a neighborhood newspaper advertising supplement out of the hip pocket of his slacks and leaned across the table, partly unfolding it as if to show Reynolds an item inside.

"This is interesting," Jones said. "See?"

Taped inside the folded throwaway was a white envelope.

Sweating again, Reynolds took the paper containing his payment. "Yes. I see. Good."

Smith leaned forward. "Now we have some new requirements for you."

"No," Reynolds pleaded. "No more. I can't go on like this."

Smith ignored his plea and calmly outlined for him his new instructions. Reynolds listened with a feeling like death, knowing he would weakly obey. He had to have the money. And now they had him anyway: if he refused to cooperate, they could turn him in.

*   *   *

About one hour after the coffee-shop meeting, the one who called himself Smith, wearing a summer suit and tie now, walked into a dim cocktail bar in a downtown hotel. Mona Reynolds, looking beautiful and expensive, was seated alone at a booth along the far wall.

Smith joined her.

"Hi," she said huskily, giving him a smoldering appraisal. "You're late."

"Sorry. I had some business. Are you keeping the pressure on as we asked?"

Her smile was cruel. "Tonight I plan to tell him about a trip to New York next week."

"Where you'll spend lots, right?"

"Oh, my yes. —You know, this is *my* kind of work: being paid to spend money."

Smith did not smile. "It doesn't bother you? Maintaining this kind of financial pressure on your husband?"

"He's a penny-pinching creep," Mona clipped. "We have lots of money in those trusts, if he wasn't too cheap to give up the tax shelter to get to some of it. Why should I suffer because he has this *illness* about saving for his old age?"

"Precisely," Smith said with a little smile. And he handed her an envelope thick with money.

"Goodie," Mona purred, putting it in her purse. "Something for *my* old age."

"Aren't you going to count it?" Smith asked.

"Not now," Mona said. She added, "You know what I want now."

"Tell me."

Her voice lowered. "I want to go to bed with you."

"Room six-oh-five," Smith said, and got up and walked out. Mona followed almost immediately.

"Adventurer, *this is Houston*," the radio signal hissed.

Flying right seat inside the sealed crew compartment, Christie Hart scanned the banks of instruments and computer displays before replying. They were right on the line, timing of the maneuver within nanoseconds, and all three onboards agreed. Christie touched the transmit button. "Houston, *Adventurer*," she replied.

"Adventurer, *we'll run the midcourse correction sequence one more time.*"

Behind Christie, in the third chair, H. O. Townsend muttered over the closed cabin intercom, "Balls."

Christie looked at command pilot Buck Colltrap, seeing the same strained irritation on his face. There was a slight air-conditioning malfunction inside the simulator, and all three of them were hot, sweaty, and wrung out after three hours of constant nervous tension.

Colltrap touched his transmit button to speak to the training crew outside: "Jack, this is Colltrap. We hit the maneuver on the money. This was supposed to be a one-hour tuneup. It's now going into the fourth hour. What's the story?"

Davidson Myrick's replacement as chief of crew training operations, Jack Schaeffly, stiffly refused to break from simulator protocol. "Adventurer, *Houston*," he came back in his flat, nasal twang. *"Our No. 2 computer indicates short burn of two seconds, over."*

Again on the closed intercom, Townsend said, "One nice final little runthrough just to keep us sharp before we go to the Cape, they said. Then this SOB starts feeling his Wheaties and feeding horse manure into the computers to keep us drilling half the night. He can keep manufacturing simulation errors from now till hell freezes over."

"What do you suggest?" Colltrap asked, also on intercom. He was angry too, holding it icily under control.

"What say we just open the hatch, go out there, and beat shit out of the sucker?"

Colltrap seemed to ponder the idea for a moment as if it had been seriously suggested. "Negative," he said finally, and touched his transmit control. "Houston, *Adventurer*, standing by to copy new computer reset parameters."

"*Roger*, Adventurer. *Stand by for update.*"

Christie took a deep breath and attended to the computer resets. Waiting for data, she looked into the deck below where her twisted-wire amateur radio antenna was taped to a window, her two-meter handi-talkie and extra batteries in a nylon sack nearby. She would not be the first amateur radio operator in space. Owen Garriott, W5LFL, had had that honor, and others had followed, using personal ham gear to make random contacts with eager fellow amateurs operating low-power two-meter stations back on earth. Christie, however, would certainly be the first to beam back feeble signals in the 146-MHz frequency from deep space.

Today was supposed to have been a short drill, and her personal schedule allowed Christie time to do some final testing of the fine-wire antenna bent in a roughly circular configuration and designed to operate through one of *Adventurer*'s windows after being taped in place. She would use a standard Icom two-meter handi-talkie and a small linear amplifier to boost output to about thirty watts. When *Adventurer* was positioned so that the line-of-sight signals would reach Earth—and when Christie had time—she would provide many lucky hams with the longest-range VHF "QSO" in history.

Today Christie was supposed to have had time to test her ham gear by making a few contacts through the radio frequency energy-muffling effects of the surrounding building. But not now. Jack Schaeffly's interminable simulated problems had worn them out and left Christie no time for play.

"Adventurer, *Houston*," the radio crackled. "*Stand by for computer update.*"

It was another hour later when they finally climbed out of the mockup, and Jack Schaeffly, cool and calm (and looking a little officious), met them at the bottom of the ladder.

"Good drill," he said with his cool smile.

Buck Colltrap bellied up to him, nose-to-nose, like an angry manager confronting an inept umpire. "You God damned *jerk*," he snarled, using the hardest language in his vocabulary. "We're supposed to be sharpening up for final countdown and injection into orbit, and you've wrung us out instead. What the hell are you trying to do? Get us so fine we'll get up there and screw up?"

"A little extra training never hurts," Schaeffly said.

"Myrick didn't even have this runthrough scheduled."

"Myrick," Schaeffly replied frostily, "is no longer in charge."

Christie and Townsend exchanged glances. But Colltrap, still in an uncharacteristic rage, said it for them first: "Is that what this is all about, Schaeffly? Proving you're in charge now?"

"If you have a complaint, commander, take it on up to LeRoy."

"I intend to." Colltrap walked off angrily.

Christie followed slowly, a little discouraged. This was supposed to be a gathering high, the buildup to the great flight, and Schaeffly's bureaucratic nonsense had hurt their crew effectiveness, taken away that pleasant edge of readiness and replaced it with fatigue and anger.

Didn't he know better? It was almost as if he wanted to sabotage them. *Calm down, calm down,* she told herself. *He just feels insecure and needs to establish his authority. No harm done. Don't start seeing bogeymen before the scary part even gets under way.*

She glanced at her wrist chronograph, something she had caught herself doing a lot in the past number of hours. Every time she noted the time, she subtracted it from the timetable uppermost in her mind: *It's launch to orbit minus twenty-two hours right now.*

She wondered how apprehensive Colltrap and Townsend really felt. She wished she didn't have the little compartment of fear down deep inside.

But then, she told herself, if she weren't apprehensive, she would really be crazy. And that made her feel somewhat better.

She hurried. Don would be waiting, and this evening they would have dinner at their favorite spot, then go back home for a few hours alone. She would call her father, too, to reassure herself there had been no aftereffects from the mugging, and to tell him again she loved him. And then an Air Force jet would take her and her fellow astronauts to the Cape. She felt a pang of love and regret; it was going to be so long . . . out there.

Inside the headphones of Soviet cosmonauts Alexi Picaran and Valeriy Zubakov, the final numbers of the countdown tolled mechanically. *Sixty seconds,* and the final status light rundown showed clear. *Fifty seconds,* backup pumps energized, recorders on. *Forty seconds,* all controls auto, gyro functions check. *Thirty seconds,* computer reset functions and electrical backups, check. *Twenty seconds,* launch extender arms activated and retracted. *Ten.*

Sweat trickling down his face inside the plastic dome of his helmet, Alexi breathed deeply, trying to calm his rising heartbeat. A glance at Commander Zubakov showed him intent on the digital readout scrolling past his eyes on the overhead data console. *Does he have a heart at all?* Alexi wondered.

It was a thought unworthy of a patriot and finely honed Soviet space scientist, he reminded himself sternly, and he banished it.

Alexi was a veteran of four space missions, including crew on the first *Mir* space station long ago. At forty-four, he was second only to Zubakov in longevity within the active ranks of the service, and in space time. Selection as crew member on this cosmic voyage was the highlight of a life which began as the son of a peasant farmer and proceeded through years of effort—for notice by proper officials, for demonstrating his loyalty in the military, for struggling to excell in his late-starting formal education and training. Alexi had spent his life fighting to become all that he could be, for that was what his father had taught him every man must do, and he was pride-filled to be part of this venture.

And yet, at this instant as the countdown went past *five*, and he saw his commander's hand tighten slightly on the backup manual firing control in case of failure by the Earth computer ignition system, he felt nervousness, uncertainty, awe . . . fear. He was thinking of Irina, his wife, and their two children, and the grandson who had just been born. *He will be walking before I return to hold him.*

If I return.

He banished that unwanted thought, too.

Excitement filled him as the count reached *three*. He braced himself. This he was doing for his family, for his motherland, for history, he reminded himself. There was no more time for brooding about the unknown perils ahead . . . or about the odd tension and preoccupation which had so seemed to change his commander, the intrepid Zubakov, seated close beside him.

Everything, he told himself, would be as planned, and his name would be known for all of history.

Zero, and with a thumping vibration, the solid rockets fired and jolted the spacecraft away from the docking station *Lenin* and onto its escape course.

Alexi realized through the vibrating racket that an unfamiliar sound was roaring in his headphones. Alarmed, he looked at his commander. Zubakov held his arms above his head, and his face and neck were distorted through the visor glass of his helmet.

"We fly!" Zubakov was shouting in exultation. "We fly! We fly!"

New York: drizzling rain. In the Beekman Place apartment, the two businessmen finished discussing the telephone call they had just received. On the couch of the sumptuous apartment, their Iranian colleague sat comfortably barefooted, oiling a .45-caliber automatic.

"You'll go to Houston," one of the businessmen told the other. "Make sure our contacts are solid and that no last-minute glitches take place."

"*Ja.*" The second man nodded stolidly. "There is only now the counting down, is it not so?"

"Yes," the first man said with grim satisfaction.

On the couch, the Iranian diplomat slammed the receiver of his pistol open, then let it hammer closed with a cold, menacing clack of steel on steel.

"Can't you put that thing down for five minutes?" the British businessman exploded.

The Iranian's chocolate eyes studied him with contempt. "If any phase of this operation falters, my good friend, you may be very glad to have me and my weapon at your side."

seven

It was not yet 7:30 A.M. Monday morning when Hart angrily slammed his car to a halt beside the Houston police car in his professional complex parking lot, hurried through still-dim halls, and walked into the gaping doorway of his office suite.

The outer office was a wreck: furniture overturned, books and clerical materials out of the reception desk strewn everywhere, magazines thrown from the corner rack. Two uniformed policemen were poking at table surfaces with their little fingerprint dusting kits. The chief of building security, a rumpled, middle-aged man named Johnston, watched morosely. He was wearing the building security gray slacks and shirt, and had a useless Motorola hand-held radio on his belt.

Seeing Hart, he hurried over. "Doctor, I can't tell you how upset I am about this—"

Hart struggled to keep his temper in check. "You're not half as upset as I am. Was somebody caught this time?"

Johnston nervously licked his lips. "No, sir. The ingress was noted at 6 A.M. during the routine tour of the building—"

"Maybe your security is too routine! What do I have to do, hire my own guard?"

Johnston stiffened. "Doctor, our area security is the best. Given the size of this complex, we provide excellent—"

"Excellent? *Excellent?* They killed someone Friday night and weren't seen. They broke in again last night and weren't seen. Do you expect some kind of medal because they didn't break in one night over the weekend?"

Johnston gave him a cold, old-cop stare. "No need for sarcasm."

"I'll tell you what there's a need for. Some God damned security in this building! Jesus Christ!"

The door to his inner office swung back and Bud Slagerfeldt walked in. "Thanks, Fred," he told Johnston. "I'll get back to you."

The older man stuffed his shirttail into his pants, started to say something else to Hart, and then turned and walked angrily out. Hart turned on Slagerfeldt. "What did they take this time? Was anybody hurt or killed this time, or do we declare a moral victory?"

"You were a little hard on old Fred."

"It's a little hard on me, being broken into every other night! And the night they don't break in, they clobber me in the parking lot."

"Temper, temper."

"My ass!"

Slagerfeldt looked at him keenly, his eyes on the small bandage covering the stitches high on his forehead. "I guess you've got cause to be upset. I only learned about the mugging in the parking lot late last night, going through some of the routine squad car reports. —Do you really think the people who broke in here were involved in hitting you in the lot?"

"How the hell should I know? You're the cop."

"How do you feel? Physically, I mean."

"My head hurts."

"Good thing you had that little gas gun."

"Yes."

"Of course it's a violation of city ordinance to carry a concealed weapon like that."

"Fuck you."

The detective grinned. "Yeah. Well, you can see what they did in here. I'm afraid they pulled out a lot of filing cabinet drawers in the other office and rifled your desk."

Hart pressed past him and went through the inner doorway to confront the dismaying mess beyond. It looked like *all* the file folders had been pulled out, their contents strewn everywhere in a ghastly jumble. His desk drawers had been taken out, too, and evidently overturned on the floor, then thrown aside.

"It will take a week to get some of this straightened out," Hart groaned. "Some of it we may never get refiled in the right places."

Slagerfeldt followed him in through the wreckage. "What are they looking for, doc?"

"I don't have any idea," Hart lied.

"Have you made somebody mad at you lately?"

"You mean, is this revenge? I can't think of anyone."

"You shrinks do deal with some weird people."

"So do you cops. But I can't believe any of my patients might have done this."

Slagerfeldt's lips turned down. "Of course there's always the chance that it's a series of coincidences . . . the burglary and killing Friday night, the attack on you last night, this new break-in."

"Do *you* think it's coincidence?" Hart demanded.

"No. Do you?"

"No."

Slagerfeldt pounced. "Then what are they looking for?"

"I have no idea."

The detective lit a cigarette, seemed to consider something, then made a private decision. "Look at it this way. You have a burglary and your secretary is killed. Then this guy Myrick jumps or falls . . . or gets tossed . . . off his apartment balcony. And you were treating Myrick. Then *maybe* somebody tries to take your wallet, or *maybe* somebody tries to kill you and make it *look* like a mugging. Now you get broken into again. What does all that suggest to you?"

Hart decided he didn't have to act like a complete idiot to protect Myrick's confidentiality. "Theory: someone knew Myrick was seeing me. They feared he would tell me something—God knows what—that would get them in trouble. They were so desperate that they killed Myrick. Then they came here, broke in, looked for something in his file. Didn't find it. Worried about what I might know. Decided they had to take me out, too. Came back and searched the office again."

"It sounds a little like *Miami Vice*, but I'll buy it as a working hypothesis. So I have to ask you: What did Myrick tell you? What did you have, or what do you know, that somebody would kill for?"

"Nothing. —And that's the God's truth, Lieutenant."

"I believe you. I almost wish I didn't. If I suspected you were withholding information, it might give me someplace to go."

"Do you think Myrick might have been murdered?"

"Officially, no."

"Unofficially—?"

"You're *sure* you don't have anything worth stealing that relates to Myrick in any way?"

"I had an audio cassette. It was a recording of my last hour with Dave. Charlene had it. But the killer took that Friday night."

"Was there stuff on the tape—?"

"Bud, I've gone over that hour in my memory a hundred times. Except for some odd therapeutic problems, I can't think of anything that would incriminate anyone."

"Not even Myrick?"

"That may be the line a reporter from the newspaper is on."

Slagerfeldt's eyes narrowed. "Who?"

"Blyleven is his name."

"That prick. He thinks he smells dirt to splatter on NASA, I guess. He's a damned pest."

Hart was surprised. "He's talked to you, too?"

"Yes, but he doesn't know anything. He asked me about you. Somehow he learned Myrick was seeing you. He said he had met Myrick once, and got the impression he had never had a sick day in his life."

"Bud, he told me he played golf with Myrick sometimes."

Slagerfeldt sighed. "Well, reporters lie to get info sometimes. —You're *sure* there's nothing here—was nothing here—that would justify all this mess?"

"Nothing."

"Okay. I'll keep on keeping on." The detective turned toward the door, then looked back. "This has got to be really horseshit for you, with your daughter just arriving down there at the Cape for the space shot. You don't need something extra to worry about."

"She wants to go, Bud. She's lived her life for this. I'm scared. But she wants it."

"I wish nobody was going."

Hart was quietly astonished. "This is probably the most significant event in the history of our race. This is the contact that poets and philosophers and scientists have dreamed about for ages. When we get out there to Mars and find that beacon, we may find information—history—further instructions—that will make everything that's happened to us before seem like child's play."

"So we race, and the commies are already ahead of us, and those assholes in Europe and all the religious nuts and Third World countries would like to see both of us fall on our faces. Is it worth it?" Slagerfeldt cocked his head in sincere puzzlement. "Is it *really* worth this kind of rhubarb and hassle?"

"Bud, it's worth anything. It really is. This is—what was the name of that old book?—*Childhood's End*."

Slagerfeldt sighed like a very old man and started to walk out. Then he remembered something and turned back again. "By the way, I'm sure you know that Myrick had been in a private hospital in Dallas just a couple months ago? A hospital that specializes in head cases?"

Surprise made Hart's nerves tingle. "No. What hospital?"

"Parkview Limited."

"I never heard of it."

"It's small."

"He went for psychiatric treatment, you say?"

"Asthmatic bronchitis and depression, their records say."

"He didn't tell me."

"He was in there four days, over a long weekend. They say he was discharged after some hypnotherapy and attitude discussion. Gave him a prescription for an inhaler. He was improved when he left, they said."

"Hypnotherapy?" Hart echoed.

"I looked it up." Slagerfeldt's eyes were like mercury, unreadable. "It seems things like asthma often get worse because of stress. A little hypnotherapy and sometimes you get your attitude readjusted a little so you can cope better, and it makes you less prone to asthma attacks. But I'm sure you know all that. It's your line of work."

"I didn't know he had been treated in Dallas or anywhere else."

"Was that what he came to you for?"

"What?"

"He came to you for asthma?"

"No. Just . . . a little nervous tension."

"No big crisis in his life? No enemies breathing down his neck?"

"Bud, you asked all this before. The answers are the same. No."

Slagerfeldt shrugged. "No harm trying. I'll be in touch."

Left alone, Hart looked with renewed dismay at the unholy mess. *What was someone looking for?*

He was nonplussed about the information concerning Myrick's treatment or treatments in Dallas. A complete history had been taken, and Myrick hadn't so much as hinted at any recent trip to Dallas and Parkview Limited. Why had Myrick held out? If he had held this out, what else might he have hidden? And— it kept nagging—what had that break in the trance signified, when Myrick momentarily talked gibberish?

Try as he might, he couldn't make it make sense.

But he *had to make it make sense.* In so few hours, Christie and her companions would launch. And then it might be too late, if there was a basis in reality for his galloping fears.

What was he forgetting? What wasn't he seeing from the right set of assumptions, to bring sense out of this? *Plus or minus seven days . . . mission failure . . . program in . . . are you silver. . . .* It was driving him crazy with fear and frustration.

He was getting nowhere, and time was running out. He couldn't go to NASA or anyone else with suspicions based on nothing.

Nervously he started stacking files haphazardly on the desk. There was no way he would be able to see patients today, or perhaps for the rest of the week. They would all have to be called and referred to one of two other good men in the complex. When the temporary receptionist came in, she was going to have a lot of telephoning to do.

After leaving Hart's office, Detective Bud Slagerfeldt went to a pay telephone and got through to his superior. He explained what he wanted and why he wanted it.

"Bud, I understand your concern," his superior said when he had concluded. "But we can't spare a man for surveillance of that kind on the basis of what you've told me. We couldn't spare anybody for a stakeout right now if you were talking corporate president or Akeem himself. Sorry."

"Give me a cadet out of the training class, then," Slagerfeldt said.

"We've got no cars."

"Put him in one of those junkers we've got in the motor pool, waiting for auction."

"You want this bad, don't you?"

"Yes, sir. Real bad."

There was a pause. Then: "Okay. You'll have a trainee and a trash cruiser and a walkie-talkie. But not indefinitely, do you hear me? Just a few days. A week at the outside."

"Great," Slagerfeldt said, and hung up.

Hart returned to his office after lunch to see how the cleanup was going. Things in the outer office were beginning to look normal again, and his temporary had almost finished contacting patients scheduled for appointments over the week.

Johnston, the security man, came back.

"I talked to Mr. Billinghurst," Johnston said. "We're going to change all the locks on the offices. *All*. And add two more nightwatchmen."

"Fine." Hart started for the inner office.

"Oh, doc?"

"Yes?"

"When the boys ran their broom under the counter, there, they found that thing I left on the counter for you."

Hart looked and saw a dusty cassette tape on the empty counter.

"It was on the floor all the way in the back, out of sight," Johnston added. "I suppose it's old, but I thought I ought to call your attention to it."

Chilled, Hart examined the cassette. On the pale green front label, in his handwritten block printing, was the identifier: MYRICK: SESSION #4.

He understood. When Charlene was killed, this tape had somehow gotten knocked to the floor and out of sight. The ransacker had been frustrated on that visit, and again last night, not finding what he (she?) had been looking for.

This tape.

And now he had it.

"Doc?" Johnston said. "You okay? You kinda lost your color there."

Hart regained control of himself. "I'm fine. Thanks for finding this for me." He slipped it into his suit pocket.

He had to play it. It might tell him everything his memory had let through the cracks.

But finding it was not an unalloyed blessing. If his fears were correct, somebody had already killed for the information he now possessed.

eight

Wednesday. They had been in the orbital docking vehicle atop its rocket on the launch pad for almost five hours, and it was getting old.

After a long silence, the radio voice came: "*Zeus, this is Mission Control.*"

"*Zeus*, go ahead," Commander Buck Colltrap said, his face calm behind the spherical plastic mask of the helmet.

"*Zeus, ah, be advised the winds aloft continue to gust at thirty knots and we have decided to scrub for today, over.*"

"Roger, understand scrubbing the launch for today," Colltrap said, and reached up to start loosening the connectors on his helmet.

"*Stand by for hatch opening. Prepare to leave the spacecraft.*"

"Roger," Colltrap repeated. He unfastened and removed his helmet.

Beside him, Christie Hart got her helmet off, tugged the torso restraining straps loose, and flexed an arm that had gotten a little stiff. Behind her, H. O. Townsend muttered, "Damn. Damndy damn damn damn!"

"You can't engineer the weather," Colltrap observed with a trace of weariness.

"At least we didn't get scrubbed by a computer malfunction, like yesterday," Christie observed.

"And now," Townsend drawled, "having looked at the bright side, let's all go beat our heads against the bulkhead for a while."

Outside they could hear the first sounds of the gantry team coming off the elevator to reopen the hatch that had been sealed at 0530. Colltrap and Christie went through the power-down routine, watching arrays of light-emitting diodes dull and go dark.

"If we make it tomorrow or Friday," Colltrap said unnecessarily, "we'll still have the good window for LFO."

"The Launch From Orbit window will still be open," Christie pointed out, "but every day's delay puts the Russians that much farther ahead of us."

"Yes, Christie," Colltrap said with that irritatingly superior, super-cool test pilot voice he used sometimes. "But we've got more than a week's slack in our new intercept course. You know that."

"Yes," she replied, feeling testy. "But what happens if they change course and are there when we swing into Mars Orbit? What happens if we're on the ground and *they* arrive and come down to join us?"

"You know very well what happens. Every contingency has been covered."

"All I know," Christie responded, "is that we have nothing remotely resembling a weapon on board, and we've told them that, and they've issued their version of the 'peace in outer space' line, too."

"It's not just a line," Colltrap said, continuing in his lecture-hall tone. "Both sides thoroughly subscribe to the Geneva Space Doctrine of 1990."

"And both sides are still putting up more spy and antimissile satellites," Christie pointed out.

"That's another matter."

"*How?*"

Metallic clanking in the hatch area broke off their conversation. Realizing they were all a little cranky from the long wait, tension, and disappointment, Christie and her teammates grinned sheepishly at one another as they finished unstrapping and prepared to clamber out of the vehicle.

Getting heavily out of his seat, H. O. Townsend started thinking about the steak he was going to have.

Christie thought about Don and her dad, and how disappointed they must be; she would call them as soon as possible.

Buck Colltrap, momentarily fuguing into an altered mental state, wondered if the .38 caliber revolver hidden in his personal effects locker behind them would be secure, realized that his instructions provided no contingency for worrying about such a matter, returned to normal cognitive patterns, and forgot that the other thoughts had ever been in his mind.

Richard Hart had stayed home from his office reorganization to allow himself total concentration on television coverage of the launch. Like millions of other Americans, he experienced disappointment when the day's scrub was announced. Unlike other Americans, who didn't have a daughter on board, he also was aware of intense relief.

But now she would have to go tomorrow.

After calling the office to make sure his temporary was on duty and there were no emergencies, Hart returned to his home stereo system and reran the office cassette back to the marked area to play it still another time. He had played it oftener than he liked, and he still had no clue.

As he started the tape, the sounds from his office

last Friday filled the headphones he slipped over his
ears:

   *"Remember that you can change. You can—and will—
find the dreams becoming less frightening, and in the days
ahead you will find the daytime fears also becoming easier to
handle. In a short time—a day or two, perhaps, from this
hour plus seven days at the most—"*

   "Plus seven days? Crew. Unforeseen. Program in. Program in. Program in. One hundred. Sixty-eight. Sixty-eight.
Are you silver? Are you silver?"

   "Explain what you mean."

   "The mission will fail. My role is crucial."

   "No, Dave. The mission will succeed."

   "You don't understand! It will fail! Sixty-eight! Sixty-
eight. Are you silver?"

   *"Dave! It's all right! Close your eyes. Relax again. . . .
It's all right. Close your eyes."*

   The tape fell silent for a moment, and he remembered Myrick obeying, breathing more slowly again,
returning to trance. Then his own voice resumed:

   *"In the days ahead, you'll feel better. The dreams, no
longer necessary, can fade. You know, Dave, that you will
not die, you will not cooperate in your dying, you will not
kill anyone else, you will not go crazy. You understand these
things?"*

   "Yes."

   Hart switched off the tape. The living room was
silent. He rubbed aching eyes and tried to see something he was missing.

   He couldn't find a thing.

   Davidson Myrick had slipped out of one altered
state into another, and back again. It was a unique
event in Hart's experience, and he wished he could
understand precisely what had taken place psychologically.

   But theory wasn't as vital now as meaning. If
there was meaningful information in the recorded

mishmash, it was so obscure that he couldn't get even close to decoding it. Fate had given him another few hours, if MarsProbe was somehow in danger. He had played the tape until he had it fully memorized now. But he seemed no closer. Was he missing something crucial, or was his theory about the value of the cassette a dumb, melodramatic fantasy on his part?

The mission will fail.

The key, if there was one, had to be in the numbers. *One hundred. Sixty-eight. Plus seven days.* But they meant nothing to him.

"God dammit," he said aloud to himself. "You can't waltz into NASA like a hysterical daddy, and violate professional confidentiality, and tell them they've got to stop a trillion-dollar mission because you've got wet pants on the basis of *nothing*. You've got to have some facts. There's something you're missing on this tape. There's got to be, if anything is really going on here."

He was tempted to call the office and cancel the day's work, then call Kecia and cancel their evening's date. But his head hurt, and he knew that more than once in the past he had found the solution to a complex problem by *looking away from it*, doing something else for a while so that his unconscious mind could work at its own pace and make lateral connections that logic would never have found.

Maybe it would work this time, too.

So thinking, he changed clothes. A little later, he went down to the garage and drove off for work, avoiding the white Oldsmobile with a man in it that was parked illegally in the complex driveway.

In the bowels of the space center near Houston, NASA Director Warner Klindeinst faced three members of his inner circle: Project Director John Selmon;

Chief of Operations LeRoy Ditwhiler, and Chief of Crew Operations Jack Schaeffly.

"Then we definitely are a 'go' for tomorrow morning?" Klindeinst asked.

"No reason why not," Selmon said. He turned to Ditwhiler. "Any negative thoughts, LeRoy?"

Ditwhiler shrugged. "Purging is on schedule. *Adventurer* is still parked up there ready to blast off. I say go."

"No crew problems, Jack?"

Schaeffly blinked sharply, as if jerked back from some private reverie. "What?"

"No crew problems?"

"No. None." Schaeffly's jaw set and for an instant he had an odd glint in his eyes. "Fine. Everything is fine."

"Those little midcourse correction parameter changes that Boyd Reynolds wanted programmed in?"

Ditwhiler nodded benignly. "We had a technician inside the *Adventurer* earlier today, and we sent up the computer updates with that stuff as a part of it. No problem whatsoever."

Klindeinst hesitated. Ten thousand details nagged at his mind. But MarsProbe had been in the planning and preparation stages for so long—so many of America's very finest minds had worked on nothing else for years—that he could not think of a single detail that they needed, at this late stage, to worry about. Every contingency had been covered months or years ago.

Sometimes it seemed as if things were too beautifully planned, that their preparation and engineering was going so smoothly that they would be lulled to sleep while some gigantic major error passed by right under their noses.

But that was irrational worry, Klindeinst reminded himself. There could be no staged rehearsal for this venture, and there was no provision for backup.

Everything that could be anticipated, had been anticipated. The stakes were incalculably great: the first nation to reach Mars, locate the radio beacon, and plunder whatever scientific riches those unknown forebearers had left would lead Earth into a new epoch. For second place in this race there would be eternal also-ran status in history, in the future, in the can of worms that continued to be this planet's jumbled political wars.

MarsProbe *had to* succeed. It was as simple as that.

"No problems, then?" Klindeinst asked, repeating himself.

No one spoke. Every man in the room looked confident.

God, I wish I didn't know about all the untested systems, all the things that could go wrong! Klindeinst thought.

He remembered all the way back to 1970, and Apollo 13, when an O_2 tank exploded on the way to the moon. The general public had never realized how hairy that was, how narrow the odds on getting the crew back alive. What if something no one could control—some freak like that—took place six *months* out on the way to Mars? What if a pebble sailed out of space and holed the skin of the spacecraft? What if—

Klindeinst shut off that part of his mind. Sometimes you just had to trust your technology—and luck—and take the balls-out risk.

That is to say, his crew of three fine young people had to take the risk.

"Anything else?" Klindeinst asked aloud.

In all likelihood everyone in the room was having thoughts similar to Klindeinst's. But no one spoke.

The meeting broke up.

"Wow," Kecia Epperly murmured that evening when Hart picked her up to go out to dinner. "You drove the *real* car."

Hart held the wide white door of the Corvette for her. "All this can be yours."

Kecia got in with a flurry of skirt on long bare legs. "Oh, Richard, not tonight. I've had a day."

Walking around to the driver's side, he felt a stab of angry resentment. *How long are you going to keep trying to discharge the tension by making jokes about it? She's never going to marry you.*

Tonight he hardly gave a damn. *One hundred. Sixty-eight. Silver. . . .*

"The wait this morning before the scrub made me nervous," Kecia said as they drove toward the country club.

"That makes two of us."

"What now?"

"I talked to her on the phone a while ago. They try again in the morning."

"Scared?"

"Her? No. Me? Hell yes."

Kecia nodded sympathetically. "It's all well and good to talk about progress for humankind. But that's your *baby* up there. And you love her a lot."

"I do. And it's all well and good to talk about humankind, but part of me just wishes it wasn't happening. I want that little fart close to me. And safe."

"But she's going."

He sighed. "Yes."

"What do you think they'll find up there?"

"I don't know," he admitted.

"You don't think there's a message in those one-to-five pulses, and that's all there is? Some people are still saying—"

"I know. But the best minds in the world have been at that tack for years now. They've amplified those pulses, analyzed them, modulated them, massaged them with computers, tried to convert the changes in polarization to audio frequencies—done all kinds of things none of us can even begin to understand."

Kecia nodded. "And it still comes just—pulses."

"In a pattern sure to show that it isn't accident. Yes. I think they form a message that says no more than, *'We were here. Come learn from what we have left for you when you're smart enough to detect our signals and make the trip.'*"

Kecia shivered a little and hugged her bare arms with red-tipped fingers.

Hart chuckled. "Me too."

They drove on in silence.

He could tell she had had a hard day with her students. There was turmoil in her department, and without tenure she was feeling pressure from both factions in a power struggle, too. Characteristically, she had cautiously sided with a minority of faculty members who took the unpopular view that an English Department still ought to be concerned about good composition and spelling.

She was from Nebraska originally, had moved to Austin with her husband before her divorce, had attended graduate school there after the breakup. In addition to teaching and working on her first book, she was by hobby a computer hacker, and had had some articles in computer magazines.

Hart had said once, "I'd like to read them."

"The articles I wrote about computing? Unless you're a nut like me, they wouldn't make any sense at all."

And that had ended it. The hobby was one of the areas she held to herself, private, unshared. He did not know how many such areas there were.

She lived alone and evidently was not seeing anyone else. She said her university assignments and daily work on a novel left little time for anything else, even her computer hobby. *He* was her hobby, she had told him once.

It had taken her a long time to get over her divorce. There were days when she thought she wasn't over it yet. "Some days I'm just fine. Then I go to sleep and when I wake up in the morning I'm depressed and sad, and I know I've been dreaming, but I can't remember what."

Nearing the country club, Hart wondered if she was one of those divorce casualties he met in his practice, the ones who never quite got over the loss. He hoped, of course, that she was not. Loving her this much, being patient, hurt.

Kecia broke the silence. "Did you hear from Joe Blyleven today?"

"No," Hart said, surprised. "Do you know him?"

"I do now."

"How? Explain."

"He came to school. Wanted to interview me."

"What the hell for?"

Kecia's chuckle was rueful. "Not about the novel I'm writing. He learned somewhere that you and I are best friends. He wanted to ask me about your relationship with Davidson Myrick."

"Jesus! That prick!"

"I told him to go away."

"What's *with* that guy, anyway? He's got an unhealthy fixation on Dave Myrick's death, and the fact that I might have been seeing him for therapy. Listen, if he bothers you again, let me know. I'll call his boss down there."

"I think I got rid of him rudely enough. But he's fixed on it, all right. He said it's a great yarn, a man so obsessed with his work, like Dave. He said Dave even had a huge photo-mural of *Adventurer* framed on the wall of his living room."

"That's no story," Hart said. "The story—which I

hope Blyleven and his ilk never find—is that Dave evidently spent some time in a small mental hospital up in Dallas not long ago. If Blyleven ever finds out about *that*. . . ." He left it unsaid.

"Myrick did that? And didn't tell you?"

"That's what Bud Slagerfeldt told me."

"Geez, I wonder what he was doing up there."

"I'd give a lot to know."

"Think you might call and find out?"

"I'm thinking about it."

They reached the club. The sun was setting behind the eighteenth fairway, and the western sky was haze-streaked and lovely. As Hart helped Kecia out of the car, she pressed against him and lightly kissed his lips. "I love you," she whispered.

It would be all right, he thought, walking in with her. Everything would be all right.

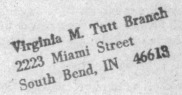

nine

"We have a nominal docking orbit," said the voice on the PA speakers in Mission Control.

Controllers standing at dozens of consoles whistled and applauded, and Project Director John Selmon started around the room, passing out cigars. Operations Chief LeRoy Ditwhiler took one, but had another of his own already smoking in his clenched jaws.

Dr. Boyd Reynolds stared at the big screen on the far wall, seeing its presentation change from the distant, hazy Florida sky where the rocket had vanished. The new picture presented a complex of orbital path lines with the position of the orbiting docking station superimposed.

Over the big screen was the newly installed mission clock. In brilliant blue figures it showed:

PRESENT TIME................ 1701 GMT

ELAPSED TIME

DAYS	HOURS	MINUTES	SECONDS
0000	00	31	05.23

The crew of *Zeus* was on the way to rendezvous with *Adventurer*. The mission had had a flawless beginning.

Jack Schaeffly walked by and smacked Reynolds on the back. Schaeffly looked pale and overdrawn, but his tight smile was genuine. "We're on the way, my friend."

"Great," Reynolds managed, mustering a smile.

Even this moment of triumph could not erase from his mind the black realization that he had sold mission secrets. Who did they represent? He didn't know. All he knew was that he was a traitor. *How can I live with this?*

Only last night he had had his latest disastrous telephone conversation with his wife Mona. This time she was in New York, doing theaters and the stores.

"Transfer funds to my checking account then, Boyd. I won't come all this way with my friends and be mortified because you're too cheap to allow me a little spending money!"

Despairingly he tried to reason with her—explain how deeply they were getting into financial trouble. "I'm not a young man anymore, Mona. I have to plan retirement—"

"And my life doesn't count? Nothing matters but your selfishness?" And on. And on. And on.

He loved her, miserably. He thought she was right. If he had just been more successful, he could have given her everything. He had promised her everything. If she was disappointed in him, she was no more disappointed than he was in himself. He had failed her. And she was right in wanting to be her own person, establish her own life, have the dignity of self-actualization. He had read all the feminist books.

He had called the bank three hours ago, when it opened, and transferred the funds. He would cover his own account by cashing in CDs . . . the last of the CDs. When Mona came home he would explain it all to her again, go over all the financial figures. He simply hadn't made their plight clear; it was his fault.

She would understand, Boyd Reynolds thought

hopefully. It was just that he had failed in the past to make their situation clear to her. She was a good person . . . a good wife. She had just been under a lot of pressure.

And at least, Reynolds thought, the mission was now safely under way. There would be no more demands for stolen computer information from those two men who called themselves Smith and Jones. He was finally free from that pressure, and safe.

Two hours later, in his office, self-deception came crashing down with the soft blinking of his telephone.

"Dr. Reynolds," he answered briskly.

"Doctor," the sickeningly familiar voice said, "this is Smith. We want to see you tonight. What time can you meet us?"

More than a half-million miles out in space, the Russian spaceship was performing flawlessly. The moon had already filled the viewports with its blindingly stark terrain during the near pass, and had begun to shrink toward the dimensions seen from Earth as it was left behind.

Earth—home—was a great pale blue soccer ball diminishing in the blackness of space.

Alexi Picaran was just rising weightlessly back to the flight deck from the exercise chamber when the radio message came from home that the Americans had achieved orbital docking. He felt a strange and unexpected burst of gladness—that soon someone else would share this dread infinity with him and Valeriy Zubakov, fellow voyagers—and compassion . . . for he knew how they would soon begin to feel.

Alexi was not afraid. But with each passing Earthday the immensity of this journey, the sense of isolation, grew stronger. Was man really meant to make such journeys of discovery? He wondered if the great Spanish and Portuguese explorers of earlier centuries had felt thus. Of course this was necessary, and he was pride-filled to be part of such a mission. He owed it to his motherland and to himself; he could do no less and ever face his own young son with pride. But the loneliness was already far worse than he could ever have imagined.

Valeriy Zubakov, his commander, watched him strap himself into his station. "The Americans are hopelessly behind us," Zubakov said.

"I wish them well," Alexi said.

"You talk like a fool."

Alexi looked quickly at his commander, whose face was beet-red with sudden anger. "Please?"

"You are a fool," Valeriy Zubakov repeated, filled with rage that seemed almost ready to overflow into violence. "Wish them disaster. Wish them to be lost in space. Do not wish them well. They are the enemy. Has the deep black already addled your mind?"

"They are fellow humans, fellow cosmonauts—"

"They are the enemy and you will obey me!" Zubakov shouted, slamming a gloved fist onto a control console, inadvertently throwing a dozen minor switches and making a firework of warning signals explode red and yellow all across the overhead monitor panels.

"Reset," Alexi said urgently, his fingers flying to the mis-set switches.

His commander stared at the explosion of warning lights. A computer klaxon began racketing behind their console chairs, adding to the chaos. Zubakov, usually so coldly controlled and quick to respond to any emergency, did nothing.

Alexi's quick fingers reestablished normal operating parameters. Nothing major had been harmed, and the spacecraft's momentary yawing action, caused by interruption in the operation of stabilization gyros, was halted. The warning lights blinked out one by one and the klaxon fell silent.

Without a word, Zubakov threw his headset

down—or rather out, for it floated across the cabin and bounced sharply against the far viewing port—and wheeled out of his chair. Headfirst he swam down through the doorway into the exercise area.

The radio crackled: *"Malfunction indicators 71, 77, 83, 41, 06. Report status at once."*

Alexi shakily touched his throat mike. "Malfunctions corrected. Status normal."

Normal? he thought with deep foreboding. What could be called normal? Valeriy Zubakov's outburst had unsettled him. It was totally uncharacteristic.

The Soviet psychologists had drilled and tested them endlessly to prepare them for the mental and emotional rigors of this cosmic voyage. But Zubakov was already acting strangely. Had the psychologists overlooked something?

Alexi shrank from the suspicion. It could not be true. For if it were true, there was nothing whatsoever that he could possibly do about it.

Alexi's fear stirred, and grew. . . .

In a closed, security-guarded office in Zurich, three men met. One was German, one French, one Greek. Each man had more wealth and power in his own right than most people dreamed of. But the power of the secret conspiracy they represented within TransOrbital, the Common Market's space program for Mars, was far greater.

"The United States probe will leave orbit tomorrow," the German said. "Everything is in place?"

"The one minor annoyance, which has been corrected," said the Greek.

"Then all is well?"

"The year of preparation has paid off. Our plan is working to perfection."

The Frenchman slowly shook his head. "A malfunction—a warning or an illness—would have been enough to stop them."

"You know," the German said, cold-eyed, "how our invaluable friends in the Arab world feel about that."

"But for so many to have to die."

"It is sad. But our Arab friends may be right: only catastrophe can assure major delays for both superpowers, and guarantee that our role will never be learned."

"So many know a part of the operation," the Frenchman worried on. "If we were revealed—!"

"Many know a small bit, but only a very few of us see the total picture, understand how things mesh. You worry too much, my friend. No one is in position to begin to unravel the entire skein."

"Then you believe we are safe?"

"Yes. And both the American and Russian expeditions are doomed. It is inconceivable that any agency could save them now."

Wearing jeans, a sportshirt, and deck shoes, Hart met Kecia at her apartment Thursday evening. They had agreed to eat in, and she looked comfortable and pretty in lavender shorts and an off-white jersey. They embraced.

"You look tired," Kecia told him with a sympathetic smile.

"I'm not handling my anxieties as well as I might like," he admitted.

They went into her living room, tall oyster-white walls, fireplace, contemporary furniture, stacks of books. She curled up on the couch and he sat beside her, taking her hand.

"You figure they'll leave orbit tomorrow?" she asked.

"Oh, yes."

"And you're scared."

"Totally."

"You know she wants it badly, Richard. She chose it."

"I know," he sighed.

She squeezed his hand. "Well. —Chinese?"

"Good."

She called a nearby Chinese carryout and, while they waited, opened a bottle of well-chilled Chardonnay. The food was delivered in steaming plastic containers. It was good but Hart couldn't eat much.

The major television networks all had special prime-time coverage of the day's events, including the blastoff from Cape Canaveral, the orbital rendezvous maneuvers, and a live transmission from inside the docked *Adventurer*, showing the MarsProbe crew going through prelaunch inspection procedures.

Christie looked heartbreakingly tiny and beautiful. She looked very young and fragile to Hart, and he got a thick lump in his throat.

CNN carried other live pictures, taken from the central docking module, showing *Adventurer* out at the end of the precarious-looking structure of girders and cables, lights glowing in the cabin windows against the deep black of space.

"She'll be fine," Kecia said.

"I know. I know."

"You're a pretty extraordinary family, Richard Hart. She got every gene in your inheritance that's made all of you successful. You're all winners. And you're all strong." Kecia hesitated, a little frown touching her forehead. "Sometimes I wonder if some of you haven't been too strong for your own good. You don't compromise much. That's kind of scary. But if anyone can take on this kind of trip and come back whole and fulfilled and happy, it's Christie."

Hart thought about it. "Nobody in our family, back through the generations, ever became president, or indelibly changed history. But I guess the one thing that's been passed along from one generation to the next has been the idea that you take what you were given, and become all you can be. You face your life and make it the best you can. My father gave me that, and I gave it to Christie. I guess, if I'm scared for her now, I have only myself to blame."

Kecia chuckled. "Are you saying you should have been a wimp, so she would be a scaredy-cat?"

He threw up his hands. "I'm just scared shitless for her. Leave it at that."

"This isn't any fly-by-night operation. They've covered every contingency they could imagine. That spacecraft has more redundancy built into it than anything that ever flew."

"I keep thinking about Dave Myrick," he admitted.

"That he was more ill than you thought? That some mistake of his might be programmed into the flight planning somehow?"

He tried to articulate the vague worries that kept swirling, trying to intensify. "He came to me a nervous, hounded, troubled man. I thought he told me everything. Then I learn later that he was in a hospital up in Dallas not long before he came to me. Why? What was he doing up there?"

"Couldn't you just call the hospital and inquire?"

"No. If there's something fishy and it involves them, a call would only alert them."

"You think they have something to hide?"

"Hell, I don't know. Probably not. Maybe I'm seeking spooks and gremlins just because I'm unsettled about Christie. But Dave Myrick died, and then there were two break-ins—and a murder!—at my office, and maybe that mugging in the parking lot wasn't a mugging at all. Dave had a really strange, unexplainable hypnotic episode in my office during that last visit on the day he died. I taped it. I think the break-ins were part of a search for any tape or written record

I made of the session, just to be sure nothing remains that could reveal something."

"I don't understand. Reveal *what*?"

"I don't know!" he admitted disgustedly. "I found the tape. I've played it over and over. It makes no sense. But he talked about the mission failing. He was tortured by thought of mission failure—that somehow he would be responsible. What if"—he hesitated before saying this aloud for the first time—"what if Dave really did know something? What if there's something fatally wrong with MarsProbe? With *Adventurer*? What if he blocked it out of consciousness? What if something that happened to him in Dallas blocked it out? What if he didn't die by accident, or suicide, but was murdered to make sure he never remembered the fatal flaw?"

Kecia uncoiled her legs in a quick motion of dismay. "My God, Richard! You sound like you're thinking sabotage! Or some kind of maniac conspiracy!"

"I know how crazy it sounds," he admitted.

She watched him, troubled. She didn't speak.

"No one would have thought those assassinations at the U.N. were possible before they happened in 1989," he said doggedly. "No one would have believed the things that happened in London a year ago. No one would have thought we would be hearing radio signals from another planet. No one would have thought MarsProbe would ever happen, or that the Russians would have a head start on us, or that half the people on the planet would want both of us to fail, for one reason or another."

Kecia took his hand. Her fingers were chilled. "Richard, is there *anything* you haven't told me about this? Or that detective?"

"Not really. It's hunch—intuition, something my child senses that I can't quite put together rationally." He met her eyes. "But I really am scared, Kecia. I have this feeling that something enormously important took place with Dave Myrick in that last session, and I can't figure out what it is."

"What are you going to do?"

"I don't know. I've thought about going to Dallas—talking to them at that hospital. But maybe that's crazy."

"If it would make you feel better, I think you ought to do it."

"I'm thinking about it."

She moved into his arms. "Hey. Kiss me. Maybe I can make it all better."

Smiling, he complied. But then all the tension broke through and he held her at arm's length. "You know," he told her, "you are just so important to me. Let's talk about getting married, okay? I mean it. I'm too old for you and you're still a little screwed up from your divorce, and we're both scared of failing again, but to hell with it. We've both lived all our lives being nice and careful and responsible. And what the hell has it gotten us?"

She giggled and hugged him again. "Oh, my Richard."

"I mean it."

She turned serious, fixing him with magnificent, somber eyes. "I know you do, Richard."

"And?"

"I'm sorry. I just can't. Not yet. I'm scared. You're right about that."

"I'm trying not to press. I'm not an ogre. I won't totally invade your life."

"I know that. You're not the one I'm afraid of."

There was nothing to say to that. He kissed her fingers and wondered how a grown man could feel so vulnerable. Half of him was here, stuck, and half was out there somewhere with his daughter, while he tried to tell himself he was imagining the fear. . . .

Later, Kecia made it clear that he was welcome to stay the night, as he sometimes did. He was too tense, too mixed up. He drove home, entering the lower level of the parking garage.

Two police cars, blue-and-red gumball machines winking on their roofs, were parked in the lower level. Attendants were just pushing a gurney into the back of a hulking yellow ambulance nearby. Hart parked and walked to the elevator station, where the policemen stood talking with security guards.

One of them recognized Hart and touched the brim of his cap in salute.

"What happened?" Hart demanded.

"Huntington," the guard told him. "Died."

Huntington was one of the regular security guards, a middle-aged man who had often commiserated with Hart over the ups and downs of the Oilers. "What happened to him?" Hart asked sharply.

The guard shrugged. "Nobody knows. He was alone on this level. We found him on the ground. I guess he had a heart attack. There weren't any marks on him."

Hart shook his head and rode the express elevator to the top floor, the car's security camera looking at him as he went.

When he reached his level and left the car, he was thinking that Huntington had probably had a bad heart for a long time, and it had finally caught up with him.

Then he reached the door of his apartment and instantly, with deep shock, saw another possibility.

The door to his apartment, left firmly locked, was ajar.

ten

Friday dawned overcast and muggy. Hart was up early, tensely reviewing his plan. A quick trip to his office assured him that all was well and he could plan to contact his regular patients and begin seeing them again sometime next week.

He did not tell the office temporary to schedule any appointments just yet, however. There were things that took priority.

By ten o'clock he was on the road. The highway from Houston north to Dallas ran wide and fast, interstate all the way, and the Corvette ate up the miles.

He kept the radio going. *Adventurer* had not yet launched from orbit, but systems were being activated and the LFO was estimated for early afternoon.

Meanwhile, the world had had an opportunity to react to the orbital docking and imminent beginning of America's voyage to Mars.

The Grand World Council, formed by sixty-two of the Earth's most backward nations after the dissolution of the United Nations removed their accustomed soapbox, had already scheduled a conclave in Algiers to start next week. Their agenda, surprisingly including

items condemning the Mars launch by their usual
champion, Soviet Russia, was being revised to include
a dozen or so diatribes against the United States's
effort. Demonstrations and riots were ongoing in Ethi-
opia, Iran, Greece, Chad, South Korea, and most of
Central America. The Ayatollah pronounced both
space launches as the work of the devil, and promised
renewed terrorism against children of the world in the
name of the deity. The Gulf of Sidra became a beehive
of activity as the Libyan junta sent its speedboats and
fishing vessels out on full military alert. Meanwhile, in
the western world, religious fanatics from the far right
fell strangely silent on finding themselves in the unac-
customed position of agreeing with unbaptized hea-
thens.

It would have been funny, Hart thought, if it did
not so well demonstrate why any advanced culture capable of putting a beacon on Mars would probably
consider Earth a planet of clever, tool-manipulating
apes.

Was there any chance that the expeditions would
bring back knowledge and insight so vast and hum-
bling that humankind might actually be shocked into
getting together? Some religious leaders talked of such
a hope. Hart in his darker moments feared that the
opposite would be true—that the achievement by the
world's advanced cultures would only give them another leap of centuries forward, while the Third World
continued in the tenth century. If that happened, today's bitter hostility could only escalate. He could see
the advanced cultures finally banding together out of
this experience. But only to practice genocide on the
less-developed.

The bitterness was already there, this adventure
bringing it out like nothing else ever had. Terrorist
bombs had exploded yesterday in Paris, Chicago, San
Francisco, Melbourne, Moscow, Vienna, and London.

An excursion boat off the coast of Sicily was missing and feared sunk by a renegade two-man submarine, and four terrorist organizations in the Middle East were clamoring to take the "credit." Even the unmanned space launch planned by the European consortium had been roundly condemned. The have-nots had never been so extreme in their blanket opposition to the developed countries. Mars and everything it stood for had become an incendiary rallying point for all the hate in the Third World.

In an extraordinary space conference held in Belgrade almost a year ago, the "West"—in this case including the Soviets—tried to short-circuit some of the violent reaction by openly comparing notes about their competitive plans for Mars. They pledged "cooperation" in the race, introduced some of their top planners, and assured the world that all information would be shared. It did no good.

The consortium used the lectern to question the safety of crewed flight, and argued that its own unmanned robot lander was safer, cheaper, and more humanitarian. Russia had a knee-jerk response: only its probe could represent all the peoples of the planet. The United States talked about free enterprise. Both major nations introduced the commanders of their flight crews, and the two men were pictured worldwide, clasping hands and grinning at each other.

But that rhetoric and show biz didn't work either. Four bombs went off near the convention center, killing two dozen people, while peace and harmony were being pledged inside.

At the heart of the worldwide extremism seemed to be the thought: *Any attempt to contact another civilization is against the will of God.*

And besides, anything that comes out of it should be given to us because we want it.

Hart wondered where it would end.

This morning, however, while half listening to the ongoing reports from space and trouble spots around the globe, he had more pressing business on his mind.

In retrospect he knew he had been very foolish last night, barging straight into his apartment after finding the door jimmied and ajar. Surprise and anger had overruled caution.

Inside he had found no one, no lights, no obvious signs of commotion. But then, remembering, he had walked to the cassette deck of his stereo system.

There he found the tape door canted open, the cassette of his session with Myrick gone.

The guard downstairs had had no heart attack, he thought. Perhaps an examination would find a small puncture wound, or the mark of a hypodermic needle. The guard had been killed as a way to gain entry to this apartment.

They had wanted this tape very badly, and now they had it.

So they knew exactly what had transpired in the session, and what he knew.

Hart started to call security. Some instinct stopped him, and he thought it out. If he called, Slagerfeldt would be here. His withholding of information about the tape would then come out. Slagerfeldt and the police wouldn't be able to do anything, but Slagerfeldt would slap security restrictions on his movements, probably have him watched.

Hart couldn't afford that.

He paced the floor while the TV console played muted-sound pictures of *Adventurer*, in its orbital docking cradle. Reviewing things.

Maybe he was overreacting and maybe he wasn't, but he had nothing to lose now by pursuing the slender clues he possessed about Davidson Myrick prior to his death. They—whoever *they* were—now knew anything he knew already. If he was in unexplained peril, checking things further wouldn't do much to make matters worse.

They had his number. He could either sit tight and impersonate a sitting duck, or he could try to find out what in the hell was really going on.

If Davidson Myrick had been sick, his sickness could in some unforeseen way have affected crew training for MarsProbe. If Myrick had been murdered, it could have been because someone feared he would tell Hart—or someone else—details about whatever had made him a mentally ill man.

Myrick had been tense and nervous, and plagued by asthma, known to have partially psychosomatic causes. He had gone to Dallas to a private hospital and had come out so depressed, so nervous, so plagued by bad dreams and tremors, that he had secretly started seeing Hart despite the blow to his ego that seeking continuing counseling posed for a man of his personality, and despite the danger to his professional reputation if he were found out.

The break-in was the final step in convincing Hart that he had to go to Dallas, see the facility for himself, try to talk his way into Myrick's records there in an attempt to make sense out of the puzzle.

Of course there was risk, maybe damned serious risk. But there was something radically wrong somewhere, and he had to try to track it down. His love for his daughter demanded it.

The "Parkview Limited" of Bud Slagerfeldt's file was actually called Parkview Limited Hospital, Inc. It consisted of a single four-story brick building on a street of professional buildings just off the Central Expressway not far north of Dallas's gleaming downtown.

There was no lobby inside the glass front doors, only a small foyer with a few plastic chairs, just one of them occupied at the moment by a gangling, nervous-looking youth in jeans and a dress shirt open at the collar. Farther access to the building was blocked by a walnut-paneled wall with a sliding window for a receptionist. The door beside the window looked stout, and it had an electric lock in it.

The receptionist, a young man with wavy brown hair and a small mustache of the type much cultivated by homosexuals, slid back his glass window and peered out at Hart with boredom fringing on hostility. "Can I help you?"

Hart recited his rehearsed story. Giving his correct name and professional address, he truthfully said he was seeking information about a patient who had previously been treated at Parkview Limited. Shared information, he said, might help understand his patient's case.

The man took scrawled notes on a form of some kind. What was the patient's name? When had he been treated here? Approximate dates, then? His attending physician or psychologist's name? Not many of the staff were here on Friday afternoon. He would see what he could find out. Please wait.

Hart waited. Traffic rumbled by on the tree-lined street. Inside the reception window was the receptionist's computer terminal. It had a telephone number block-printed on adhesive tape and stuck on the side of the keyboard. Hart made note of the number, then walked over to one of the vacant chairs against the wall and sat down.

Blinking furiously, the skinny man looked over at him with a friendly grimace. "New patient?" he asked in a gentle, bemused tone.

"Visiting," Hart told him.

The man cracked bony knuckles. "If you're here about the stop-smoking program, I can tell you: it really works, boy."

"Is that so? Are you being treated for a smoking habit?"

"Yes, sir. I'm waiting for my therapist now. I've just had two treatments and I'm just about cured already. I haven't had a cigarette in a week and a half, and I don't even want one."

"That's remarkable," Hart said encouragingly, noting the twitchy hand movements, darting eyes, film of pallid sweat on the face.

"Yes, sir, boy. Don't even want one. It really works. I can recommend it."

"How do they help you stop?"

"Well, films, for one. And hypnosis, of course, with the help of one of them new psychedelic—no, that's wrong—psycho—uh—"

"Psychotropic?" Hart offered.

"Yes, sir, that's it, boy. Psychotropic. A psychotropic drug. It's harmless, and all, but it really helps you get hypnotized."

Hart was going to ask what drug the youth was being given, if he knew, but the receptionist appeared again in the windowed office and sat down, looking bored again. Simultaneously the electric door buzzed and opened, and a lank, gray-bearded man of about forty came halfway through the doorway, peering at Hart with wide, red-rimmed eyes. The man wore wrinkled khaki pants and a blue-and-yellow–striped sportshirt, and the plastic nametag stuck on his left chest said he was MAXWELL, J., PH.D. He looked anxious, perpetually nervous, with a little tic.

"Dr. Hart?" he asked tensely. "Hi. I'm Jess Maxwell. You had a question about a patient?"

Hart repeated his story. Maxwell listened with nervous intensity. "Yes," he said when Hart concluded. "I took the liberty of checking with the association about your credentials. Now if you have identification. . . ?"

Hart showed him a driver's license, a professional card, and the state membership card. Satisfied, Maxwell took him through the electric door and back along a narrow, tiled corridor past a number of glass-doored offices to his own, in the far corner of the first floor with a dingy window overlooking a dumpster trash receptacle. The office was sparsely furnished in the kind of "homey" chairs and tables many professionals used, presumably to keep clients relaxed during therapy. Another computer terminal glowed on a credenza behind a small desk.

"Now," Maxwell said, sitting in the most-worn easy chair and letting Hart take anything that was left, "I'm sorry to say that the psychologist who dealt with Mr. Myrick is not in this afternoon. As a matter of fact, he has left the hospital and is now in private practice in Plano."

"Perhaps if you gave me his name—?"

Maxwell nervously ignored that, and instead reached for a brown manila file folder. "As a professional courtesy, we've pulled our file. Tell me, doctor: How is Mr. Myrick getting along, and what course of treatment is he now undergoing?"

"He's dead," Hart said.

Either Maxwell was shocked or he was a fine actor. "Dead!"

"It was all over the news, doctor. Don't you follow the news?"

Maxwell looked pale. "He wasn't my patient . . . I've been busy."

"Well, Dr. Myrick had an accident. And to close my file, I want to make a record of his stay here, and his treatment, et cetera."

"Of course . . . of course . . . oh, dear me!" Distracted, Maxwell handed over the file folder.

The record was in standard form, biographical information, health history, family record, insurance

data. A summary of the initial interview was included
and at a glance it appeared to report nothing Hart did
not already know. Later pages noted details of a cursory physical examination by an M.D., and several
pages of interview notes showing counseling to calm
Myrick's nerves and talk to him about diet, allergies,
and activities designed to calm his nerves. Nothing
special.

Hart handed the folder back. "Thank you. I believe this record dovetails with the limited information
I have in my possession, and I can close my case record."

"I'm very sorry to hear about Myrick's death,"
Maxwell said with every sign of sincerity. "I didn't
have his case, but still. . . ."

"Your record shows no indication of hypnotherapy," Hart said.

"Well, it may be that the attending psychologist
performed a light induction at some point, but as the
file indicates, our job primarily was to rule out physical
complications and provide some guidance as to stress
reduction."

"Were psychotropic drugs attempted?" Hart asked
as innocently as possible.

Maxwell reacted sharply. "Certainly not! Does the
file indicate any such usage?"

"No. Just wondering. I spoke with a gentleman
outside whose problem appears to be much less severe
than Myrick's was, and he told me he's being treated
with such drugs for a smoking habit."

Maxwell stared, his Adam's apple bobbing. Then a
light dawned across his face. "Oh! Oh, I *see*. Con-
fidentially, doctor, we sometimes tell problem patients
that we're giving them a psychotropic that will help us
hypnotize them more deeply. We've found it makes
them more susceptible to trance-induction procedures."

Jack M. Bickham

"But," Hart pursued gently, "in fact—?"

Maxwell grinned broadly, relaxing. "In fact, what they're given is essentially a placebo, something over-the-counter like Nytol. They believe they're being given the latest medical technology, and the placebo thus relaxes them, and makes them much easier to hypnotize in preparation for a normal antismoking program."

"It's misleading, but it works?" Hart said.

"Actually, we're quite above-board with it, quite ethical." Maxwell dug a thin brochure out of a desk drawer. "Look here in our pamphlet."

Hart glanced at it. As one of the highlights of the antismoking hypnosis, the brochure clearly stated:

Using the latest psychotropic placebo!

"It's harmless, and it helps," Maxwell added.

They talked another few minutes. Hart saw he was not going to get anything further.

"You're in private practice," Maxwell observed as the conversation wound down.

"Yes," Hart said, preoccupied.

"This is my last day here. I start my own office in Fort Worth next Monday. It's a big financial risk, but I think it's worth it."

Hart thought he understood why Maxwell was both so tired and so nervous. He was taking a big step. "You'll find it a challenge, and very gratifying," he said.

"I hope so," Maxwell said with a boyish grin. "I've wanted to try it a long time."

"I wish you luck."

Maxwell nodded thanks and stood to lead him out of the office and back down the hall toward the entry foyer. Hart glanced at the names on some of the office doors as he passed them, and the name on one of them leaped out at him with such a surprise that he almost exclaimed aloud.

"Anything wrong?" Maxwell asked, holding the electric door and offering a handshake. "You look a bit pale."

"No, I'm fine," Hart smiled, recovering. "Long drive, no lunch."

"There's a very nice cafeteria two streets over."

Hart got the directions, thanked Maxwell warmly, and went out and climbed into the now baking-hot Corvette.

Driving south on the Central Expressway, he absorbed the shock of his discovery, and what it might or might not mean.

One of the things Davidson Myrick had demanded during the last session was, *"Are you silver? Are you silver?"*

It had made no sense then. But now perhaps it did.

Myrick, Hart thought, hadn't been talking about "silver" as a color, or as a metal. In thinking of Myrick's words, Hart now automatically capitalized the word.

For one of the office doors inside the hospital had read: SILVER, J. S., PH.D.

Myrick had been asking if Hart was Silver, a therapist at Parkview. Hart had induced trance. Earlier, he would bet anything, Silver had done so. And this realization instantly brought Maxwell's story about psychotropic placebos into question. Some of the new mood-altering and consciousness-changing drugs were frighteningly efficient and powerful, many of their effects still not fully understood. Medicine was moving very slowly on the use of the latest ones; they were capable of helping many, but the control they tended to give sometimes was frightening.

And Hart was willing to bet now that Myrick had been given one of them.

Why would they be so anxious to hide the fact? They had M.D.s on their staff. Dispensing psychotropics—from Valium on up—was perfectly legal for them.

Answer: Maxwell had been told to deny the use of real psychotropics no matter who might ask. Why? Because their use in routine hypnotherapy was questionable practice, at best.

Then, however, a new thought—one that had been cooking before rising to consciousness—now surfaced in Hart's mind: *Had they been programming Myrick at Parkview to do more than calm down and avoid asthma attacks?* And if so, *what*?

But that was really too far-out to consider.

He headed south and soon left Dallas, driving back toward Houston on a surprisingly empty interstate highway, and he was about halfway there when the other driver tried to kill him.

eleven

It was a white Oldsmobile.

Hart was on cruise control a shade over sixty-five, his radar detector quiet, on a long, curving stretch of highway that ran through gently rolling hill country punctuated here and there by a grove of stunted trees, a truck stop, or distant derricks: cattle country, with a few old well workovers marked by portable rigs. The rise in oil prices had mildly reactivated the industry in the Southwest, and a few companies were going in to rework existing holes, intent on coaxing out a few additional barrels with some of the new cleanout and fracturing techniques. The return of the derricks added variety now and then to the grasslands that seemed to roll to infinity under the hot afternoon sun.

Hart's thoughts were not on the ruined energy business. He was anxious to get back to Houston. He wanted to find Bud Slagerfeldt and see if he knew any more than he had revealed earlier about Davidson Myrick's stay in the Dallas hospital. Myrick was a key to so much, and now Hart was convinced that *something* had happened to him in Dallas, starting the chain of events that had ended in his death.

The radar detector installed in the Corvette did a

nice job picking up fixed patrol radar traps well in advance of their detection effectiveness, and twice Hart slowed when the unit flashed red and bleeped intermittently, indicating a distant signal. In both cases the warning came from an approaching truck with a cheaper detector that emitted a dirty signal of its own, or from some other anomaly Hart didn't understand. Both times he resumed speed when the detector fell silent without increasing in frequency of warning bleeps.

The Whistler couldn't warn a driver of a moving patrol car approaching with its radar turned off, the trooper remaining "silent" to detectors until he flicked the unit on at close range for instant speed reading. It could not do anything about a patrol car riding up swiftly from the rear and making an old-fashioned visual clocking, either, so Hart automatically drove with careful attention to the highway far ahead, and regular glances in the rearview mirror.

He was aware of the white car a mile or so behind for a long time. It maintained its position, evidently with its cruise set at a figure very close to his own.

Hart listened to the radio. Christie was still in *Adventurer* and locked to the orbital launch platform. He worried about her and thought a lot about Kecia, too. His love for both of them hurt.

A Stuckey's cafe stood atop an overpass crossover a mile ahead. He slowed, pulled off, gave the Corvette 16.5 gallons and himself a cup of black coffee that tasted like it had come out of the same tank that held the fuel. Pulling back onto the highway he headed south again, being passed first by an eighteen-wheeler as he accelerated, then by a dangerously swaying old camper with campground stickers on the rusty back bumper.

Glancing in the rearview mirror as he reached speed, Hart saw another white car, closer this time. Or was it the same white car? Unlikely. No one had followed him off at the Stuckey's.

On the off chance that it was an unmarked patrol unit, he touched the cruise control and slowed to the legal limit. The white car—an Oldsmobile—moved up within a dozen car lengths, then fixed its speed with his. It wasn't a patrol car.

Hart accelerated again, resetting about sixty-six. The white car fell back only slightly, again matching his speed. A random radar signal from somewhere ahead on the highway bounced off the car behind him and made his detector bleep. Fatigue and irritation made him thoughtlessly depress the accelerator to put a safer interval between the cars. The speedometer rolled smoothly up through seventy-five and then to eighty, which he held for a half minute, topping a long hilltop and starting down the far side, where the highway—empty for miles except for the two vehicles that had passed him, now a mile or more ahead—curved west and then south again toward a hazy far horizon.

He let the Corvette coast down to his cruise setting and reached to retune the radio. Simultaneously, in the rearview mirror, he saw the white Oldsmobile leap over the hilltop behind him and hurtle on, closing the gap between them at an alarming pace.

The Olds was doing over a hundred. Hart held speed and carefully stayed in the right-hand lane. The Olds filled his rearview mirror. *The crazy bastard was going to hit him from behind.* Hart sawed the steering wheel sharply to the right, hitting the graveled emergency lane.

The Olds rocketed past, swerving *to the right*, almost hitting him anyway. Hart swung back onto the regular pavement, the rear wheels chittering from stress, and had a few choice words for the lone male visible behind the wheel of the Olds. Maybe the man was drunk. Or—

There was no time for idle speculation. The Olds swung wildly back onto the regular pavement just ahead of him, forcing him to swing sharply left, into the passing lane, to avoid another collision. Taillights blazed red as the Olds was braked sharply, skidding, forcing Hart to swing again into the open right lane. By instinct, Hart floored the accelerator and the Corvette shot past the larger car and in front again.

Whatever the reason, the maniac was trying to run him off the road. Hart had heard of things like this— crazies out for thrills, or to get even with a world they were mad at. He thought of pulling over and simply stopping, but the idiot might simply plow him from behind. And some crazies had guns.

In the instant that Hart used to get this far, the white car shot up alongside him again. He glanced over, and what he saw further chilled him. The driver was young, certainly not more than thirty, and he did not look crazy. He was wearing a neat summer suit and tie, he had pale blue eyes and yellow hair, and the look he gave Hart in that fraction of a second was cool, nerveless, intent on killing him.

The driver expertly swung his wheel. The right front of the Olds crashed into the left side of the Corvette with a crunch of tearing metal and the sickening hollow sound of parts of the Corvette's plastic body shattering. The impact knocked the Corvette off-line and onto the parking lane again, and just ahead was another state road passing across an overpass. The Olds pressed on over. Hart laid on the gas and got a car-length ahead. But he was on the exit ramp. He couldn't swing back onto the highway. The exit sign said thirty. He was doing twice that.

Shit. Nothing for it but to try to maintain control on the exit road. The Corvette swung up the exit, curving right, and ahead was an empty, weedy intersection with a narrow paved road running east–west. There was a stop sign. The curve of the exit ramp favored turning right, or west. Nothing out there except some brushy hills and a couple of distant oil rigs. The Olds was all over the rearview mirror, and closing.

Hart called on the expertise he had gained driving in rallies when both he and the Corvette were considerably younger. Dirt flew and tires howled protest as he took the right-hand curve accelerating through seventy and hit the two-lane blacktop in full acceleration.

The Olds had lost a little ground on the curve, but the rearview mirror showed it righting itself and slightly closing the gap in pursuit. Then Hart went over a little rise in the road, the Corvette becoming very light on its springs for an instant, and down the other side. The tach was too high and the speed was somewhere over one hundred. Hart was badly scared now.

It was a farm-to-market road, recently repaved, vacant as far as the eye could see, curving between hilltops of grass and brush, the low sun burnishing the windshield. Where, oh, where were the troopers when you needed them?

And what did the driver of the white Oldsmobile have under his hood? The Corvette was doing over 110, and the Olds was closing slightly. Risking a glance in the mirror, Hart saw that the driver had his arm out the window, holding something. There was a tiny puff of smoke from his hand, instantly gone. Hart's blood congealed. The maniac was shooting at him.

He punched the Corvette to the floor and it downshifted, screaming. A low, dry creekbed area caused a sickening brief skid which he controlled, and then came a sharp rise over a grassy hillock with a workover rig, trucks, derrick, tanks, and slush pit—a temporary little lake to catch the liquid trash of the workover—off to the right, a few sleepy cows in the field to the left. Then he topped the rise and right on the other side was an intersection with a dirt road and beyond the intersection this road turned to dirt, too.

The Corvette bolted over the crossing road and hit hard red dirt at about 115. A maelstrom of noise—dirt chunks, small rocks, and debris hitting the under-side—instantly became deafening. To the rear, the Corvette threw up an incredible plume of blinding red dust, and Hart just managed to see the Oldsmobile plunging into it.

The dirt road hadn't been so much as graded for a while. It had shallow holes and long ruts in it, and chunks of big rocks here and there, and crumbling ditches on both sides. Hart's car was all over the sur-face, narrowly under control.

The road went down across a one-car wooden bridge over weeds and dead mud, then up the far side and on a curving trajectory to the left, where it forked sharply, the main branch going farther left, a gated dirt pathway to the right leading to an old oil well—an-cient permanent derrick, pump going slowly in the dusty sun, tanks, the remains of a slush pit high-banked, muddy red water glistening inside.

Hart couldn't see the Olds at all in the enormous dirt cloud trailing the Corvette. He touched the brake slightly, getting a small skid for his trouble, and drifted hard through the left turn, seeing only then that the road curved sharply right again, skirting the oil lease.

He had to brake harder. The car responded more nicely this time, and he came around the second curve on slightly higher ground so that he had a moment to glance back at the dirt cloud he had laid behind him.

Just as he did so, the Oldsmobile appeared out of the curving cloud at the first left turn, the entrance to the oil lease. The flying dirt had concealed the curve from the Olds driver. Hart clearly saw the front wheels turn hard left, the brakes lock up. But the car was going too fast. It simply maintained its line of direc-tion, crashing through the flimsy fence and hurtling on up the grassy lease path.

It clipped one of the small oil storage tanks, bouncing crazily left, and there was a spurt of yellow flame. For a moment it looked like it might be brought under control, but it was still going very fast, throwing red dirt and weed clods all over the place. It hit the grass embankment on the back edge of the slush pit and went up its side like a ski jumper. At the moment it reached the top and became airborne, something inside exploded.

The red fireball inverted and hit the oily water of the old slush pit upside down, blazing, starting to sink. Intense inky smoke gushed skyward.

Hart stopped, stared, began shaking all over. Going back was out of the question. He put the Corvette in gear again and queasily pulled out onto the dirt road, going on. He was drenched in sweat and sick at his stomach, the rancid Stuckey's coffee wanting badly to come up.

The plume of dense black smoke was still visible, a long stain against the sky, when he found his way back to the Interstate a half hour later. At the next gas station, he pulled in.

"Hey, buddy," the old attendant said, "you have an accident?"

Hart examined the shattered plastic on the left side and a missing wheel cover. The car was pink from the dirt, not white anymore. "I guess I can get it fixed," he said, trying to sound casual. He was still shaking badly.

"Yep," the old man said, rubbing a grizzled chin. "Not like those kids on the spaceship. If they have a flat now, there sure ain't no gas stations out where they're headed."

Hart stared at him.

"You didn't hear?" the old man said, spitting tobacco juice on the oily tarmac. "They blasted outta orbit a while ago. They're on their way for sure now, boy."

twelve

Detective Bud Slagerfeldt, still wearing his fishing pants and shirt and clodhopper shoes, glumly examined the damage to the Corvette, using a flashlight in the dimness of the apartment's garage.

"He did a number on this side of the vehicle, all right." Slagerfeldt turned close-set eyes to Hart, standing nearby. "And you told the patrol how it happened?"

Hart, still a little weak in the knees some seven hours after the high-speed pursuit, nodded. "They took it all down. They were a little irritated that I didn't stop near the spot and call headquarters."

"Why didn't you?"

Hart's face heated. "Two reasons. One, I was fixed on getting out of there. Second, I didn't think of contacting anyone but you until I was back here, and calmed down a little."

"There will probably be a hearing, possibly even some kind of state charge."

"Because I saved my own ass?"

"Calm down, calm down. Jesus, what a temper."

"If I'm charged because some son of a bitch tried to kill me—"

"If they find a stiff in that car where you say they will, something has to be filed to clear the air because you're the only witness. It's for your own protection, to exonerate you. So cool off."

"Okay, okay," Hart said, fuming.

"Now suppose you fill me in on everything else."

Hart took the detective up to the apartment and told him all of it, from the beginning. Slagerfeldt made notes and seemed to forget his irritation about being called in from a long weekend.

"I suppose you know," he said when Hart had finished, "that you've been obstructing justice."

"I was protecting a client."

"The client is dead, doctor. And so is your secretary. And so—almost—were you."

"I was wrong. But I'm telling you all I know now."

Slagerfeldt sighed. "You amateur detectives. Jesus. You're as bad as my bookie. You never give me anything but bad news."

Hart found himself grinning despite his frustrated anger. "Maybe both of us like to keep you on your toes."

"On my ass, you mean. Now let me make sure I got this right."

Hart waited while the detective flipped back through the notes he had taken in his leather-jacketed note pad. Finally Slagerfeldt said, "You don't have any idea who this sucker in the Oldsmobile was?"

"No."

"Never saw him before?"

"No."

"We'll see what the state boys dig up on him, then. Now. Why was it you went to Parkview?"

"To try to find out what happened to Dave Myrick up there."

"Because you decided the break-ins and the mugging were all to search the Myrick files and see what you might know."

"Yes."

"Because somebody had something to hide that Myrick might tell you."

"Yes."

"And when they got that tape of yours—the one you didn't condescend to tell me about—you saw Parkview as your only lead."

"Yes again."

Slagerfeldt pursed his lips. "Maybe you wouldn't have gotten to try it if our motor pool wasn't filled up with junkers that won't start half the time when they're needed."

"What does that mean?" Hart demanded.

"Nothing. Never mind. From what you've told me, the trip was a waste of time anyhow. You got nothing."

"What about Dave asking if I was Silver, and then finding out there's a Dr. Silver on staff up there?"

Slagerfeldt studied him with drooping eyes. "What does that prove?"

"It could prove that something strange was done to Dave's mind up there!"

"And it could prove nothing. What do we *know*?"

"All I know," Hart exploded, "is that my daughter is aboard *Adventurer*, and there are some damned strange things going on."

Slagerfeldt leaned back. "This hypnotherapy they're doing up there. Isn't that stuff just for the whackos?"

"No, it isn't." Hart controlled himself and carefully explained a bit about the history of hypnosis in psychotherapy: the ancient origins of the technique, a little of what was understood about how it worked, how Freud himself had first used hypnotic techniques until—perhaps as part of his rejection of the seduction theory—he had dumped hypnosis in favor of analysis, with all its attendant weaknesses. Hart even went into often-ignored practitioners of hypnotic techniques during the early parts of the century, when analysis was all the rage, and tried to explain to Slagerfeldt about the work done by such men as Milton Erickson.

"You don't 'go to sleep' under hypnosis," he explained. "You aren't even hypnotized by the therapist, so much as you go into your trance on your own, with him as a facilitator. Athletes, writers, actors, all talk about getting 'in the zone,' or words to that effect, when they're really functioning. They're talking about a heightened, changed mental state—something awfully close to hypnosis. There's nothing very mysterious about how it often works, even though we don't really understand the mechanisms very clearly. The mind clears, relaxes, focuses; distractions vanish; the mind shows its power over body functions; the unconscious is given freedom; suggestions are accepted, habits changed. —Hell, Bud, it's no magic act, but it *works!*"

"But I always heard," Slagerfeldt said, "that you couldn't make someone do something under hypnosis that they wouldn't do ordinarily."

"That's true. But if a trance can alter a person's perception of reality to some degree, then actions that otherwise would be viewed as unacceptable, or impossible, might be considered."

"Are you saying you might be able to hypnotize somebody to think they could fly, so they dove out a window?"

"No. But I might be able to so enhance their sense of balance, and their confidence in it, that they would walk a wire over a safety net."

Slagerfeldt shook his head. "This is deep shit and I don't think we're getting anywhere."

"Just one other thing."

132 Jack M. Bickham

"Okay."

"For at least two decades both the East and the West have been experimenting with mind-altering drugs. Some of these are available only to medical doctors under controlled circumstances. But I've read reports of psychotropics that would make your hair stand on end. With one of those, it *might* be possible to hypnotize someone so deeply that they would do something totally uncharacteristic, as part of a post-hypnotic suggestion pattern."

Slagerfeldt's eyes narrowed sharply. "So you're saying that it *might be* that someone could drug a person, condition them under the drugs, and plant the suggestion that later, on some signal, they would do something catastrophic."

"I don't know. But I think we have to consider the remote possibility." Hart felt tension clamp his guts. "And if someone got to Davidson Myrick, then they might have gotten to others inside NASA, too."

"And with the right cue—"

"You call it a trigger. And yes. With the right trigger, who knows what somebody over there might do at a crucial—wrong—moment?"

Slagerfeldt stared at the undraped windows looking out over the Houston skyline. Minutes ticked by in silence. Finally he stirred, stood. "I hope this is all BS. You're to sit tight. From here on out this is my baby. I've got a friend who works for the Bureau. I'm going to spoil his weekend, too, if I can find him. If anything you seem to suspect is true, we've got a real problem. It could involve NASA."

Hart walked him to the door. "You'll let me know what they find out about the Olds driver?"

"Yes. You'll contact me at once if anything else happens here?"

"Yes."

Slagerfeldt shook his head. "You should have confided in me from the start, doc. I thought you were smarter than this."

"We all make mistakes. Look at the horses you bet on."

"Hey. I had one on the nose Saturday." Slager-feldt limply shook hands. "Of course," he added, "it only paid two-forty."

Hart closed and carefully locked his door. Then he inspected his balcony windows, feeling foolish but making sure all the locks on them were shut, too. He hurt all over from the physical beating he had taken during the high-speed chase in the 'vette. He limped to the telephone to call Kecia, then hesitated.

He was a target now. Even if his vague ideas about *why* were 180 degrees out of phase with the truth, he was still in danger. He could not bring Kecia into it. He had to stay away from her.

Having thought it out, he dialed her number.

"Hi! I was about to start calling you!" She sounded bright and cheerful, glad to hear from him. "You're all right?"

"Never better," Hart told her. "I went to Dallas today, looked over that clinic up there."

Her voice tensed. "No problems?"

"Nothing," he lied. "I didn't get much information either, though. Just routine stuff. They've got an elaborate computer system in-house. I wished you were there for that part, so maybe we could just bust into it and check everything for ourselves."

"Might not be that simple, my friend."

"Yeah. I copied a number down. I think it's a Dallas phone exchange. I don't suppose you hackers can break in over AT&T long lines, can you?"

"Hell, we can try, doc. What's the number?" He gave it to her. "That's a Dallas exchange, all right. Hey, why don't you come over and we'll play with the computer awhile . . ." Her voice lowered . . . "and then just . . . play?"

He wanted to. But he had made his decision. "Too late tonight, Kecia," he said briskly. "I'll get back to you in a day or two. Okay?"

There was a moment's surprised pause. Then she said in a different tone, "Okay. Sure. Stay in touch."

He heard the hurt in her voice. He wanted to shout that it wasn't what it seemed, that he was making space between them right now for her own protection. But if he explained, she would be right over here and he wouldn't have the willpower to make her go.

Better this way.

"See you later," he said, and hung up.

And wondered if he was going to get any sleep at all that night.

In the lobby of the Park Lane Hotel in New York City, Mona Reynolds clung to the arm of her lover, Jeff Hensen, and managed a hectic smile for the man whom unwelcome coincidence had just brought back into her life.

"They say it's a small world, Phil," she murmured. "And my goodness, isn't it true!"

Phil Underwood was pale, faint spots of emotion spotting each cheek. The three of them stood there an instant, the two men tall, good-looking, dapper in dark summer suits, and Mona capable of turning any male head in her cobalt cocktail dress that bared creamy shoulders and long legs at midcalf.

"I suppose it's not so strange, Mona," Underwood said finally, the pain in his eyes denying his smile. "This was our favorite hotel, too."

He looked so weak, so sad. Mona wondered what she had ever seen in him. "Are you in New York for long, Phil?" she asked.

"I leave tomorrow."

Mona turned to Jeff Hensen. "I'm going to the powder room, darling, and then we can be on our way. It was nice seeing you again, Philip." She turned and hurried away, elegant hips swaying.

Jeff Hensen uneasily eyed his rival. "Nice meeting you," he said, breaking off.

But Underwood, the pain and rage bright in his eyes, was not quite finished. "You seem fond of one another."

"I think she's wonderful," Hensen said honestly.

"You poor bastard," Underwood said.

Hensen's face heated. "What the hell kind of crack is that? I love her. She loves me. We're going to be married."

"Really?" Underwood's smile was ghastly. "When?"

"As soon as she can get out of her marriage."

"Ah, yes. That."

"We're going to be married," Hensen insisted stubbornly.

"I have some literature from the Hemlock Society," Underwood told him. "There are many less painful ways to destroy yourself."

"She's a wonderful woman! Everyone says so!"

"Yes. I daresay you could collect letters of reference for her from hundreds of men."

In the powder room, Mona bathed her hot face with a cool paper towel and examined her image in the mirror. She looked flushed, upset. Damn Phil Underwood anyhow!

She hated him now. He was like all the rest of them, wanting to take her freedom, control her, make her a possession. Only Jeff was different. Maybe.

For years she had tried to be a good wife to Boyd Reynolds. She sat home, vegetating, staring at stupid TV shows while he sat across the room poring over scientific volumes. He was weak . . . dependent.

When she wanted to go out, he said he had to work, and if she went without him, he pouted for days, making her feel even more guilty. But when she stayed home, he didn't even talk to her. He didn't care how she looked, how the passing years frightened her, how dull he was, how much she hated it when he rolled over in the morning with that big ugly thing sticking straight up in the air, and stuck it in her, and came, and then rolled off and went in without a word to shower and go to work.

How she had hated it!

How she hated him, and all the men like him.

But Jeff was different, she thought. The way things were now, they could only meet far from home, as here in New York, or in Denver or San Francisco. But as soon as she had a little more money saved from the payments those people were giving her, she could tell Boyd to take a flying leap, file for divorce, be free. And then she could have Jeff, or, if Jeff turned out to be like the others, she could at least be free to do whatever she wanted without guilt.

Mona considered it a godsend that Jones and Smith had contacted her. It was a dream deal. She could spend money the way she had always wanted to, make Boyd squirm, and be paid into her own account on the side while having so much fun. She suspected that they were making Boyd give them dumb little computer formulas from the labs, but she was sure her husband was not important enough to know anything really significant. No one would be hurt except Boyd, and he had it coming.

She went back out to join Jeff. To her relief, what's-his-name was gone.

"Hi," she beamed. "Now let's go have fun!"

The Earth was the size of a ball now, the kind Alexi Picaran had played with in the small, frozen yard of his home as a child. It was very beautiful. Alexi was lonely and worried.

Beside him, his commander, Valeriy Zubakov, stabbed at a computer input console with an ungloved right hand. Zubakov had grown more remote, more nervous and angry, with every passing shift. His eyes were puffy now from lack of sleep, and his face twitched. He looked, Alexi thought, very, very bad.

Alexi wanted to reestablish friendly contact . . . perhaps get his commander to talk and unburden himself of some of the pressures that were causing him to deteriorate at such a shocking rate. *Something* had to be done, and poor Alexi was at a loss as to what to do besides attempt to be friends.

"What routine, my friend?" he asked with interest.

Zubakov's fingers continued to fly over the small keyboard, making digits flow swiftly across the ruby-colored strip-screen above. "All must be in readiness," he snapped. "If emergency comes, the onboard computer must have this program."

"What program?" Alexi asked, feeling greater alarm.

"The program. The program." Zubakov stabbed more keys. "The time is here."

Alexi could have wept. None of this was expected . . . had been anticipated . . . nothing in the years of training. His commander had always been a model of control, of sanity. This deterioration was terrifying.

Alexi had tried, in veiled, careful language, to talk to the communicators back on Earth during Zubakov's sleep cycles. They had soothed him, believed not a word of the vague hints he could explain and convey . . . had even had Dr. Rachtiroff, chief psychiatrist of the mission team, speak to *him* in long, soothing cadences about maintaining calm, facing the perils of space, trusting Soviet science-planning.

They thought *Alexi* was yielding to stress!

Now Alexi faced a real crisis, and could only act on instinct. Zubakov was still resetting switches he had no business touching now.

"Valeriy, my comrade," Alexi said huskily, "the computer interface is turned off. Our directors on Earth cannot monitor this input for accuracy."

"Be quiet. Be quiet."

So intense and frightening was his commander's expression that Alexi reached across the control panel himself to flip the switches that would transmit the parameter changes back to Earth for verification.

"No!" With a hoarse scream, Zubakov slashed at Alexi's hand with his own, preventing him from throwing the switches.

"But Valeriy—!"

"Be still! This must be done! You have nothing to say about it! The corrections must be made!"

Alexi leaned back, numb with worry, obeying by force of a life's conditioning. After all, he told himself, Valeriy was the commander. He was the final authority. He had his reasons. Alexi had to be calm, reason through them until he understood.

Zubakov abruptly slammed a green switch on the overhead panel and pulled two coiled cords out of sockets on the side rack.

"What are you doing!" Alexi cried, really concerned now. "You have just cut off all communications with our controllers on Earth!"

"Prepare for engine burn," Zubakov said hoarsely, wild reddened eyes pivoting from panel to panel as he punched buttons, pulled small levers.

"No engine burn is scheduled! We are on course!"

Zubakov keyboarded a swift, intricate command. Lights dimmed. "Prepare for firing."

To his utter horror, Alexi saw his commander's hand move toward the firing sequence controls. Control center had ordered no course correction burn. None was indicated. They were on the path, on course. No correction was contemplated for weeks at the earliest.

Any burn now would be against all the regulations, all the training, all sanity.

It could only mean disaster for them.

"*No*, Valeriy!" Alexi cried, seeing at last that Zubakov had gone mad. "You must stop—!"

He grabbed Zubakov's arm. Zubakov made no sound, but he had the strength of four men. He threw Alexi's hand away, reached down on his far side and came up with something—a grayish object so unexpected, so alien in the environment of the spaceship, that Alexi simply did not recognize it for a fraction of a second.

"We must make the correction burn *now*," Zubakov said, his voice cracking, his left hand holding the Makarov pistol on Alexi. "You will not interfere."

All Alexi knew was that his life was invested in this mission, that he owed success to himself, his family, his mother country. He became the total of his training and devotion, and lunged to seize the pistol.

Zubakov squeezed the trigger. The pistol emptied itself of all eight 9-mm. rounds in a single ghastly explosive burst. Alexi Picaran was hurled out of his chair against the far bulkhead, red fountaining in a thick, weightless spray. Three bullets did not hit him. They instead shattered instruments and gauges in the walls and ceiling, filling the compartment with flashing shards of plastic and metal. Some of these blasted into Zubakov's face, penetrating to his brain. Blinded, screaming, Zubakov groped for the firing sequence buttons. His hand first fell on the controls to explode the emergency exit hatch. As the hatch fired, the pressurized atmosphere of the cabin exploded into the near-vacuum of space.

With his dying breath, Zubakov hammered his hand onto the firing sequence buttons. The Russian ship, two dead men at the controls, rocketed off course, turning in a vast arc toward the chill distant yellow of the sun.

At precisely the same hour, in Vienna, a world-renowned psychiatrist carefully examined his chronometer and walked out of his study to an adjacent private office. His fine old home was silent as a tomb. His wife and children had been accidentally killed during a skirmish between Austrian and Hungarian border guards a decade earlier.

The doctor turned on a light in the dark interior office and walked to a corkboard where color photographs were pinned side by side. One was of the Russian spacecraft, the other of *Adventurer*.

The time carefully penned in on the bottom of the Russian spacecraft photo had just passed, according to the doctor's timepiece. He ripped the Russian photo off the board, crumpled it thoughtfully, and dropped it in the basket nearby.

The time printed on the bottom of the American photo was near.

thirteen

On board *Adventurer*, the overhead panel displayed a miniature version of the clock in faraway Mission Control:

PRESENT TIME. . . . . 1702 GMT

ELAPSED TIME

DAYS	HOURS	MINUTES	SECONDS
0002	00	32	11.18

Beyond the windows, stars in unbelievable number shone with a heartless brilliance. Occasionally an attitude-control jet hissed from the nose, wing root or empennage of the spacecraft, creating a brief constellation of firefly particles. Automatic environment control mechanisms hummed or sometimes ticked hollowly, and far back toward the hatch leading to the cargo bay, gentle wide-spectrum lamps beamed on beds of algae and other edible vegetable matter beginning to prosper in their baths of controlled nutrient fluids.

On the command-level flight deck, Col. Buck Coll-

trap occupied the command seat on the left, with
Christie Hart beside him. H. O. Townsend had drifted
up from the level below to don the third set of headphones while the Earth news summary was sent up.

Word of the Soviet space disaster had become general knowledge in the middle of the night, U.S. time.
By American morning, the whole world knew.

The president had issued a statement extending
sympathy to the Soviet government and friends and
families of the dead cosmonauts. The president spoke
simply and with feeling, recalling his country's shuttle
disaster of 1986. It sounded like he had struck all the
right chords.

Russia had given few details of the accident. Amateur trackers and monitoring stations from other countries all agreed that the Russian craft had fallen
mysteriously silent several minutes at least before an
explosive decompression and freak firing of main engines which sent the spacecraft on a broad, curving
trajectory that would end in a fiery plunge into the
sun.

In Bonn, West Germany, the Common Market
consortium TransOrbital, through a high spokesman,
issued a progress report on its Ariane Plus vehicle program: the consortium's unmanned probe would launch
in September with a predicted ninety percent success
factor and no risk to human life.

Renewed demonstrations by religious groups had
already broken out in New York, Chicago, Los An-
geles, Dallas, Atlanta, and a dozen smaller cities in the
United States, and in London and Birmingham, En-
gland, and Melbourne, Australia. The leader of Libya
called for an immediate recall of the imperialist American spacecraft and diversion of funds to the Third
World. Guatemala attacked Mexico.

Meanwhile, the news summary concluded, two
tornados had done little damage on the outskirts of

Kansas City last night, and America's own Mars venture, *Adventurer*, was said to be "on line, on time, and on the money."

"Ah," Townsend drawled as the three of them removed their headphones, "those NASA PR types are silver-tongued devils."

Buck Colltrap turned sharply. "When did you come up?"

"Few minutes ago, pardner. I wanted to hear the news."

"Are you on the duty roster for this shift?"

"Nope. I just—"

"Then I suggest you return to the galley," Colltrap bit off, his eyes never leaving the computer display in front of him.

"Well, pardon *me*," Townsend muttered, and drifted belowdecks.

Colltrap glared at Christie. "What are you staring at?"

"You," Christie said candidly. "Aren't you acting a little weird, O sainted commander?"

"There's no room for clowning up here, Hart. Aren't you on schedule for some of your amateur radio work anyway?"

"Yes, any time I want to start now. But if you need any help with the status checks scheduled for this hour—"

"I can handle them alone. You're excused." Colltrap turned angry eyes to the instrumentation arrayed in front of him and over his head.

Sighing, Christie unstrapped and dove headfirst down the hatch into the compartment below. Her tiny ham radio setup was ready and waiting, the spacecraft window oriented toward the Earth for the directional two-meter signals. Townsend was hanging glumly onto an overhead pipe, staring into nothingness.

"He's just cranky," Christie told him.

"It's not like him, Christie. If he's this uptight a day out from our own moon, what'n hell is he gonna be like six months from now?"

Christie smiled. "Tired and calmed down, I betcha."

Townsend brightened under the warmth of her charm and floated over to the galley area. "You want a hot fudge sundae?"

"Not even a toothpaste tube of Jell-O, thanks. I'm scheduled for an hour here on the ham band and then it's my exercise time."

Townsend opened a compartment and removed an unappetizing-looking tube of gunk, removed the tip, and inserted it into his mouth. Squeezing the tube, he made short work of the contents. He made a face as he disposed of the tube. "I wish they'd figured a way to stow enough chow for us not to have to go back to the early-day type of stuff."

"Well, in a few more days we can start dining on some of the wonderful things in the hydroponic gardens."

"Right, right. Algae and lettuce. Yuk."

Christie put on her lightweight headphones and boom mike, checked the connections into the little Icom hand-held in its rack on the wall, made sure the coaxial cable fittings to the loop antenna were secure, and turned on the VOX. "QRZ Earth, QRZ Earth, from KU5B on board the spacecraft *Adventurer*. KU5B transmitting five-two, listening eight-two. QRZ?"

The din that racketed back in her headphones was stunning. Thousands of stations down on her home planet—hams like herself who did radio, TV, and computer communications as a hobby—called back simultaneously on her listening frequency, which had been cleared of normal local repeater operations during her scheduled hours of listening. By rules of the game established by the American Radio Relay League and

used on earlier shuttle flights, all the call signs heard
by her recorder would qualify for a special card from
her, attesting to the station's feat of talking to Mars-
Probe in deep space. She had signed hundreds of
cards prior to her departure, and would periodically,
as recreation periods allowed, radio back the call signs
that she actually had noted in her small logbook. Cards
for these few lucky hams would be filled in at New-
ington, Conn., the ARRL headquarters, and mailed
out. Everyone else would have to wait years until
Christie's return and analysis of her cassettes for additional call signs.

It wasn't likely that the state of radio art would be
advanced much by Christie's hamming, although amateur experiments had had surprising results before.
Her "space DXing" was good public relations and
good recreation for her, something she and her fellow
crew members would badly need before this grueling
journey was over.

"Okay, stand by," Christie transmitted after
furiously entering calls in her log. "Please stand by,
please stand by. I QSL the following stations: Delta
Lima Six Oscar Romeo, Whiskey Five Oscar Uniform,
Whiskey One Alpha Whiskey, Whiskey Seven Poppa
Hotel Oscar, Juliet Hotel Three Sierra Sierra Novem-
ber, Victor Kilo Three Delta Echo, Whiskey Five No-
vember Uniform Tango—and hello, Gillie Joe—Golf
Four November Zulu, and Kilo Hotel Six Tango Tango.
This is Kilo Uniform Five Bravo aboard the spaceship
Adventurer, listening one-forty-six, eight-two. QRZ?"

The callback practically knocked her headphones
off.

Christie was intent on following her plans and
having all the fun possible . . . and not thinking about
the fact that Buck Colltrap had been uncharacteris-
tically surly with her, too. He would get over it, she
thought.

He'd darned well better!

Hart called and finally tracked down Detective Bud Slagerfeldt Saturday afternoon.

"What's the problem?" Slagerfeldt sounded irritated.

"I wanted to know what happened with the man who chased me in the white car."

"They still don't have a firm ID."

"But they did find him."

"What was left. The body was badly burned and busted up. But it could have been worse; he was thrown clear of the explosion, which left us most of his billfold—full of fake identification—and enough skin on his fingers to let us run a national fingerprint check."

"What if you can't identify him?"

"We'll do our best to get the ID. If we fail . . . we fail."

"Bud, he tried to kill me."

"So you told me."

"What is this, anyway? Don't you know he probably trailed me from Parkview in Dallas? If you can tie him to those people in any way, it proves Dave Myrick was brainwashed up there some way, and probably killed when he started to get out of line."

There was a pause. Then the detective said, "You're building this theory up fast."

"Bud, I don't know of any other set of assumptions that might explain any of this."

"Maybe. Oh, by the way, stay home. The patrol is sending some people over later today to take a detailed statement from you."

"Am I being charged?"

"Not that I know of. But if you get smart with them and withhold any information, there's no telling what they might do."

"I'll level with them," Hart said, "just like I have with you."

"Smart."

"Bud, tell me what your friend with the FBI had to say when you filled him in on all this."

"Well, I haven't had time to locate him yet."

Hart was stunned. "Haven't had time!"

"Doc, I'm a busy man."

"Listen! What if this goes a lot deeper than we've seen so far? You know as well as I do that half the crazies of the world want MarsProbe to fail. What if Myrick's emotional instability was caused by somebody wanting to sabotage the flight? What if that guy who followed me was part of that kind of conspiracy? What if the Russians are behind it, and now that their own ship has blown up, they're going to intensify their efforts to wreck our mission too?"

"Or what," Slagerfeldt countered tiredly, "if it was a suicide after all?"

"Bud, damn it! Dave Myrick was totally committed to MarsProbe. Why, Joe Blyleven told a friend of mine that he was in Dave's apartment once or twice, and the main item of decor—a huge wall mural in the living room—showed *Adventurer* in flight. Is that the kind of man who kills himself on the eve of the mission?"

"Blyleven said that, did he?" Slagerfeldt commented thoughtfully.

"Yes, and I'm sure you saw it when you were in his apartment, too. A man doesn't *decorate* with his job and then take his own life, abandoning the biggest project of his life."

"Well, maybe so."

"So are you going to give this a little more priority, or not?"

Slagerfeldt's exhalation was audible, and it sounded wearily disgusted. "Doc, I've got two fresh murders and a particularly nasty rape on my hands, not to mention a shooting in a liquor store robbery and a missing child who just happens to have a city councilman for a grandpa. I am doing my fucking best on this case. I can't spend all my time chasing crazy speculations."

"Okay, Bud," Hart said bitterly. "You aren't convinced it's any big deal. If I want any more of this checked out, I need to do it myself. Right?"

"Doc, I like you. I don't doubt someone is out to get you. But I think you're seeing connections where there aren't any. Let me handle it my way."

"Thanks," Hart said angrily, and hung up.

When the patrol people came—two bulky men with an even bulkier old Uher recorder—he answered everything as honestly as possible. They went over and over details such as his speed, the Oldsmobile's estimated speed, damage to his Corvette, insurance coverage, things Slagerfeldt hadn't thought important. They worked very hard at it and it was past 5 P.M. when Hart finally closed the door behind them.

He thought for the dozenth time of calling Kecia. He couldn't. He had to keep her out of it for her own protection. Fuming over a magazine he wasn't really reading, he wasted almost another hour.

He couldn't concentrate on anything but Myrick, Parkview, and everything else that had happened. It all kept coming back to a growing fear about Christie.

What had Myrick's entranced outburst meant?

The telephone rang and he hoped it was—and then that it wasn't—Kecia.

It was.

She sounded bright and upbeat. "Hi. I just thought I'd check in and see how things are going with you today."

He filled with gladness that he immediately had to stifle. The best way to protect her was to keep her in the dark until the danger surrounding him had played its course. If his theories were all wrong, there was no sense alarming or endangering her. If he was right, she needed the safety of distance that couldn't be guaranteed if she knew the truth.

He said cautiously, "I haven't been doing much, just reviewing some cases. How about yourself?"

She reacted to the cool tone of his voice, her own enthusiasm damping sharply. But she sounded like she was determined to stay cheerful. "Well, I've been doing some hacking. Remember that telephone number at the clinic you mentioned to me?"

"Yes."

"It's a Dallas number, all right. I dialed it up and tried to see if I could get into their computer, see if there was anything I might find to help us understand about Dr. Myrick's treatment there."

"Is that legal?" He knew the answer.

"Of course not. Anyway, I'm sorry to say I didn't get very far. I got the computer prompt, and tried a few common security system entry codes. But it told me it was open to external lines for data input only, and access was by internal keyboard system only. So I guess you can call in to put information in, but it won't let you get in to look at anything unless you're in the building and keyboarding directly into the hard disks."

"Too bad," Hart said, and then he had an alarming thought. "Is there any way they might tell that you called, and trace your number?"

"No way. I took a little AT&T detour through San Antonio. Besides. The computer up there disconnected automatically when I asked for entry into the data files; no time to try an auto trace."

He breathed more easily. "Well, thanks for trying anyway, Kecia."

"So I guess if we really wanted anything out of

that system, we'd have to go up there and sneak into the computer on the spot."

"Not likely," he told her. "I have trouble remembering how to work the Apple at the office."

"No problem, doc. I managed to steal the internal password, which is CLINIC. So all a person would have to do is go to an online terminal, type in 'clinic,' punch 'Return,' and follow the instructions that came on-screen."

Hart was astonished. "That easy?"

"Hey, there aren't five people in Texas who could have stolen that password like I did. I'm one of the best hackers—"

"Sorry. —But unless you're in the clinic, it doesn't help."

"Hey." Her tone changed again. "Let's talk about it. I'll buy you a pastrami on rye and you can watch me starve my bod on a glass of iced tea."

He wanted to. Oh, how he wanted to. But he just could not put her at risk. There was some possibility that the man in the white Oldsmobile had had colleagues. Somebody could be watching him right now. He couldn't guarantee that there would not be another attack on him.

He couldn't guarantee anything.

He said, "I appreciate the offer, Kecia. But I'm really busy right now. Getting the office ready to resume practice, and so on."

"Well," she said after a pause, "how about if I come over?"

She was not making it easy. He had to keep her away. "I've got to tell you the truth, Kecia," he said, hating this. "I'm . . . feeling a little crowded right now."

There was a brief silence, then: "Oh."

A little exhalation of breath, little more. Soft surprise. And hurt. "Is this because I wouldn't talk about matrimony the other day?"

He almost broke his promise to himself, but he made himself go on. "That's as good an explanation as any."

"So if you can't have it your way, you don't want it at all."

Oh, Christ! Is that really all we understand about one another? "That's as good an explanation as any right now, Kecia." His voice sounded constricted . . . dead.

"All right." Her voice became crisp and businesslike. "Take care, Richard. Talk to you later."

"Kecia—" But she had already hung up.

It made for an evening that was just about as miserable as any he could remember. By 10 P.M. he was ready to do virtually anything to press on with what he had begun to think of as "the case." He considered his options. The first was to do nothing and he rejected that instantly.

A little later he began to see an easy way to pursue the clues he had about Parkview and Davidson Myrick, but this safe course had little chance of turning anything up.

The other scheme that began to grow in his mind was a little crazy. It also would bring results through risk.

At midnight he went into his extra bedroom and rummaged amid stacks of neatly cannibalized newspapers, journals, and magazines he continually collected.

One pile had to do with Christie and MarsProbe from the moment he had known she was on the team. He remembered back in February there had been a major supplement in the Houston *Post* about the entire mission team—pages of small pictures and brief biographies, emphasizing the size of the support group, its intellectual resources, and its diversity.

He found the piece, got a couple of 3×5 file cards, and carefully copied down, in tiny block printing, the

names of the team members that the newspaper had
called "The Select 50."

By that time it had started to get late. He turned to
CNN. They showed some television footage taken
from *Adventurer*, boring deeper into space. There were
a few seconds of Christie at her little ham radio rig.
She looked happy and excited, and so youthful and
beautiful she made his throat ache with love for her.

If there was the remotest chance that she could be
in danger, and he might have a key to defusing the
danger, he had to follow up on it. He might be a fool,
but he could live with that. He would never get over it
if he did nothing, and something happened that action
on his part might remotely have prevented.

He returned again in memory—all he had left
now—to the moments in his office when Myrick's eyes
had opened unexpectedly and he had spoken with
such terror and urgency. Myrick had said, "*The mission
will fail. . . . My role is crucial.*"

He had not said the mission might fail, or could
fail. He had said it *would* fail, certainly.

Was there some clue he had overlooked or failed
to understand? What did the number one hundred
mean? The number sixty-eight? What had been signified when Myrick said, *program in*?

He had gone over the same questions dozens of
times. Feeling worn out and thwarted, he returned his
attention to the TV set and watched dully as an interviewer plodded through a talk with a NASA scientist
about MarsProbe's ongoing mission.

"And you say this is one of the—and I quote you,
doctor—relatively routine portions of the early mission
profile—unquote. Could you explain that, doctor?"

"Certainly, Rick," the scientist said with a lean
smile. "Launch from orbit was achieved, and our
tracking confirms a nominal flight path configuration.
The crew will conduct experiments routinely now until

the first scheduled midcourse correction maneuver, which is scheduled for plus seven days."

"So," the interviewer said, "at plus seven days—"

He went on talking, but Hart didn't hear his next words.

The meaning had just exploded like a thunderbolt in his brain.

In working with Myrick, he had used the phrase *"plus seven days."*

That had been the moment when Myrick's eyes shocked open.

The phrase "plus seven days" had been the trigger.

Myrick had been saying the mission would fail *in seven days.*

Sick sweat bolted out of every pore of Hart's body. He reviewed again. The more he thought about it, the surer he felt.

Something was planned to happen to *Adventurer*, and it was supposed to happen seven days after launch. Next Thursday. Five days from now.

Myrick's death did not mean the threat was wiped out. It only meant someone had eliminated him to prevent his continuing treatment, which might result in recalling how and why a disaster had been somehow built into the mission. And two attempts had been made on Hart's life for the same reason, to make sure there was no one who might reconstruct the scenario from any hints Myrick might have given him.

Was he crazy, constructing a fantasy scheme to explain his normal anxieties about Christie's safety? But a fantasy did not explain Myrick's death, or Charlene's. Or the attempts on his life, or break-ins at the office and theft of the tape.

Good God. Who would concoct such a grandiose and bizarre scheme? The Russians, to make sure their own spacecraft won the race? The Third World? Religious maniacs?

That didn't seem to matter much right now. If he was right, they would try again to kill him. And he was the only one likely to be able to make any progress toward unraveling the skein because no one else really seemed convinced that anything was amiss.

If he was wrong, and there was no conspiracy, his plan of action couldn't result in much real danger to him or anyone else.

If he was right, his life was in danger anyhow.

He turned the TV set off and started nervously pacing the floor. He stayed up late, reviewing details of his plan. Kecia came back into his mind, and he hurt. The clock ticked. *Five days.* He was scared stiff. But if he was right, only he could make a difference now. And he knew what he had to do.

fourteen

Sunday a little after 2 P.M., LeRoy Ditwhiler, chief of operations for MarsProbe, leaned back in his chair at the Johnson Space Center. Tenting his fingers, he studied his visitor. "I understand your concern, Dr. Hart. It's very difficult for family and friends of astronauts on any mission, and this one is very ambitious. And I understand Christie is your only child?"

"Yes," Richard Hart said. His color did not look good to Ditwhiler, and he had obviously missed some sleep: his eyes were slightly puffy and the lines of tension were drawn clearly around his mouth. Impeccably dressed in a dark suit and tie, he looked his reputation as a top professional man—a psychologist, Ditwhiler remembered—practicing here in Houston.

But Hart's nervous call and request for a Sunday meeting, and his obvious worry, were common stuff. Ditwhiler had seen it often in those close to space crews.

Unwrapping a fresh cigar, he decided to sympathize and try to calm Hart down. "Every precaution has been taken, doctor. And the crew is healthy and relaxed on a nominal flight so far. There's nothing to worry about."

"I wouldn't have asked to see you on a Sunday if I didn't have some basis for concern," Hart told him.

Ditwhiler calmly lit his cigar and leaned back, intent on letting his visitor talk out his anxiety. *Hey, look at me. I'm practicing psychology on a psychologist.* "Tell me the basis for your concerns, doctor, and we can talk about them."

Hart frowned. "In the protocol for the mission, do you have a program sixty-eight?"

"Sixty-eight?" Where had *this* come from? "No, doctor. We don't identify computer programs that way, nor do we list activities by number in that fashion. Where did you hear about some kind of program with the number sixty-eight?"

Hart ignored the counter-question and gave him another: "If someone in ground control said, 'Program in,' what would that mean?"

Ditwhiler sucked harsh smoke into his lungs. "It might mean we had a certain bit of data—possibly a subroutine of some kind—loaded into a computer. But we don't use that term and I don't think I've ever heard it before. —Where did it come from?"

Hart hesitated, clearly troubled and baffled. Ditwhiler felt a little sorry for him. Hart went on doggedly, "Are key members of the mission control team here given regular psychological evaluations?"

"They're not required to take psychological tests once they're on the job, if that's what you mean. Why?"

"I worry about incorrect instructions—or wrong data—being sent up to *Adventurer.*"

So that was it. Ditwhiler relaxed. "Doctor, I'm sure you realize it's perfectly normal to experience a lot of anxiety at a time like this. But I can assure you, every man and woman out there in control right now—or at any other time—is not only highly trained and intelligent, but emotionally as sound as a rock. I would bet my reputation on any of them."

Hart winced, as if the cheerful words confirmed his worst fears.

"Look," Ditwhiler said, standing. "I need to visit Mission Control about now anyway. Walk down with me. Look it over for yourself. You'll feel better."

Hart silently went along with him. They reached the control level and went through a door that put them on an observation catwalk above the working level of the mission's central nervous system. More than two dozen technicians sat or stood at computer/television consoles; banks of lights and status indicators winked continually. Two dot matrix printers were spitting out reams of endless mathematical copy, and three engineers at a nearby work station were poring over these data and comparing figures with nominal projections. The big screen showed the interlocking orbits of Earth, its moon, and Mars, with the distant sun as a referent. *Adventurer*'s path was marked by a bright green line that appeared to have just left the orbit of the moon and progressed an inch along a thirty-foot trajectory pointing to Mars. Over the big screen, the clock display constantly changed final digits:

PRESENT TIME. . . . . 1920 GMT

ELAPSED TIME

DAYS	HOURS	MINUTES	SECONDS
0003	02	50	16.11

"You see?" Ditwhiler smiled, patting Hart on the back. "You should pardon the pun, but—everything running like clockwork!"

In Moscow, only two men remained after the top-level secret meeting. They were perhaps the two most powerful men in the Soviet Union.

"You believe the reports from the KGB are correct?" asked the first man.

The second man stood at the window, looking down on Red Square. Families strolled, enjoying their Sunday evening. The air was warm. He was filled with shock and anger. "Only one or two more aspects must be examined," the man said. "But yes. I believe the reports are true."

"How could a conspiracy of this magnitude escape our attention? I tell you, Sergei, this is a blow like none we have ever taken!"

"No one will know beyond these walls. As soon as the final items have been checked, we will meet again and decide appropriate actions. The people responsible for the death of our cosmonauts, and the failure of our mission, will pay."

"What of the Americans?"

"What?" The second man turned from the window. "What did you ask?"

"What of the Americans? If this information is true, their own astronaut team is flying into a disaster like our own."

"Yes. There is no doubt. They are doomed."

"Should we warn the United States? For humanitarian reasons—"

"And reveal the methods and procedures by which we have uncovered this plot? No. Let the Americans take care of their own."

"But the merest suggestion, Sergei. A hint, placed at once in the news. . . ?"

"No," the second man repeated firmly. "The American effort is doomed, just like our own. After their spacecraft has been destroyed, both nations will begin again on an even footing. Our country will still have a chance to be first to the Mars beacon."

"Do the Americans have any suspicion of possible disaster?"

"We think not. As you know, all their spacecraft transmissions are being digitized and encoded on this mission. We have not yet broken their coding, so we know little except the systems data, which are all normal."

"Then they probably are unaware, and their astronauts. . . ?"

"Must die," the other man said. "It is regrettable, but almost certainly their fate. Our national interest must come first. The evil things we have learned must remain our knowledge alone."

When Hart left the Johnson Space Center, he felt curiously calm. He had done everything he could, short of putting his plan into effect. He drove home, reviewing it.

He tried to be coldly rational in analyzing the possibilities. At the Dallas clinic, the receptionist had given him only a quick, bored glance, and was highly unlikely to remember the face of one of hundreds of routine visitors each week. Friday had been the last day for the only other person who had seen him there, Maxwell, J., Ph.D., and Maxwell would be over in Fort Worth tomorrow morning, engrossed in starting his own private practice.

Hart had to try it. The thought drummed in his mind: *four days*.

Bud Slagerfeldt called Hart's apartment that evening to report that a fingerprint identification on the Oldsmobile driver had come up with the name of a syndicate enforcer whose base of operations was New Orleans. When Slagerfeldt got Hart's apartment telephone recording, he stiffened:

This is Dr. Hart. Business requires me to be away for a day or two. Please leave your message at the tone, or contact my office number for a professional referral in case of emergency. Thanks.

Slagerfeldt used the radio to call the police cadet

who was supposed to be watching Hart and staying with him wherever he went. "Where are you?" Slagerfeldt demanded.

"Outside the building, lieutenant."

"Why aren't you with your subject?"

"I am, sir. He's in the apartment."

"He is *not* in the apartment. I just called and got a recording."

There was a moment's silence before the trainee came back. He sounded nervous. *"He hasn't left, lieutenant. I can see both of his cars parked in there on the first deck of the lighted garage from where I'm parked."*

Fuming, Slagerfeldt drove to the tower, found the manager, entered Hart's apartment with the aid of a master key. Hart was gone. The garage security man, when located, said yes, he had seen Dr. Hart enter a taxi from the inside elevator entrance.

"I didn't see any cab," Slagerfeldt's surveillance man said, mystified.

"Idiot," Slagerfeldt grated. "Jesus!"

He hoped Hart had spotted the tail, and with some sort of quixotic independence had just gone out to have a drink or meet a client, or some woman. At least no one had taken Hart out of the building and there was reason to hope his disappearance was momentary, and harmless. But it was disgusting to screw up so badly, and, in view of the new information about the Oldsmobile driver, a little scary.

Slagerfeldt liked the doctor. It was unlikely that a syndicate enforcer had been working entirely alone. There was at least one more local connection. He—or she—had to be found. Hart was not likely to find the other person. But that other person might find him.

For the moment, Slagerfeldt felt helpless. That was galling. "This," he said aloud, "is all I need."

The academy cadet tried to make a joke based on the detective's widespread reputation for loving to bet the horses. "No winners today?"

"I had one bet in New Jersey," Slagerfeldt told him.

"The horse didn't win?"

"There's a little lake in the infield at the track there. My horse got crowded and jumped the rail—ran straight into the lake. He bogged down. Before they could get him out, the son of a bitch drowned."

The cadet tried to keep a straight face, but cracked up.

"Keep laughing," Slagerfeldt snarled. "That sense of humor will help you a lot on the shit detail you're on, starting in the morning."

By the time Slagerfeldt left the apartment tower and drove angrily to headquarters, Hart—carrying a billfold stripped of ID and filled with almost $3,000 in cash—was on a bus for Dallas.

fifteen

On Monday morning, Hart used a pay telephone in south Dallas to call Parkview Limited Hospital. He told the girl who answered the telephone that his name was Richard Hennings, and that he wanted to check in for treatment of a smoking addiction. He gave her a fictitious Denton address and laid it on thick about having a week off, and wanting to become an in-patient before his month-old abstinence from cigarettes ended in nervous surrender to the old habit.

The girl asked a lot of questions and then quoted rates. There was a vacancy and he could check in today if he wished.

He wished.

After stalling the hour or so it would normally take to drive in from Denton, he then took a taxi to a corner near Parkview and walked from there, carrying his overnight bag. The male receptionist of the previous visit was gone, replaced by the young woman who had answered the telephone. She gave him a long form to fill out and he obeyed, using his cover story: self-employed, living alone, cash payment.

The girl took the papers back, went away for a

while, and then came back to open the inner door for him. "Dr. Silver is waiting for you," she explained. "This way, please."

Following her elegant legs down the hall, Hart counted his blessings. He had had a yarn ready about wanting Silver as his doctor because of fine things he had heard about him. Having Silver handle the entry interview made it easier.

The girl led him into a private office about a dozen feet square, no windows, fluorescent lights imbedded in an acoustical ceiling, beige walls, bookcases stuffed with journals, a desk and swivel chair, two facing chairs, a standard psychiatric couch against one wall. A thick-set man, about sixty, with a monk's fringe of gray hair, gold eyeglasses, and eroded features, turned from a computer terminal as Hart and the girl entered.

"Dr. Silver, this is Mr. Hennings, the new patient I spoke with you about?"

Silver gave Hart a soft handshake. His seersucker suit was rumpled and his eyes tired. He smelled of defeat. "Thanks, Jennifer. I'll buzz you. Mr. Hennings, I'm Jake Silver."

Shaking hands, Hart wondered what events had broken Silver, giving him the sagging shoulders of fatigue that went deeper than rest could ever cure. There was a sad resignation in the man, the mark of one who had been broken. "I'm glad to meet you, doctor."

"So you quit smoking about a month ago?" Silver asked after Hart was in a chair facing him and he had leaned back wearily in the swivel.

"Yes," Hart said, grimacing. "Twenty-seven days ago, to be exact. I was getting this hacking cough, and my allergies were kicking up—"

"Have you had allergy tests, Mr. Hennings?"

"No. It comes and goes. I don't know what I'm allergic to. But gosh, I thought the cigarettes couldn't be doing me any good—"

"Indeed they couldn't," Silver agreed.

Hart nodded and made a gesture as if diving his fingers into a shirt pocket for cigarettes that were no longer there. "I'll do anything. I need help."

Silver nodded reassuringly again and started explaining the program. Hart listened carefully.

Parkview was a small hospital staffed by specially trained psychologists and nurses, and had a two-physician resident medical staff. It specialized in treatment of relatively mild personality disorders and had had its special stop-smoking program in operation for about four years. The existence of physicians on the staff assured medical evaluation and treatment, if necessary, in addition to counseling. Parkview's antismoking program claimed a success rate of nearly ninety percent.

Hart's program, Silver explained, (if he chose to enter as an in-patient) would extend through next Saturday noon. He would then be expected to return to one of the group therapy sessions weekly for at least three months. After admission, he would be given a physical examination and the first of his private, one-hour therapy sessions. Each evening there would also be a group meeting; eight others were in the hospital at the moment for treatment of tobacco dependency. Parkview also worked with alcoholics and sometimes with other drug dependencies, but Hart's treatment would not put him in contact with patients in these categories. The hospital had a recreation room, a non-denominational chapel, a television lounge, and an exercise room with adjacent sauna and whirlpool.

All well and good. Hart could imagine a strung-out Davidson Myrick sitting where he sat now, desperately seeking hope for his tattered nerves. Who else from NASA might have sat in this chair? It was the major thing he had to find out, working from the list on the folded cards in the bottom of his shoe.

Silver concluded his litany of facts. "So are there questions?"

Hart made up a few. Would they be able to give him medication that might help? He had heard they used hypnosis. He was scared of hypnosis, but golly, if it might help, he was willing to try it. What if he couldn't sleep? Did he get a private room?

Silver gave all the right answers. "So what do you think, Mr. Hennings?" he asked finally, watching Hart closely. "Would you like to become a part of the Parkview family, and beat this damned thing once and for all?"

Hart hesitated, simulating a man wrestling with a scary—and costly—decision. It was not entirely an act. Once he committed, he thought, he was in their control, locked behind that electric door and God only knew what other security measures. Myrick had done it, and ended up dead.

"Yes," he said finally. "I'm ready."

Silver stood and shook his hand. "Jennifer will handle the financial details, and then we'll have an orderly check you into your room. Congratulations, Mr. Hennings. You've just made a life-changing decision, and I know you'll never regret it."

Hart hoped not.

Kecia Epperly walked out of her small faculty office at the university, heading for her morning class. A graduate assistant named Diana, who was almost her age, met her in the hall.

"Professor Epperly. Hi!" Diana was bright, pretty, piquant-blonde, bouncy in a canary T-shirt and white shorts.

"Hi, Diana," Kecia murmured, and started on past, burdened by the papers she had to return.

"How are things with you and Richard these days?" Diana asked blithely.

"Tell you later," Kecia snapped, and hurried on.

She knew Diana was standing where she had been left, mouth agape, and Kecia almost felt guilty about being so brusque. But the truth of the matter was that she just couldn't handle small talk right now.

Especially gossip about Richard Hart.

Shit, she thought, she should never have mentioned him to Diana and a couple of other people in the department in the first place. But he had seemed so damned *nice*, and everything had looked so hopeful.

And now it was finished.

She was still in shock over his refusal to see her over the weekend, the coldness in his tone. She had needed a lot of nerve to let down her defenses and he had walked right in as if he owned her . . . as, during their lovemaking, she had felt he did. And then to have him suddenly switch off this way—dump her.

She walked nearer the classroom, wishing she were someplace—anyplace—else. She knew she would get over it. She knew she should have had a bailout plan in place in part of her mind, in case of this kind of rejection. But it had been so fast, so unexpected.

Was it for the best? At least this way she would feel no more pressure, have to make no ultimate decisions about her life right now. And that, strangely, felt sort of good.

It had seemed after her devastating divorce that she would never risk again. But she had been just twenty-four and the healing had finally come. Then, during the brief time with John, she had been so sure—being in love again had felt so right . . . so healing. She had gulped her fears and said she would marry him. And then, in a panic of his own she would never fully understand, he had dumped her.

So long ago! It seemed forever, as if it had happened to someone else. But the hurt remained. This time she thought it would never go away, superficially healed over, like the scar tissue over a terrible wound, but still pain-filled when touched.

The hurt was what had made her so unsure about committing to Richard, although the rational part of her knew he was different . . . trustworthy . . . wonderful.

And now Richard had dumped her, too. Just when she had begun to think she might trust again. The child in her was so hurt and surprised, just so bewildered, she didn't think she would ever feel right again.

Kecia didn't think she had ever misjudged someone as badly as she had misjudged Richard Hart. She had thought she knew all about pain, until this.

In an interior office of the federal building, Detective Lt. Bud Slagerfeldt faced FBI agent Dan Fallon across Fallon's absolutely empty gray metal desk. Slagerfeldt had laid it all out as carefully as he could, given all the holes in his information and the fact that he was now seriously worried about the whereabouts of Dr. Richard Hart. "So," he concluded, "whatever the hell is coming down, we thought you'd better know everything we know."

Fallon, thirtyish, with a face that resembled a page with no printing on it, leaned against the edge of his barren desk. "I'm not sure what we might develop out of this, but we appreciate it. And I'll keep you up to date on anything we turn up."

"I haven't given you much to work on."

"Actually," Fallon admitted slowly, "we've got a, ah, little investigation already ongoing out there."

"Relating to this stuff?" Slagerfeldt asked hopefully.

Fallon looked at a corner of the room. "Well, not exactly."

"Someday," Slagerfeldt said, "you guys are going to share some information with us on a deal like this. And I'll faint."

Fallon's lips quirked, almost making a smile. "And this Dr. Hart is still missing this morning?"

"I just hope to shit he's not in the bottom of some lake. I don't think he is. He left his building alone. But he didn't come back last night, and the girl at his office says she hasn't heard from him either."

Fallon's eyebrows knit. "You don't think somebody might have abducted him and forced him into leaving that message?"

"I'm hoping not. I'm hoping the crazy bastard is off on some wild hair of his own, trying to do a Dick Tracy number."

"What you told me of him doesn't jibe with that kind of behavior."

"He's had shocks. His patient's death. His secretary. That car chase in which he very nearly lost his ass. Now his daughter is on board *Adventurer*. His daughter, for Christ's sake! He's got reason to be on the edge and possibly not thinking quite straight. I've seen people go into the psycho ward with less provocation."

"What are you going to do about him?"

"Issue a missing person report, if he hasn't shown by five o'clock."

Fallon nodded, got to his feet, extended his hand. "Thanks, Bud. I want to get this going through channels right away. I'll stay in touch."

Fallon walked him to the elevator. Slagerfeldt rode down alone. Outside, it looked like it might rain. He wondered if it was raining in New Jersey. He hadn't figured on rain when he picked today's horses.

*   *   *

Richard Hart's room was small, enough space for an aged hospital bed and dresser and one chair for a visitor, with a bathroom that he evidently shared with the room next door. The sullen nurse told him he should hang his clothes in the closet and call her when he was in his pajamas, slippers, and robe. When Hart did so, she brought a brown envelope for any valuables he might want to check into the hospital safe. He gave her his billfold, with almost $2,000 still in it, and his ring.

"Anything else? No? All right. Fine. You can relax a little while, Mr. Hennings, and someone will be along for you shortly to take you for your entry physical."

Left alone, he prowled the little room, getting oriented. He was on the third floor. The walls were faded beige stucco, the floor highly buffed brown tile. The only picture on the wall was a mountain scene of the painted-on-velvet school. His window looked out onto a narrow concrete balcony, but there were bars over it. Beyond the bars, below, was the back parking lot, cars angle-parked under towering shade trees. He could see the alley behind the lot and a storage building and a wood stockade fence on the far side of the alley that enclosed an old residential yard in which a large black dog prowled the weeds surrounding a grape arbor, several gnarled old maples, and a rusty 1953 Chevrolet sedan.

In the spotless bathroom, his neighbor had left shaving articles and a soggy towel on the side of the institutional bathtub/shower. There was a small window over the commode, and by standing on the water closet he might have looked out onto the same parking lot if the glass in the high window hadn't been opaque.

He returned to his room. The feeling was of entrapment. A small part of him wanted to panic and yell to get out. He controlled it and had a little talk with himself.

After a while, a large black man in a white cotton uniform appeared. He was not more than twenty, and built like a football player. He said his name was Lawrence and he had come to take Hart for his physical.

"Lawrence," Hart said, padding down the hall beside him, "you're built like a moose. Where do you work out?"

Lawrence gave him a slow, broad grin. "I play a little football over at SMU."

"I guess that explains it." They entered the elevator and it started down. "How much do you weigh?"

"Two thirty-three," Lawrence drawled.

"Lineman?"

"Huh-uh. Fullback."

"Starter?"

"Huh-uh. Too small."

They got out on 2 and Lawrence led the way to a glass door that said CLINIC on it.

The physical was conducted by a doctor in his sixties who didn't say much beyond professional, cheerful instructions and a few more standard questions for a form. He had the air of a man stoically going about duties required to keep body and soul together, and Hart wondered what sad professional accidents had left him working for a salary here rather than enjoying a third wife and the fruits of million-dollar investments like most of the doctors he knew.

There was a chest X ray and then some bloodwork and a paraffin cup to fill in the bathroom, and then the usual poking, prodding, and peering in the examining room.

"Your lungs sound good and clear," the doctor told him. "We'll schedule your allergy tests for tomorrow. Anything else you ought to tell me?"

"Can I get some tranquilizers?" Hart asked. "See, my nerves are pretty well shot."

"Well, we'll discuss that with Dr. Silver a little later. You just wait outside and we'll find Lawrence and have him take you back to your room."

Hart went out into the waiting area. No one else was around. The glass door into the hall was inviting. He waited for Lawrence.

Was there time to look around? Could he risk it? *Three days.*

Still no Lawrence. Hart left the waiting room and ventured out into the corridor.

No one challenged him as he shuffled along in his robe and slippers like any other patient. He went first toward the front of the building, where he found the lab, a small pharmacy, and doors marked SURGERY. Retracing his footsteps, he passed the clinic waiting room again, going by X ray. There were two unmarked doors, locked, beyond X ray, and then another shorter corridor intersecting to run across the back of the building just before this hall dead-ended in a steel fire door marked with a red exit sign.

Hart poked along the hall to the left, but found only two public restrooms and a broom closet. Going back the way he had come, he entered the other short hall. Two doors on his left were opaque glass and dark. He tried the doorknob of the first and looked into a dusty little library: stacks, a reading table and chairs, dirty windows looking out into a tree. He retreated and looked at the door across the hall. The sign said TREATMENT, and the door had no glass in it. He tried the handle. It was locked.

The next door on the same side had a similar sign, but someone had left it propped open. He peered in. The ceiling was acoustical tile and the walls buff plaster. Except for a couple of straight chairs, an end table, and an ancient glass cabinet containing some sterilized examining implements, it was empty.

Beside the cabinet was a door into the room next door, the one that was locked on the corridor side.

He crossed to the door and tried the knob. It turned. The door opened. Cold air gushed out over his bare legs and brilliant light almost blinded him. Everything in the room registered on his retina in the smallest fragment of a second: *chrome cabinets; overhead high-intensity lights like those in a surgical suite; a white-clad table or stretcher on rollers centered under the lights; tubes and hoses snaking out of some kind of glittering console. Two men and a nurse flanking the table, on which lay a still, portly, waxen-faced, unconscious middle-aged man with bare feet sticking out from under a surgery-green coverlet.*

The nurse and both doctors—or whatever they were—looked sharply at Hart as the door opened.

"Oops," he said, and hurriedly closed the door.

sixteen

He had screwed up.

There was nothing to do about it now but bluff his way through and act stupid.

Leaving the room by which he had gained access to the unlocked door, he hurried into the hall and headed back the way he had come, slippers making a flapping racket. As he turned the corner and started toward the clinic waiting room, he saw Lawrence come out scowling, peer up and down, spot him, and wait for him with ham hands on hips like an indignant line coach.

"Where you *been*, man?" Lawrence demanded. "You ain't supposed to wander around in here. You wanna git my black ass in trouble?"

"Sorry," Hart said, a shade out of breath. "I thought maybe I could find you."

Lawrence grimaced and took his arm. "Come on, man. From now on, obey your instructions, aw right?"

They had just turned toward the elevator when a door slammed behind them and footsteps sounded, followed by a voice. *"Wait a minute, there!"*

"Aw, shit, man," Lawrence groaned softly. "Have

you been snoopin' someplace where you ain't supposed to?''

The man who hurried up to face them, anger stark
in his ruddy features, was fortyish, plump, with scant
red hair and freckles standing out by the hundreds
against the angry pallor of his skin. He was still wearing the clinical jacket he had had on in the room where
Hart had blundered.

"Who are you?" he demanded, staring at Hart.

"He's a new patient, doctor," Lawrence said anxiously. "I was supposed to fetch him back from clinic,
but he wandered off—"

"He walked right in on a hypnotherapy session,"
the doctor snapped. "It's mighty lucky he didn't snap
our patient right out of his trance." He glared at Hart.
"What were you looking for?"

"I was just . . . walking around," Hart said, not
having to be a very good actor for the "scared and
worried" role he was playing. "I'm new, you see, and
my nerves are awfully bad, and gosh, I didn't really
think, doctor. I'm awfully, awfully sorry. Gee, I feel
awful about barging in that way—it scared me when I
opened the door and all those lights blinded me—I
couldn't see a thing—"

The doctor's eyes changed marginally as he took
in the meaning of what Hart was feeding him. His
chest heaved and he backed off a little. "Well, no harm
done, I guess, but I hope you learned your lesson. We
have strict rules. How would you like it if someone
barged in on one of *your* sessions?"

Hart hung his head and looked wretchedly
ashamed. "I don't know what to say."

The other man studied him for an instant, then
squared his shoulders. "Well, as I said, no harm done.
Lawrence, see that the patient gets back to his room."
He turned and hurried back the way he had come,
heels clicking on the immaculate tile.

Lawrence hustled Hart into the elevator and they started up.

"Who was that?" Hart asked.

"Dr. Heath," Lawrence said.

"Who is he?"

Lawrence's expression showed that he couldn't believe anyone could be so dense. "He just runs the hospital, is all!"

Left alone in his room, Hart sat on the edge of his bed and sorted out what had happened.

It looked like he had been lucky, and had gotten away with a serious mistake. The information he had given Dr. Heath, dropped into an apology as if by accident, had led him to ease off at once. And it was possible, Hart thought, for those brilliant lights to blind someone who blundered in from relative dimness. Possible but in this case not true.

The room was not a surgery. Yet the equipment had included both nitrous oxide tanks and mask and the materials needed for injection of something like sodium pentathol. There had been tubing on the surgical-style tray and the unconscious patient had been hooked to an IV which the nurse had been attending.

Thinking back, Hart could recall the faint sound of a man's voice coming through the door the moment before he opened it. Putting the picture together, including the droning tone of the voice he had heard but not registered until now, he had a fairly clear picture of what had been going on.

Hypnotherapy might be as relatively simple as the induction of a light trance through use of the most elementary techniques in the comfort of the office chair. If the doctor was a physician, a light tranquilizer might be administered orally before the session to aid in relaxation. In more extreme cases, Hart had heard of the use of Valium IV or even sodium pentathol—the common "truth serum" so often used in heavier dosages as a general anesthetic for surgery—or any number of other drugs that altered the state of consciousness.

Most of these were restricted to treatment of the very ill in the setting of a hospital's psychiatric wing. He was convinced the scene onto which he blundered had been such a treatment in progress. He wondered how violently ill the patient was, and what drug or drugs were being used. The use of powerful psychotropics in conjunction with hypnosis was not a procedure to be undertaken lightly, without very serious reasons.

If Dr. Heath and possibly others here were using such techniques on lesser cases in order to prove dramatic results, they were trampling not only ethics, but probably some federal laws, too. Was this why Heath had been so upset about his barging into the room, or was the explanation a simpler irritation that a patient was blundering around without supervision?

No answers were forthcoming immediately. An attendant brought him a late lunch on a tray, and explained that ordinarily meals would be taken in the patient cafeteria in the basement. Hart was receiving special treatment because he had been in the clinic during the normal lunch hour.

The meal was standard hospital-style fare, a watery patty of ground beef swimming in tan gravy, a scoop of powdered mashed potatoes, a dollop of tasteless green beans, a slice of white bread in plastic, a tiny green salad, a container of milk, a cup of coffee, and a small square of what looked like chocolate cake but tasted more like the wrapper the cake came in. Hart was surprisingly ravenous and cleaned up everything.

An hour or so later, when he was getting honestly fidgety, there was a light tap on his partly closed door, and Dr. Silver came in and sat on the visitor's chair. "So how are we doing?" he asked cheerfully.

"Fine," Hart told him. "But I think I made a fool of myself and violated hospital procedure a couple of hours ago." He gave the psychologist a nervous, engaging smile. "I hope you're not here to toss me out on my ear."

"When you wandered into the treatment room downstairs?" Silver said, unsmiling. "Yes. I heard about that. No harm done. Nothing was going on. But for your own protection, you'd better not stroll around in areas that aren't designated for your use. We do have a couple of potentially violent cases in the hospital right now, and if you walked in and got one of them stirred up . . . well. . . ." He shrugged and grimaced.

"I'll watch myself," Hart promised with evidence of heartfelt remorse.

Silver leaned back in the chair and crossed his legs, relaxing. "All your physical tests aren't back yet, and there's a standard psychological evaluation that one of our nurses will be administering to you later this afternoon. But I'm pleased to say everything looks fine so far, and I'm confident you're going to leave here a new man."

"Gosh, that sounds wonderful. But I'm nervous as a cat."

"Well, why don't you just prop yourself up there on your bed, get comfortable—you might as well take your slippers off and let your feet slide under the cover, that's it—and we can talk about it a little bit."

Hart followed instructions. Silver asked him a few more questions about his smoking, using the technique of mirroring Hart's stance, gestures and general breathing and postural reactions. Twice Silver gently urged him to slow down and take his time. Silver's voice was gentle and almost somnolent, lulling Hart into relaxation.

Inwardly, Hart resisted the induction. Outwardly he pretended at first to be a difficult subject, hard to

hypnotize, but then he began very slowly to simulate
the first signs of drifting into trance.

After quite a long time he let his eyelids slowly
close.

"There, that's better, isn't it," Silver intoned monotonously. "You feel good, you're relaxed, you see
how nicely you can do without chemicals of any kind.
Please lift your left arm slightly from your side."

Hart obeyed. There was silence. His arm began to
ache. He knew the test, and he had to hold the arm in
the air at this unusual angle as if the effort were nil.

"Now," Silver told him, "you will find when you
let your arm totally relax that it will remain where it is,
suspended in the air with no effort on your part. You
will not even need to be aware of your arm, and it will
simply remain in midair. You cannot even make it fall
if you try to do so. Now. Let all your muscles totally
relax, and your arm will not fall. Do that for me now."

Since he was not hypnotized, Hart was feeling increasing discomfort from the strained muscles in arm
and shoulder, and if he had relaxed for an instant—as
he badly wanted to do—the arm would have dropped.
But this technique was standard, to prove to the subject the power of the hypnotic induction: in trance, the
subject's arm would have seemed truly nailed in space
without muscular volition or effort.

Silver waited, and Hart's arm hurt. Much longer—

"All right," Silver droned. "You see how you are
in a trance, and you needn't be bound by ordinary
physical problems? Now you may let your arm fall and
it *will* fall, gently, onto the bed beside you. Let your
arm fall now."

With relief, Hart let his arm lower.

"Now let's talk about tobacco and the human
body," the doctor went on. "Let's imagine the effects
of poisons on your body. . . ."

It was pretty standard stuff and Silver was only

routinely expert at it. Hart let him singsong on, and thought about Christie, and about Kecia. He wondered if Davidson Myrick's lethal treatments had begun like this. How much time was left for finding out the truth about this place? The time pressure was brutal.

"And now," Silver said finally, "we can slowly begin to relax from the state we are in, and I thank you for being so cooperative. You may rest awhile. When you are ready, you may come back to normal consciousness, you may open your eyes, you may rejoin me here. You may start coming back now, and join me when you are ready. Signal by opening your eyes when you are awake."

Hart delayed a full two minutes, then made his eyelids flutter. Slowly he opened them. The light from the window was sufficiently bright to make his blinks genuine. He rubbed his eyes and stretched and gave Silver a cautious smile. "So that's what it's like?" he asked, feigning wonderment.

"You see," Silver smiled, "you are aware of the process at all times. How do you feel?"

"I feel . . . good. Better. More relaxed."

"Good." Silver stood and patted him on the shoulder. "I'll have the nurse come by after a while with that standard test for you to fill out, and then she'll show you how to get to the patient lounge and rec area. I think we've had a good start. I'll see you in the group session at seven o'clock."

"Thank you, doctor."

Silver left the room. Hart used the bathroom. He still hadn't met his neighbor. When the nurse came in, she had pencils, computer answer sheets, and a copy of a psychological evaluation instrument that Hart had administered hundreds of times himself before deciding it was more or less useless. He made a show of working hard on it.

He still hadn't located the central computer, his

primary target, and his experience on the second floor had convinced him that he needed to explore as much as possible to get a feeling for what else might be going on around here. He had to be careful. But time pressure created a throbbing pain in the back of his skull. *Three days*, he thought again, and then thought about it and corrected himself. He had only the rest of today, Tuesday, and Wednesday. The evil could come anytime Thursday, the seventh day. His time was running out.

Some two hours later, Dr. Heath summoned Silver to his office. When Silver entered, he found the hospital coordinator looking at the growing file on new patient Hennings, R.

"This man Hennings," Heath said, a slight frown creasing his freckled high forehead. "What do you think of him?"

"Pretty standard tobacco problem," Silver said. "I think we can help him and have him out of here by week's end. He'll be back for the usual outpatient group therapy—"

"His chest X ray," Heath cut in, "does not show the usual residual damage and discoloration of the heavy smoker. His lungs are relatively clean. Blood and urine appear quite normal, with no traces of nicotine or other drugs. I spoke with Nurse Burdick and the floor attendants. They haven't noted any symptoms of the extreme nervousness he listed as a primary complaint."

Silver didn't quite see what he was driving at. "He's adjusting well—"

"Then there is the matter of his blundering around where he shouldn't be."

"Surely that was just an unfortunate accident—"

"It may be, Jake, or it may not be."

Silver felt a deep chill. "If you think he might be an investigator of some kind—"

"I find that highly unlikely. However, let's take extra steps to observe him, Jake, hmm? You and I both know how much we could lose if an intruder . . . ah . . . well, enough said."

"I never counted on bad things happening," Silver complained. "They said nothing bad would happen. Now, with Myrick dead, their man killed down there in that automobile accident—"

"Shut up, shut up!" Heath snapped. "God damn it, Jake, we've been paid well enough, haven't we? Did you ever think you would be a millionaire? Just shut up! Maybe it's proved to be a little more than both of us bargained for, but we're *in* it now and there's no going back. If it comes unraveled now, the only question will be whether the authorities get us, or *they* do."

Silver made a shuddering attempt to control his nerves, and partly succeeded. He swallowed hard. "All right. I'm in control."

"Good. And don't overreact about this patient. The chances are a hundred to one that he's an innocent fool, just like he seems to be. But *watch him*. We can't take any chances."

seventeen

The onboard mission clock showed an elapsed time of five days, one hour, thirty-seven minutes, eight seconds. In Houston it was lunch hour. Time had become abstract under the merciless glare of stars on board *Adventurer* in deep space.

Tethered beside Col. Buck Colltrap in the experiment section aft of the crew quarters, Christie Hart watched him flip switches on a miniature oscilloscope connected to a wide-band radio receiver. Instantly the face of the instrument traced a multitude of incoming static bursts and impulses that shouldn't ordinarily have been there. Other instruments in the sleek graphite composite panel reported that the ship was being bombarded by intense radiation on all frequencies, from very low into unreadable portions of the UHF range.

The second day of experiments to monitor activity of the sun had chanced into a major solar eruption never before monitored so broadly from this area of the solar system.

Instead of being pleased, however, Colltrap seemed beside himself with angry irritation.

Pale with ill-controlled rage, he bit off his words being transmitted back to Houston: "We're in an anomalous arm of radiation extending out from the sun, almost like we were flying through the field of a highly directional antenna. Do you want the next readings in the infrared or X-ray portions of the spectrum? Over."

Houston came back: "Adventurer, *this is Houston. Stand by one.*"

Colltrap gave Christie a violent glance. "Stand by. Stand by. That's all they ever say back there. What do they think we are? Robots?"

"Buck, there's no great, tearing rush," Christie told him. "We've got two days set aside for this test at this time, and the biological experiments don't begin until work cycle seventeen."

"That doesn't matter! Jesus, you're as bad as they are! We could fly out of this narrow band of highest radiation at any time. All they've got to do is make a simple decision."

Christie looked into his red-rimmed eyes and gave him a little smile and a shrug. "You're right. Sorry."

"Jesus," Colltrap growled disgustedly, and bent again to the scope.

Christie continued to conceal her dismay. No one could ever have predicted that a cool old hand like Colltrap would have this kind of reaction in deep space. It frightened her. But all she could do was hope that the years of training, and his innate good sense, would reassert themselves. After she had quietly mentioned his nerves to Houston during one of his sleep cycles, they had come up with the theory that it was readjustment anxiety, and that there was every reason to hope he would stabilize in a day or so. She hoped to God they were right. In the meantime, he was awfully hard to live with in this hermetic environment.

"Houston," Colltrap snapped, his voice cracking

with tension. "Have you got further instructions for us yet?"

"Adventurer, *Houston. The computer is sending back data at this time. We will evaluate and advise, over.*"

Colltrap yanked the headset off his ears and threw it hard against the panel, where it bounced and floated off on the end of its lightweight cord. "Do they think we can just sit around all day and wait for them to get their act together?"

"Buck," Christie urged gently, "calm down! It's no big deal. Why don't you go into the exercise bay and—"

"No big deal!" Colltrap shouted at her, his eyes crazy. "No big deal! I suppose the discovery of an entirely new field phenomenon in space is no big deal? What's wrong with you and H. O. since we launched, Christie? Has every hint of discipline and scientific curiosity just gone down the tubes around here?"

Christie swallowed the angry, hurt retort. Her self-control took over. "I apologize, Buck. I guess I've been too lax."

"*You* take an extra turn on the exercise machines if you think it's such good stuff," Colltrap fumed, turning back to the experiment instruments. "I'm going to rerun these tests whether they think we ought to or not."

Christie watched, aghast.

It was nothing dangerous. They had plenty of power, and could have run the experiment a hundred times. But Buck Colltrap—cold, controlled, always on top of things and superbly capable of endless waiting or split-second action on the edge of the performance envelope—had never in his life taken an action in contradiction of orders. Now he had been told to wait but he was going ahead on his own.

Christie left him at the experiment and drifted up into the command level, guiding herself with the handholds. In the pilot's chair, H. O. Townsend was staring out at the ocean of stars.

They had entered an interplanetary region where even the faint obscuration of normal space, with its widely spaced particles of dust and molecules of matter, was missing: an area of unusual stark clarity. Nothing had quite prepared them for the startling visual acuity they had begun experiencing yesterday, and today it was continuing. Through the windows beamed the cold, fierce light of individual stars, the most intense blue-white, amber, yellow, orange, pulsing rust and crimson; tiny pinwheels of entire galaxies unimaginable distances away, winking beacons of green and blue, and to starboard the fierce yellow-white disc of Earth's sun. Townsend was staring at the cosmic array with profound admiration and wonder.

"H. O.," Christie said, tugging herself into the right-hand seat, "are you as worried about Buck as I am?"

Townsend turned on her, his eyes angry. "I don't discuss a fellow crew member in those terms, Chrissie. You want to gossip, get on your ham radio."

She gasped. Was *she* the crazy one?

Absorbing this new shock, she went to the bulkhead-window station where her miniaturized amateur radio gear was stowed. Peering out once more at the stunning panoply beyond the thick window, she told herself that Buck and H. O. were both just tense as they started to settle in for the long journey. She told herself that Townsend's nasty retort had hit her hard because *she* was still adjusting, too.

But it was more than that, and she knew it. Buck Colltrap's behavior was *not* normal. H. O. was worried about it, too, or he wouldn't have lashed out at her.

And she had been vulnerable to the unexpected because of Don.

The husband she might be losing.

Houston had been wonderful about building family contacts into the daily time line right from the beginning. With dozens of technicians probably listening on the high-density circuit, Christie had hidden her fears . . . had been upbeat, breezy. Don had sounded cheerful, too.

Underneath the surface, however, even over the metallic electronic circuits, she could hear the tightness in his voice. He had tried so hard to patch it up with her that last lovely night, and they had almost succeeded. But the fear was real, on both sides. And the anger.

She had to believe she would get safely to Mars and home again. But were Don's fears right? Would she be the same person?

And would he? Could two people who loved each other manage to stay together through this kind of stress? Had too much bitterness already come between them?

Sometimes, Christie knew, the best people tried their best, but just couldn't control all of themselves, their feelings and changing desires. Marriages died sometimes from trying too hard in the face of an avalanche of outside change and misfortune.

She shuddered. She was so scared, and it was not the thought of death out here that so scared her. It was of losing the damn guy . . . losing herself.

In Houston, monitoring devices immediately recorded the fact that *Adventurer* was repeating its electromagnetic field tests. A technician named Dover took the news at once to Jack Schaeffly, the senior officer on the floor.

"Why is he doing that?" Dover asked, puzzled and irritated.

"I don't know," Schaeffly said. He frowned at the big screen for a long moment. "It may not be significant."

Dover's eyebrows rose, but he said nothing. Going back to his work station, he wondered how the chief of training could consider a breach in discipline "not significant." Dover thought about mentioning it to one of the higher-ups, but decided it wasn't his place to do so.

In Washington, D.C., where Warner Klindeinst had flown to resume his other duties and prepare for a Friday night speech, protocol had been thick enough all morning to cut with a knife.

Now, finally alone in his private office with the visitor he had slashed through miles of red tape to see privately, he offered a cigar to Dr. K. J. Kharkhov, director of the Russian space program.

"Thank you," Kharkhov declined in impeccable English. "I do not use them."

"Real Havana," Klindeinst pointed out.

Kharkhov smiled. "In my country, Havana cigars are common."

Klindeinst put one of the hoarded cigars back into the humidor and carefully lighted the other for himself. "The fortunes of war."

As the dense smoke swirled over the large, dark mahogany desk, the two space chieftains eyed one another. Klindeinst, heavy, with his strongly Teutonic features and close-cropped white beard, looked like a Germanic statue in his expensive dark suit and military-straight dark red tie. Kharkhov, forty-four, and looking much younger with his pale blond hair cropped close, his ice-blue eyes calm, and a touch of recent sunburn rouging his cheeks and nose, could have passed for a Miami insurance salesman in his lightweight tan suit and ivory tie.

"My country is honored by your visit," Klindeinst told him.

Kharkhov made a slight gesture of dismissal. "As you know, it was scheduled many months ago."

"Yes. In view of the recent tragedy in your program, it's especially good of you to honor the commitment. I want you to know that all of us at NASA were shocked and saddened by what happened to your crew."

The Russian inclined his head. "Your message was received at my headquarters and circulated to staff. Thank you."

Klindeinst hesitated, then decided to be blunt. "Dr. Kharkhov, what happened?"

Kharkhov's eyes became hooded. "We continue to analyze data. You know, of course, that there was a cabin decompression of unknown cause, which triggered a malfunction in the engine controls."

"Were there warnings?"

"Nothing. No."

"There was a story in London that indicated some problem with communications prior to the accident. . . ?"

"The story is incorrect," Kharkhov said stiffly.

"Doctor, let me speak frankly. Certain of our experts have suggested that some breach of discipline in the crew might have caused a shutdown of communications. From what you have shared with us about your spacecraft systems designs, the probability against an accidental engine burn appears to be on the order of ten trillion to one."

"Still," Kharkhov grunted, "this is what happened."

Klindeinst carefully watched his Soviet counterpart. "Doctor. Our countries have been in competition, friendly and otherwise, for many decades now. There have been times in our space programs when we have shared, worked together, to our mutual benefit. We have a crew out there now, just as you had. If there is *anything* we should know from your preliminary findings which might help us protect the safety of our mission, I plead with you to lay national differences aside and share with us any information you might have."

The Russian scientist buried his chin in his chest. For what seemed a very long time, he did not speak. Air-conditioning hissed in ceiling louvers, the only sound in the deep quiet.

Kharkhov did know something, Klindeinst thought suddenly, with foreboding. Would he tell?

Kharkhov finally raised his eyes to meet Klindeinst's. "I can only say this, my friend. Our spacecraft did not fail."

"The *crew*, then?" Klindeinst said. "Are you saying that something went haywire with the crew? Is there something about the enormity of the voyage—or some other unknown peril—?"

Kharkhov's stony control suddenly broke, and his fist trembled on the edge of Klindeinst's desk. When he spoke, his voice shook. "Bring them back, doctor. Bring them back *now*. There are factors . . . I cannot say more, and will deny to my dying breath that I have said this much. But in the name of humanity—in the name of the love we share for our brave cosmonauts— *bring them back. Now!*"

Klindeinst could only stare in shock. "But that's impossible! We have to go on!"

"Yes," the Russian said with infinite sadness. "Of course. Please forgive my outburst. Purge it from your memory. I know nothing." He got himself back together and was again the smiling, unreadable Ukrainian. "I believe I will try one of your contraband Havanas after all."

Two days! Hart thought with a sense of rising desperation.

Late-afternoon sun slanted through the slatted blinds on the windows of the patient recreation room. On one side, three men and one woman played bridge. Nearby, two other women watched a game show on the theater-sized television set. Two boys, late teenagers, played Ping-Pong. Four other patients, three men and one woman, sat in easy chairs, reading magazines or dozing. Richard Hart leaned against an unused pool table at the far end of the room and pretended to be daydreaming.

He had been careful last night and through today. He thought his passive behavior had eased any suspicions he might have aroused with his earlier blunder into the hypnosis room. But his sense of time running out had now become almost intolerable.

Parkview, from all that he had been able to determine, was very much what it seemed: a small, privately owned hospital treating manageable cases of emotional difficulty, with a specialty in smoking problems, drug abuse, and alcohol. The teenage boys across the room were addicted to both marijuana and liquor, and last night while Hart had been attending the group session talking about smoking, a dozen kids had filtered into another meeting room for a program sponsored jointly by Parkview and AA. One or two very seriously ill patients were sequestered on the top floor, to which elevators wouldn't go without a key and to which the stairwells were blocked with locking gates. Hart had been told by another patient that people who went "up-top" were so doped with heavy tranquilizers that they dragged around like zombies anyway. The other patients were quiet, troubled, often a little depressed—in toto, not much different from patients in any other hospital.

The smoking program clearly paid many of Parkview's bills. Outpatients streamed into the ground floor offices on a regular basis. The group session last night, while not unusual, had had good attendance and was treated to an expensive video tape presentation, locally produced, about Parkview's program.

Hart had had two more individual sessions with Silver today, and was maintaining his pose of nervous hope. Silver had brought him a mild tranquilizer of some kind, and, not recognizing the tablet, Hart had palmed it beside the little paper cup and faked swallowing it.

His new floor attendant, George, had not noticed. Which was lucky, because George was an old-time attendant who didn't miss a lot of things.

George had replaced the black football player, Lawrence, late in the day. Hart regretted it because he had liked Lawrence and he didn't care for George. If Lawrence had been open, blunt, friendly, and genial, George was more like most hospital attendants Hart had known in the past—the opposite. About forty, George was a white man with thin hair and a heavily corrugated face that betrayed too many nights with too many bottles of cheap booze. His face was a doughy mask of latent brutality, his eyes inset, piggish. He was scrupulously polite and distant. Hart could sense in him a vast and bitter disrespect for the world in general, and for himself. Under the wrong circumstances, Hart thought, George could be dangerous.

Lawrence, encountered mopping the floor on the ground level, was philosophical. "They just transferred my ass, man. I guess I screwed up and I got what was comin' to me, right?"

Despite George's fairly constant scrutiny, Hart had located the central computer room. It was little more than an alcove off the treatment rooms at the rear of the first floor. There didn't appear to be any extraordinary security precautions. That had first surprised Hart, but then he had realized that nobody could guess that a Kecia had penetrated computer system security as a hacker, and had then sent him as a spy inside with memorized instruction sets that, she said, would finish opening the hard disk files.

The computer instruction codes, along with the list of names Hart had memorized from the space center directory, were rattling around in his head. He wanted badly to wait longer before trying to get to the computer terminal. But time was pressing too harshly.

He knew what he was going to have to do. The corridor door to the computers was locked after hours, but the door into the front reception area always stood open, and it looked like anyone could enter through the reception room, go through the adjoining business office, and enter the computer terminal room if they had the nerve to do so. During the day, people were always in the business office and it would be impossible. Hart had risked a quick trip down on the elevator last night—his only risk—and had found the reception desk and office behind it dark and deserted.

He had hoped he might somehow get the information he needed without trying to search the computer files of patient names. But that wasn't going to happen. He would have to risk accessing the computer tonight.

If the routine tonight followed last night's, it would grow quiet by ten o'clock, and room lights would go out. His friend George would retire to a small glassed-in area at the back of the corridor and pile up behind a desk with his porno magazines. That would be the time.

Hart watched the others in the rec room. He had learned to spot the signs of those undergoing some form of hypnotherapy: a vagueness of expression, looseness of facial muscles, slightly dreamy quality in the eyes. An untrained observer would have noticed nothing. Hart noticed.

A tall and heavyset man came into the lounge. Wearing tennis sweats and canvas shoes, he put thick hands on hips and looked around passively. His name, Hart had learned in a brief conversation this morning, was Jackson. Hart had initiated the hallway exchange of pleasantries because Jackson was the man he had found in the hypnotherapy room on the second floor yesterday. Hart hoped to talk more with him and learn something about the problems that were serious enough to warrant such deep therapy.

Jackson's eyes found him. Hart smiled encouragingly and waved. Jackson, hands jammed in the baggy pockets of his sweat jacket, shambled over. He was overweight, folds of flesh quivering under his chin, and his eyes had deep pockets under them. "Afternoon," he rumbled.

Hart held out his hand. Jackson shook it. His grip was flabby, as if not much spirit was in him. "How goes it?" Hart asked companionably.

"Another session coming up," Jackson said, and sighed.

"I'm in about smoking," Hart said. "What about you?"

Jackson patted his ample gut. "Overweight. Learning to diet."

Hart concealed his surprise. A problem with dieting was not the kind of situation that warranted the heavy therapy he had witnessed. "How's it coming along?"

Jackson sighed again. "They hypnotize me, we talk, I wake up, I'm hungry again."

It was the kind of statement that one was supposed to smile at, so Hart did. He asked, "What do you do for a living, Mr. Jackson?"

"I work at a bank in town."

"You're lucky to get some time off for this kind of treatment."

"Well." Jackson paused, considering, then said, "Actually, I'm the president of the thing."

"I see."

"We do business with Parkview. They're planning

an expansion, another facility in Richardson. I've been having this problem, and I thought I could get some help, and at the same time gain a firsthand look at how effective they are, what kind of a risk they might be for such a major loan program."

"And you've concluded?"

"I was skeptical about their capital structure at first," Jackson said, looking a bit worried. Then he brightened. "But each day I'm here, I become more and more convinced that they're a promising outfit. I came in pretty well convinced that their present debt structure simply didn't justify the kind of growth they contemplate. But they're good people. Even a bank has to take a chance now and then. As time goes on, I get more and more certain that we should lend them whatever they think they need. I'm experiencing a funny thing for a banker . . . a kind of leap of faith."

"Then you'll probably recommend approval of the loan?"

"Yes." Jackson's jaw set and he looked formidable. "And the loan committee will go along. I have ways to insist."

"Do bankers often experience this kind of 'leap of faith,' Mr. Jackson?"

"Never," Jackson said. "But this is different."

"Their financial record—"

"The bank hasn't finished the usual investigation. But that doesn't matter."

"I would have thought you'd have to see their books . . . check into their debt structure . . . credits and debits—"

"All irrelevant," the paunchy man snapped. "Figures can lie. Their plans are visionary. Time is of the essence. They deserve all the help we can provide. Their loan *must* be approved at once."

His voice sounded almost like a taped message, and Hart experienced a deep chill of understanding.

Jackson might be getting some post-hypnotic help with his weight problem during his sessions. But that was not why he had been knocked out cold and stretched on a table like a side of beef in the treatment room on the second floor.

And he was responding nicely, thank you.

Hart took a slow, deep breath. He knew now he couldn't wait any longer. Tonight he had to get into the computer and search the patient names.

Deep inside the NASA complex in Houston, Dr. Boyd Reynolds carried his attaché case through the checkpoint and the data processing lab. Entering the mainframe control studio, he ignored the two programmers busily working over keyboards on the far side of the room. He took his attaché case to the No. 3 data storage unit, opened it, connected his cable to the RS-232C ports, and punched a few buttons on the lap computer inside his case.

The codes went through instantly and the subroutine he had been ordered to copy began to unload into his case computer at a rate of 9600 baud.

A hand suddenly came down firmly on his shoulder.

He jerked around. "Don't bother me now. I—"

He stopped.

The two men standing behind him were not regular employees. They were tall, heavyset, unsmiling, gray-suited, with cool eyes and grimly set faces.

"Dr. Reynolds," the man with his hand on his shoulder said, "you're under arrest."

"That's outrageous!" Reynolds blustered, panic already rushing like sludgy ice through his bloodstream. "You must have made a mistake! I have every right to copy data to work on with my home system! I—"

"Dr. Reynolds," the man intoned, producing a wallet which opened to reveal a terrifyingly official FBI identification, "just come quietly. Please. We've been watching you for more than three months. You have the right to remain silent. You have the right—"

"No!" Reynolds cried. In the instant, he saw a life's work gone—saw what a fool he had been. "You don't understand! I had no choice! Nothing I've copied is of any significance! My wife—my financial situation—you don't understand the *pressure* I've been under—*please!*"

He cried and then wept and then pleaded as they disconnected his little computer from the mainframe, firmly took both his arms, and led him rapidly away. His cries echoed back down the steel hallway after he had gone, and the two innocent technicians remaining in the lab looked at one another with incredulity, shrugged, and went back to work.

eighteen

Late evening stretched long shadows across the fields when LeRoy Ditwhiler and John Selmon met in Selmon's office with the door closed, all telephone lines but the one from Mission Control switched off.

The two men primarily responsible for the success of MarsProbe sat in black leather conference chairs, facing one another across a small ceramic coffee table in the corner of Selmon's office. On the wall was a giant photographic print of Neil Armstrong standing on the surface of the moon. One of Ditwhiler's ever-present stogies fumed in a metal ashtray on the table, and he scratched the top of his balding, sunburned head as he studied hasty notes on a yellow legal pad.

"Then the FBI is convinced that Boyd Reynolds wasn't inputting any data that might sabotage some maneuver?" he asked.

Selmon tried to get the long legs of his lank six-and-a-half-foot frame arranged between himself and the table. "You know they've been poking around for months, LeRoy. They know what he got out, and they know nothing went in."

"Who was paying him?"

"We ought to know that within a few days, they

said. They've got somebody under cover, but some things have to be done yet before they can say it's wrapped up."

Ditwhiler angrily chewed the cigar. "God damn it, don't they know we've got a crew at risk up there? If it's a foreign power—"

"I got that much out of them. They don't think Reynolds was being paid to spy for a foreign power. At least not directly. What he was taking were new programs for manipulating enormous database files. Some American firm must have wanted the stuff badly, probably so they could steal the design and market a mainframe management program of their own."

"I don't buy that for a fucking minute. What about what Kharkhov told Klindeinst?"

Klindeinst had briefed them during a conference call. He was convinced that the Soviet probe had been sabotaged, and that *Adventurer* might also be facing unforeseen disaster. He was conferring with top officers of the CIA at this hour.

"We can't be sure we're in danger," Selmon said now. "We agreed to continue the mission pending further information."

"But holy shit," Ditwhiler groaned. "What if somebody *could* sabotage the Russian probe and ours at the same time? What about those reports that their crew went bonkers? What if they've gotten to *our* folks somehow?"

"We have to hope that's impossible. In the meantime, I've asked Trudy to find Dr. Hart, Christie's father. I told you about his visit Sunday. He was worried sick. Now I think maybe he knew something."

"Of course he sounded crazy then," Ditwhiler observed.

"We have to hear his evidence, the basis of his suspicions, and we have to get our own people and the FBI on whatever he's turned up—and fast."

"Any luck finding him yet?"

"Not yet." Frown lines filled Selmon's forehead. "Recordings at his office and home."

"We don't have forever."

"Tell me about it," Selmon snapped. Then he repented the outburst. "Sorry, LeRoy. I'm on edge."

Ditwhiler dismissed the issue with a wave of his cigar. "What do we do in the meantime? Right now?"

"I've had a talk with our systems analysts. They're reviewing everything, looking for weak links. Also, I'm tightening up our communications protocol. I've issued orders that no comm channels are open to anybody but Burns, Jurgensen, Murphy, Schaeffly, you, and me. The order is already in effect. I added your and my names because I intend for one or the other of us to be on duty down there around the clock."

"Hey," Ditwhiler said morosely. "Overtime money."

Selmon nodded at the joke, which referred to the killing overtime hours so many of them had been putting in for many months with no sign of being paid for it. "While they're tracking down Dr. Hart, I'll take the first turn in the control center."

"Maybe Hart will show up for the radio schedule between family and crew members."

Selmon shrugged. "I checked a few minutes ago. The others we invited are already here. He isn't."

"If he does show up—"

"I'll be here. We'll talk."

"What time do you want me to come on tomorrow?"

"It's past eight now. How about in twelve hours?"

Ditwhiler looked skeptical. "Can you hang in there until then?"

"If the coffee doesn't run out."

They broke up the session. Neither man smiled on the way out. Both were thinking roughly the same thing: *I hope Kharkhov was talking through his hat.* But both were also thinking that men like Kharkhov didn't do that.

Aboard *Adventurer*, Christie Hart faced the TV camera with determined optimism. "It's going fine, honey. Everything is right on the time line and all equipment is working perfectly."

There was a slight transmission time lag, and then her husband Don's voice came back through the headphones: *"Are you sure you don't want to reconsider and let me come along?"*

It was said just right, lightly and easily, but it struck her with a sharp pang. How she missed him already! "Honey, I would," she said aloud, "but it's like we decided: somebody has to stay home and take care of Pete." Pete was the parakeet.

When his voice came back, it had a tinge of that flat, hurt quality that she knew he was trying so hard to combat. *"Okay. Well, it was hot today, about a hundred. I've got a bridge game at the club Saturday night. Dean and Hank and Jessica."*

"Sounds like fun," Christie said lamely. Henry's wife Jessica was a smashing blonde with a reputation as a flirt . . . or worse. Into Christie's mind leaped a shocking picture of Don and Jessica together, not at the club, not playing bridge, not with anyone else around—*oh, shit!* "I hope you bid a grand slam," she said shakily.

"I'll bid one for you."

They went on through the scheduled time. She told him about the electrical field experiments, assuring him there was absolutely no danger, and adding that they were leaving the anomalistic field behind and returning to normal space. He told her small gossip from the office and said again how much he enjoyed watching her on news television broadcasts from the spacecraft. They were upbeat and cheerful and thoroughly dishonest.

She said, "We're pleased with how we're holding the time line," when she meant, *Oh, Donnie, I'm so scared of losing you—I want you so much right now—if you screw Jessica I'm going to die.*

He said, "Everyone is proud of you," when in his voice she heard the meaning: *I'm keeping a stiff upper lip, married to a pop culture icon and being called "Mr. Hart" all the time.*

She said, "Space travel is really different from what I expected in some ways—even more exciting—" when she was thinking: *Already I ache for you. I ache to feel you against me. I ache to feel real air touching my skin, the tug of gravity giving everything a rightside up, crowds at a shopping mall, your arms around me.*

Their voices rattled hollowly, cheerfully, back and forth.

She could do this thing. But the homesickness and the fear were real, growing, constant. She just wasn't tough enough, she told herself. She just loved him too much.

And almost all the journey gaped ahead. Would they reach Mars okay? Would the lander perform adequately, as charted? What would they find? Would the lander engine get them into Mars orbit again?

Would they find their way back home?

She tried to be tougher—stay in the here and now. "I guess I'd like to talk with Dad, now, honey," she said.

There was a slightly longer pause. *"Well, Christie, uh, your dad isn't here right now. I guess he had a late emergency of some kind."*

"Don, you sound funny. Has something happened to my father?"

"He's fine. Just fine. No problem. Uh, he said to tell you hi, and he's sure sorry that earning a living interfered with his rec time tonight."

It sounded like her father. Christie relaxed. For a moment she had worried. But she realized that she

might be prone to worry about everything out here.
She had to watch that.

A few minutes later, when the contact was concluded, Don Dillingham left the private booth and
watched while a communications specialist fitted H. O.
Townsend's wife with the headphones and boom
mike, then closed the door to leave her alone in a simulation of privacy. Every word was being monitored
and recorded. But the booth was a nice touch, giving
one the sense of being unobserved during talk with the
loved one.

John Selmon walked over and put a hand on
Don's shoulder. "You handled her question about her
father just right. Thank you."

"Where *is* he?" Don demanded, worried.

"We'll track him down. Not to worry."

But Don was worried, and he didn't like it a bit.

The man in the room adjacent to Hart's was
named Ellingson, and he was being treated for a drinking problem. Once he realized he had a next-door
neighbor, the lonely middle-aged man was hard to get
rid of. He sat in Hart's room until past 10 P.M.,
nervously talking about baseball, the weather, his
grown children, fishing, and the record store he had
once owned. Hart felt sorry for him.

"When will some of your family visit?"

"They won't. Only one in Dallas is my ex-wife,
and she says she never wants to spend any time with a
drunk again."

"You're not drunk now."

"I know . . . I know."

"Have you told your ex-wife you're in here for
treatment, and you never intend to be drunk again?"

"Yes."

"What did she say?"

"She said, 'You will be, buster. Once a drunk, always a drunk.'"

Hart winced. "Great to have that kind of support."

Ellington stared sadly into the corner. "She was so sweet when we were young. She loved me so much. Now she hates my guts. Well, she has every right. Everything has been my fault."

It was so common in his own practice that Hart nearly slipped into a therapeutic role and pointed out to the lonely man perched on the edge of his bed that it took two people to destroy a relationship. He remembered his disguise here at Parkview just in time, and simply shrugged and looked sad in return. The less said, he thought, the sooner his neighbor might return to his own room.

At ten, the lights in the hall flickered and dimmed, and the announcement came that any visitors must leave at once. A handful of people trooped down the hall on their way outside. Ellingson talked another minute or two, and went back to his own room. Hart, still in his pajamas, climbed into bed and waited, his pulse thumping in his ears.

He figured he should wait at least a half hour.

He waited an hour.

By that time the floor was silent, the lights in the hall dim, his own room lights all the way off except for the tiny nightlight on the wall near the door. No one had looked in, and if last night's experience was a criterion, no one would until about 2 A.M.

Which was plenty of time.

Slipping out of bed, he went to the closet and silently opened the metal door. He pulled his trousers on over his pajama pants and stuffed the pajama top in before fastening his belt. He left his feet bare. Quieter.

It took only seconds to mound his bedclothes up over the pillows to simulate a sleeping person. Then, heart pumping away, he slipped his hall door open and looked up and down.

The lighted nursing station at his far left appeared deserted. If someone was behind the tall counter, he or she was well out of sight and probably reading. George, the new attendant, was in his little alcove just beyond; Hart could see his long legs extended out into the doorway of his cubbyhole where he was probably propped up with another bit of porn.

The doors along the hall were uniformly cracked open about four inches, and all were dark. To the right were only more rooms and the red glowing EXIT sign at the far end, over the metal door.

Hart stepped out and walked to the far end of the door and gently pushed the metal door open and went out onto the back stairway. He was astonished at how easy it seemed. He went down the steps quickly but quietly, and within two minutes was opening the door to the first floor, and the computer area.

No one showed in the darkened corridor. A security light glared in the reception area far to the front. He made his way along the hall, peered in the reception area, saw no one. *If they catch you now you can't talk your way out of it anyhow.* Boldly he walked through reception and the little business office behind it, and entered the room where the computer terminals were. Screens glowed gray, with single access lettering lines vivid green across their tops.

He went to the far terminal and sat down. His hands were so sweaty that his fingers slipped on the keyboard as he punched in the data access code already displayed on the screen. He wanted a cigarette so badly he could have bitten his fingernails.

But he was committed. He ran through the computer entry instructions he had learned from Kecia and found the way to get a list of patient check-ins. When he punched the "Return" button, he got into a brief dialogue with the machine onscreen.

LIST PATIENT NAME ONLY (LAST, FIRST, MI)?
Yes
START DATE FOR LISTING (MM/DD/YY)?
06/01/94
END DATE FOR LISTING (MM/DD/YY) (RETURN FOR CURRENT DATE)
Ret.
FOR ALPHABETICAL LISTING, TYPE A. FOR
CHRONOLOGICAL, TYPE C
A
READY FOR ONSCREEN LIST? TYPE Y TO BEGIN.
Y

Immediately the list of patient check-ins began to stack up on the screen, the names scrolling out with astonishing speed. Hart stared at them, comparing them with the long mental list he had done his best to memorize. He was sure he would recognize a familiar name, and for all the common ones he had also memorized a first name and middle initial.

There could be a mistake, but he doubted it. And if he was on a fool's errand, it was far too late to worry about it now anyway.

The names, bright green on gray, kept stacking up. Hart realized that he should have specified only patients checked in for treatment overnight or longer, but he didn't know how to do that.

Intensely aware of the passing of time, he stayed glued to the screen. *Come on, come on!*

The *Jones . . . King . . . Limnetz* names went by, and *Mason, S. W.,* scrolled out. Hart was beginning to doubt the wisdom of any of this when the next name started.

He read it with a little tingling shock of discovery.

"Bingo," he murmured softly, aloud.

"Right," a big voice said close behind him, making him jump with shock. "Bingo. Right." A heavy hand descended painfully on Hart's shoulder.

He turned, caught in the grip of George, the hulking attendant from his floor. Panic gusted. He pulled free and rushed for the door.

He managed two steps.

Then George moved violently and his big fist crashed into the back of Hart's neck, and Hart plunged into layer after layer of gauzy, deepening blackness.

nineteen

A three-piece combo was playing in a dim corner of the cocktail lounge, and a few couples were dancing, when Mona Reynolds breezed in past the bar, briefly looked around, and headed for the booth where her two friends were waiting. She looked smashing in a bright aqua sundress, her hair loose on bared shoulders, her spikes clicking confidently on the parquet floor.

"Hi," she smiled breathlessly, sitting down opposite the two men who called themselves Smith and Jones. "Did you miss me?"

"Thanks for coming, Mona," Smith said.

"I just got back from New York a couple of hours ago and got your message on the machine."

Smith nodded. "We appreciate your coming right over. We—"

"I would have been here sooner, but do you know that husband of mine wasn't even at the airport to pick me up? I suppose he's got some silly so-called emergency, or else he's spending all our tax money on another of those all-night conference calls with the people out at the Jet Propulsion Lab." Mona paused and looked at the two men. "Wow, aren't we both *grim* tonight. What's it all about? Why the hurry-up telephone call?"

"There's no easy way to say this, Mona," Smith said quietly. "Your husband didn't meet you at the airport because there's been trouble."

Mona's hectic smile began to fade. "Trouble?"

"He's been picked up."

She leaned forward, the smile gone, cords standing out in her neck and betraying her most carefully kept secret, her actual age. "Picked up? What do you mean, 'picked up'?"

"We don't know any details. We just know they arrested him at work earlier today."

Mona's voice shrilled. "*Arrested?* Boyd? Oh, my God!"

"Keep your voice down, keep your voice down!" Smith leaned across the table. "Now listen. —*Listen,* God damn it! —Are you listening?"

"Yes." Mona's voice trembled. Her eyes were wet, frightened.

"We don't know what the charges might be. Whatever happens, you can't be implicated, and neither can we. You *must* keep your head and protest your innocence no matter what those federal boys try to throw at you."

"At me? You mean they're going to arrest *me,* too?"

"No," Smith said patiently. "I don't think so. They have no way to link our, ah, arrangements with your husband's situation. But they may try to fake you out—trick you into making a stupid confession. That's what we're here to tell you. *Stay silent.* Act stupid . . . shocked. Whatever they pull, you know nothing. And you never heard of us. Is that understood?"

"Y-yes," Mona choked. She had begun to tremble, and with her self-assurance and pride extinguished, she looked pitifully old, like a little old lady all made up for a play, wearing a dress borrowed from an inge-nue. "But if they arrest me, too—"

"They have nothing on you. You must remember that. And remember something else, too, Mona. — Mona?" She had begun to stare dazedly at the danc-ers. Smith grasped her wrist.

"You're hurting me!"

"You'll say nothing about us or our arrangement. Do you understand me, Mona?"

"Yes," she whimpered.

"Because if you do," Smith said quietly, with a tone that brimmed potential violence, "it will be the last time you ever betray good friends. *The last time*. Do you hear what I'm saying, Mona?"

Mona Reynolds stared, horror creeping into her eyes along with the shock and fear. "You wouldn't hurt me."

"Just remember to keep your mouth shut."

Mona started to reply, perhaps to plead. She never got the chance. Suddenly a pair of tall men had appeared beside the booth.

Smith looked up at them with dulled surprise. "Yes? Can we help you?"

Jones, beside him, nodded to the two newcomers and put his large hand over Smith's wrist. "It's over, Jerry. Sorry. You're under arrest." He glanced at Mona. "And you, too."

Smith's eyes rolled. "You're one of *them*? You son of a bitch! You bastard! Six months, we worked to-gether—"

"I think," Jones said, getting to his feet, "you don't want to say any more, Jerry." He inclined his head to the two newcomers. "Take him." He turned to Mona. "Come quietly." He reached for her arm.

"I haven't done anything!" Mona shrilled, twist-ing away. "I'm innocent!"

"Charges will include aiding in the sale of classi-

fied materials and accessory to an act of espionage,"
Jones told her. "Please come quietly, Mona. You don't
want a scene."

Mona stared. Standing in the aisle beside the
booth, Smith looked suddenly small in the grasp of the
two FBI agents. He fixed Jones with a baleful glare. "A
double agent. A God damned undercover man. A traitor to people who trusted you. I hope you love it."

Jones ignored him, and succeeded in grasping
Mona's wrist. She resisted. Jones expertly hauled her
out of the booth and to her feet. She sagged against
him, almost fainting, her glittery heels falling over on
their sides. The other two men led Smith out first, and
Jones followed, half supporting Mona. She recovered
partly as they reached the lobby, and her hysterical
screams echoed back through the bar, turning heads.
Then the outside door closed and she could not be
heard any longer.

Hart swam upward, trying to get out of the
darkness of his dream, and there was pain in his chest,
the hammering of his heart. He knew time had passed.
He was confused, disoriented, on the edge of a distant
panic. He could not think straight. He thought he was
home in his own bed, having a nightmare. But the
darkness was different, it had a crimson cast to it, and
he realized that the crimson was the glare of brilliant
lights through his closed eyelids. *Two days*, he thought.

Drifting. . . .

There were men's voices close by. He felt nause-
ated. The redness in his eyes was stronger, hurtful. He
felt vastly peaceful, lethargic, drugged.

Drugged.

He opened his eyes, and the overhead surgical
lights blinded him. His head swam.

"He's awake," a voice said hollowly.

He had closed his eyes again in reaction to the

harsh glare. He hurt all over and tried to move. Something restrained him. He opened his eyes to slits and looked down at himself. He was clothed as before, but he was on some kind of hard surface—a table—and his arms and legs, as well as his shoulders, were securely strapped down, preventing movement. There was some tubing. . . .

He was cold and the nausea was worse. He was dizzy and confused. He had never felt quite like this, deeply chilled, sluggish, unable to will his muscles to respond. His mind darted over the surface of thoughts but he could not grasp one. It was as if he were being carried along in a muddy stream at a dizzying speed, and the thoughts were branches he might reach out and grasp, and so orient himself. But the speed was too great and the branches were in movements of their own. The speed and disorientation were what made him feel like he might retch.

He struggled. But another part of himself was lethargic, indifferent, and whispered, *Why fight it? It's nice. Go with it. Who cares?*

A thought got through the confusion. The tubing meant they had him hooked up to something, an IV.

They were giving him a drug through the IV.

That was why he was dazed, unable to focus himself.

"Mr. Hennings," a voice echoed from a great distance.

Hart wondered who Hennings was. Then he remembered. With an enormous effort of will, he managed to nod. He wondered if he nodded enough for it to be seen.

The voice said, "Tell me your real name."

"H-" he began, and remembered again. "Hennings." Saying it required enormous effort.

"Where are you from?"

"Don't know. . . ." That was true. Did it matter?

"Why did you check into Parkview?"

Hart distantly remembered. A little segment of his brain awoke, and memories flooded into consciousness: Christie; Myrick; Charlene; the probe; the need to know names.

"Hennings?" the voice insisted gently. "Why did you check in?"

He wondered if he had only remembered, or had told the voice. He decided he had only remembered. He was not supposed to tell. *Why?* He cast around in his mind and remembered something else, his funny lie: "Smoking," he said, wondering if his mouth was making the word right. "Need . . . to . . . stop . . . smoking."

"How much have you given him?" the voice asked in a different tone. Hart floated in a vast gray sea.

"Two cc's," another voice said.

"More."

There was some slight sound, perhaps some of the tubing and plastic fixtures being touched, adjusted. Then a new chocolate wave of indifference washed beautifully through Hart's whole being and he smiled. It felt very nice. Very, very, very, very nice. . . .

"Hennings."

"Mmmm?"

"What did you come to the hospital to find? Who are you working for?"

"Mmmmm."

"Hennings. You want to tell us your secret. Secrets are not healthy and you know that. You know you can trust us. You want to share with us why you came to us and why you went into our computer records."

Hart listened. The voice out of the gray sea was vast and reassuring and harmless. The voice droned on. He knew—the tiny part of his mind that was still his own—that the voice was doing a hypnotic induction. He felt his controls soften, relax, melt away. He could trust the voice. The voice was his friend. . . .

"Not telling us the truth is very painful for you, Hennings. Hiding the truth from us, or lying, makes your heart give you pain. Your chest tightens. You can't breathe. It's as if you were locked inside a black box, and there's no air in the box, and the only way you can avoid the terrible pain is by telling us, so we can help you by opening the lid of the box. You want to have the box opened. You want fresh air, sunshine. Your lungs are closing. Your heart is laboring, it's in agony. You want to tell us what we ask."

As the voice droned on, Hart felt his chest collapsing. He could not resist. He tried to fight but he had no resources. His heart thundered in his ears. He could not breathe. His chest would not work. Panic began to rise up in him. He was going to die. The black box was suffocating him.

"Tell us now, Hennings. Why did you come to Parkview? What were you looking for? Your lungs are almost crushed by the great pressure. Your heart is in agony. You will not die, but this pain will grow worse and worse and you know you cannot stand it. Tell us and let us open the box for you so you can breathe again."

There was nothing but the pain, the asphyxia. He had never experienced anything like it. All he had to do was tell them what they wanted to know. . . .

But with the tiny fragment of his mind that was whole, he fought it. The pain wasn't real, he tried to convince himself. The wracking chills that were making him tremble, and the sweat pouring out of his body, were all from the drug . . . from the hypnosis. *He* knew hypnosis, didn't he? Couldn't he fight it, drug or no drug?

"Hennings. Tell us now. The pain is too much for you and you must tell us now."

Steel bands had closed on his lungs. He felt a blackness rising up in his head, his throat felt like it was bursting.

"More," the voice said impatiently.

"If I give him any more—"

"More!"

Hart was failing. He was going to tell. He told himself he would hang on just another minute or two, maybe they would go away, perhaps he would find a branch and be able to climb out of the river that was somehow in this black box.

Then a new wave of soft, velvet euphoria washed through him and he thought, *More of the drug hitting,* and reality was a vast watercolor, rain hitting the colors and making them wash together and then slip off the canvas so there was only whiteness, and he knew nothing.

"He's unconscious," Dr. Heath said without emotion.

"God damn it!" Silver exclaimed angrily. "We almost had him!"

"His heart rate went past a hundred and eighty. Look at him; he's drenched. If he hadn't passed out, he might have gone into a coronary."

"What's his pulse now?"

"Coming down."

"He's breathing normally again." Silver walked around the table on which the patient Hennings lay corpse-pale, still connected to the IV through which the drug had been administered. "What went wrong? How the hell did he resist?"

Heath shook his head. "He isn't a mill-run patient. His ability to resist proves that. He understands hypnosis. Even with the drug aiding us, he was able to fight."

"How long until he regains consciousness?"

"It may be hours. His system has to throw some of it off. It's excreted through the kidneys, so with the glucose solution left in, possibly by morning."

Silver paced. "I'll get the truth out of him or kill him in the process."

"Oh, he'll talk eventually," Heath said. "But it may take three or four more sessions. He's very strong."

"Then we'll give him three or four more sessions—whatever we need."

"It could kill him," Heath observed neutrally.

"What choice do we have?"

"None. However, we can't let him stay here in the hospital. We have to get him out and take him where we can attend to him without risk of discovery."

"Where we took the others?"

"Yes."

"Can we get the van to take him out now?"

Heath shook his head. "It would raise too many questions, having him vanish in the dead of night. No. We'll keep him in his room through the morning tomorrow. We can say he had a psychotic episode—I'll prescribe Nembutal capsules in sufficient dosage to keep him snowed under. We'll remove him in the van on the pretext of placing him in a major hospital. Then after we move him, we can let him come up enough to resume the IV. It's quite compatible with Nembutal, as you know."

Silver's teeth clicked wolfishly in frustration. "Can we afford taking so long to get the truth out of him?"

"By tomorrow night this time we'll have the truth," Heath said calmly. "Never fear."

"And then—?"

"Why," the doctor said even more softly, "then we see what we must do."

"Will you contact the people in New York?"

"No, you fool. Do you want them to know we've had trouble?"

Silver stared for a moment at Heath's expression, and experienced a chill based on a more primitive fear. At times like this, Silver wished he had never wanted the money so badly. He hated some of the things that had happened, and wished he could get out. But he could not get out now, he thought. A man with the jungle morality of Dr. Heath would let no one out alive.

Certainly this man Hennings would not get out alive, regardless of what he finally told them when the drug and hypnosis broke him.

twenty

Aboard *Adventurer*, Christie Hart sat in the command pilot's chair, the Comm circuit opened only to her headset. Behind her somewhere, H. O. Townsend was working out on the exercise equipment with the zeal of a maniac. Buck Colltrap was supposed to be in his sleep cycle and Christie nervously wished he were.

"That's right, Houston," she said quietly into the tiny boom mike. "He's been out in the cargo bay for about thirty minutes." She glanced at the status indicator lights on the side panel. "My internal monitoring equipment says he's inside the lander, powering up computer and engine control status indicators. Over."

There was a pause before Houston's reply came back, and it was considerably longer than the lag time necessary for radio signals to carry across the ever-widening gap between the spacecraft and its home planet. When the voice finally did come back, it was no longer the voice of Leonard Murphy, but that of Jack Schaeffly:

"*Ah, roger,* Adventurer. *Understand Buck is doing an EVA in the cargo bay, and checking out status of the lander. Say again what H. O. is doing, over.*"

Christie had a moment's disorienting feeling that everyone was crazy but her. But she responded first to the query. "H. O. is in the exercise area on the stationary bicycle, over."

"Roger that, Adventurer. Stand by one."

Christie leaned back in the contoured chair and stared numbly out at the vast, cold panoply of stars. Barring unforeseen faulty status indicator lights or some other emergency, the flight time line called for them to make their first follow-up checkout of the lander in about four months. Townsend had already been out in the bay shortly after they opened the cargo doors for additional spacecraft cooling to make certain the vehicle that would transport them to the surface of Mars had not been damaged during blastoff from Earth orbit. The three-volume flight plan, encased in its tight red plastic covers on the shelf behind her head, did not mention EVA to the lander again until Volume 3. For Buck Colltrap to be out there now was crazy. Or was *she* going crazy?

"Adventurer, *Houston.*"

"Go ahead."

"We need a readout on the number two telescope relative to flight path and Polaris, over."

Business as usual! Biting her tongue, Christie punched up the figures and read them back. Houston acknowledged and fell temporarily silent. After a minute or two, Buck Colltrap's voice, raspy and out of breath, came back on the internal communications override: *"Lander checkout complete and returning through the bay to the hatch."*

"Roger," Christie said.

H. O. Townsend, face and upper torso drenched in sweat, drifted partway up into the flight deck area. "Is he still out there doing that crazy shit?"

Christie removed one earpiece. "He's on the way back in."

"What does Houston say?"

"They wanted a readout on the big telescope."

Townsend's usually cheerful face was grim, his eyes bleak. "They're just not buying our reports. They're grasping straws—telling each other he's just too conscientious—instead of facing the issue . . . what we're probably going to have to do."

Christie looked at him. "Do? What are we going to have to do?"

Townsend showed absolutely no sign that his thoughts were even unusual. "Mutiny."

"*What?*"

He met her gaze with as cold and somber an expression as she had ever encountered. "Isn't that what they call it?" he asked. "When the crew takes over the ship from its captain?"

Indicator lights showed that Colltrap was back inside the spacecraft's controlled environment.

"You'd better go clean up," Christie told Townsend. "You're due in command in less than ten minutes."

"Think about it," Townsend told her, and sank back down out of her view.

Houston came back on frequency and asked some more technical questions about the status of the telescope experiment. Was H. O. right? Christie wondered. Was she up here with a crazy man, and was Mission Control going to put its head in the sand? She didn't know what more she could say to them. Earlier in her shift, alone on the deck, she had reviewed everything with them, all Colltrap's bizarre behavior. What more was there to say? She struggled with a feeling a little like asphyxia: events were closing in on her and she felt helpless.

A few minutes later, Buck Colltrap came onto the command level, smoothly using the handholds. He seemed calmer than he had been in days, and even smiled at her.

"It's magnificent out there," he told her. "These windows restrict the view. Out there, with half the universe over your head . . . it's awesome."

"The lander is all right?"

"Fine." Colltrap eased calmly into the right-hand seat. "I'll take over, Christie, and you can go ahead and start your next freetime cycle on the ham radio, if you like."

He seemed the old Colltrap—in control, logical, considerate, calm, kind. Christie was thrown for another loss by the abrupt change. But she nodded thanks, gave him a brief grateful smile in return, and went back into the area where her little ham handitalkie and antenna, taped to the window, remained oriented in the general direction of Earth.

She glanced at the notes taped to the bulkhead to make sure she was in one of her scheduled air times, and that this period was to be on the announced frequency. It was tomorrow, she verified, that she would switch without prior notice to a seldom-used frequency at the top of the two-meter ham band for just a few minutes. That was to escape the perpetual din of the pileup on this frequency and give assured contacts to the radio amateurs sprinkled throughout NASA. She knew a few of these technicians, and they deserved a little fun and special treatment.

She turned on the battery-operated linear amplifier, flicked on the recorder, and donned her headset. Pencil in hand, she turned on the VOX.

"This is KU5B aboard the spacecraft *Adventurer*," she said. "QRZ?"

A world of amateur radio operators was waiting. When the VOX dropped out and let her receiver come on, it sounded like thousands of them yelling their call signs, piled up on top of one another, making the frequency howl. Grinning, Christie started expertly picking out some of the strongest—or luckiest—call signs for her log.

Hart tried to awaken, and saw blurry daylight in his room. He could not keep his eyes open, and drifted again, vastly tired, euphoric, helpless.

There was something tremendously important that he had to remember at all costs . . . that he must not reveal at any cost. He drifted, trying to collect enough tattered remnants of rational cognition to identify the thing he must remember, but not tell.

He remembered. It was the name of the other NASA figure he had found in the hospital computer . . . another person besides Myrick, programmed as he was now sure Myrick had been programmed to do harm to MarsProbe.

It seemed in Hart's drugged mind that he should try to figure out why anyone would want to harm *Adventurer* . . . hurt Christie . . . and he felt a stab of fear at that thought . . . but he drifted again, and came back later from the deeps to think that he should also wonder *who* would want to injure people like Myrick . . . and the other name . . . injure Christie and the *Adventurer* crew. But it was too hard, he could not maintain concentration. He could scarcely move.

He dreamed. He was with Davidson Myrick again. Myrick's eyes were startled open, staring into a vacuum of horror, and he was saying *"Program in. Program in. One hundred. Sixty-eight. Sixty-eight. Are you Silver?"*

What did all that mean?

Silver. . . ?

Silver. He remembered Silver. God, he was in a mess. He had to get his mind together. He had to resist the prybars they were trying to insert into his brain, and keep his secret. He had to get himself together and get the hell out of here.

But dreams came . . . Kecia . . . childhood experiences, confusion.

Later, *voices*:

"I'm going to catheterize him, nurse. And then if he rouses, I want you to give him the capsule. He mustn't be allowed to have another psychotic outburst in here. He's a very sick man. We're going to have to transfer him after lunch. But for right now he must be kept sedated, understand?"

"Yes, doctor."

He heard them enter the room. There was some moving around of his body, and then distant, sharp discomfort as the tube went into him, and then relief. He didn't much care. He pretended to be asleep. And then he really was asleep.

And then he was staring with open eyes, half-focused, and the nurse was bending over him with a capsule between her fingers, and a little paper cup. "Take this and swallow it, Mr. Hennings."

The capsule went between his teeth. She touched the cup to his lips and water flowed in. He swallowed. *He almost swallowed the pill.* He didn't. He managed somehow to get it under his tongue, and gulp some of the tepid water without the pill going down.

"There. That's good. Just rest, now."

He fell back on the pillow, out of breath, reeling with nausea. *Don't fall asleep. Jesus God, don't fall asleep. You can't let that capsule dissolve in there.*

He reached into his mouth and raked the dissolving capsule out from under his tongue. There was a bitter taste. He shoved the jellified remnants of the capsule into his pajama pocket. The taste of the stuff still in his mouth continued to create a terrible commotion in his stomach. Then he knew he was going to vomit.

With more effort of will than he thought he had in him, he shocked his eyes open. Sunlight flooded through the windows. The room was empty. The door was closed to the hall . . . the other door ajar to the bathroom.

Covers flipped back. He got his legs off the edge of the bed. The universe tilted. His stomach was in revolt. His legs felt like they were not connected. He reeled across the cool tile floor and into the bathroom and got his head over the commode just as everything in his stomach—vile-tasting acidic liquid and phlegm—gushed out of him in a series of brief, gut-wrenching convulsions.

Sobbing for air, half blinded by tears, he wiped his face on tissue and tossed it into the toilet and flushed. The water swirled and made an unholy racket and took everything down.

He crawled back to the bed and climbed back into it with an effort that would have equalled any climber of Everest.

He was soaked in cold sweat, and dazed by a torrent of disconnected, frightening thoughts and sensations. Had he just done that? Had he escaped detection? Who was Silver?

He slept.

At the Johnson Space Center, Project Director John Selmon faced Houston Detective Bud Slagerfeldt across a desk littered with telex reports covering the last two hours. Selmon had the feeling of a man in an avalanche, but he fought the new details pouring through his mind in an attempt to give the detective his total attention. For he knew Slagerfeldt's puzzle was part of the larger—frighteningly larger—problem.

"You have no idea where Dr. Hart went when he left the apartment?" Selmon asked.

Slagerfeldt shook his head. Deep circles darkened his eyes. The man looked like he hadn't had a full night's sleep in a week, Selmon thought. Slagerfeldt said, "We don't know where he went and we don't know where he is. We had a lead late last night, a body a farmer pulled out of his farm pond. But it wasn't Hart."

"My God, man! You don't think he's been killed, do you?"

Slagerfeldt's weary eyes sagged. "He was seeing Davidson Myrick. Myrick is dead. He had a secretary doing case-typing for him. The secretary is dead. I told him to leave the investigation to us, but that's his daughter out there in your rocketship, and he wasn't about to wait for anybody. I think he gave my man the slip and I think he tried to do something on his own and I think he got too close to somebody. I hope he's not dead. But the longer he's missing, the less chance there is we'll ever see him alive again."

Selmon glanced at some of the papers on his desk, then let his gaze return to the detective. "I didn't know until very recently that Dave Myrick had been seeing Dr. Hart professionally. What was he being treated for? What can you tell me about that?"

"Nerves," Slagerfeldt said.

"Nerves? Is that all you know about it?"

"Dr. Hart was long on professional confidentiality."

"Well Jesus! Myrick is dead! What possible—"

"I know Hart," Slagerfeldt cut in. "I trust him. He's . . . or he was . . . a good man. I respect his judgment. Maybe I was wrong. I respected his feelings on this."

"But if there was crucial information in Myrick's records that might lead to the apprehension of his killer—"

"There isn't."

"How do you know that, if you let Dr. Hart keep the case a deep, dark secret from you—?"

"We got a search warrant for the doc's office late yesterday. The Myrick file is now at my office. We've gone over it with a fine-tooth comb. There's nothing to help us."

"What was wrong with him, then, if you have the file?"

"Nerves. Bad dreams. Worry about the project. Loss of sleep."

Selmon was disappointed. "Nothing more?"

"Nothing more."

"Then why in the world were his visits to Dr. Hart such a big dark secret? We have psychiatrists on staff here, some of the best. Why didn't he—?" Selmon stopped, thinking about it. "Wait a minute. Maybe I see."

"He was afraid he would be yanked off the project," Slagerfeldt said.

"Yes." Selmon shook his head. "I see. And dammit, he might have been right. We can't take any chances with key personnel. —But none of that explains about Dr. Hart, does it?"

Slagerfeldt leaned back in the chair and rubbed the back of his neck as if it ached fiercely. "I've thought about what we know, and the things the doc said. I'll give you a theory."

"Go ahead," Selmon urged, wondering if it would dovetail with all the new information that had bombarded his desk in the last few hours.

"I believe the doc thought Myrick was involved somehow with somebody who either had a grudge against NASA generally, or wanted to screw up Mars-Probe. He was worried after Myrick's death because *something* made him think that if Myrick had been killed to prevent his talking, then someone else inside here must be in on the deal, too."

"He thought the enemies—whoever they might be—had more than one person set up to do harm, somehow, to the voyage of *Adventurer*," Selmon said.

Slagerfeldt's eyes betrayed an instant's keen scrutiny. "You've come to the same conclusion, then."

"I didn't say that."

"You didn't have to."

The two men gauged each other.

Finally Selmon said, "I don't have any idea what might have happened to Dr. Hart, or where he might be, or who might be involved. We're taking certain steps internally to try to assure that no one is in a position to sabotage *Adventurer*. The FBI and our own security people are actively involved. Beyond that, I can't tell you much."

Slagerfeldt stood, looking even more weary. "Okay. Fine. I wanted to let you know where I'm at on the thing. My concern is the doc. I think if you knew anything about that, you'd tell me."

"I would. Believe me, my friend, I would."

Slagerfeldt walked to the office door. "I'll be in touch if anything turns up. You have my card. You'll get in touch with me if there's anything?"

Selmon stood. "Yes."

Slagerfeldt went away. Selmon waited until he could be sure the detective was off the floor, then punched a number. "Has Dr. Klindeinst's plane landed yet? —No? —ETA? —All right." He touched the hook button and dialed again internally. One of the new security people answered in Mission Control. "Dr. Ditwhiler, please. This is John Selmon calling."

After a moment, Ditwhiler came on the line.

"We'd better huddle in my office right now," Selmon told him.

"Five minutes," Ditwhiler said, and hung up.

Actually, it was four.

Ditwhiler sank tiredly into the chair facing Selmon's desk and fired up the stub of a cigar. "Dr. K. is delayed."

"I know," Selmon said, shuffling some of the telexes again. "We have some things to talk about right now, and we can't wait for him."

"Like what now?"

"First of all, I've just had a meeting with a Houston cop. He was working on Myrick's death, seems to think there's reason to believe it wasn't a suicide or accidental."

"Not accidental?" Ditwhiler blinked. "I never subscribed to any thought of suicide. Dave was nervous and on edge, but he wasn't suicidal. But I just imagined it was one of those tragic accidents . . . he was tired, distracted, toppled over the railing—"

"Slagerfeldt—that's the detective—isn't convinced."

Ditwhiler relighted his cigar. "Do you give him any credence?"

"I don't know if I would or not. But there's also a matter of an FBI report that's just come across my desk."

"On Myrick? I didn't know they were looking into that."

"Oh, yes," Selmon said softly. "They've been looking into a lot of things."

"And?"

"They don't believe it was an accident or suicide, either."

"On what basis?"

"Personality profile. Recent activities, including the visits to see Dr. Hart. Not the behavior of a potential suicide."

"Accident?"

"There was no patio furniture on Myrick's balcony, and the AstroTurf on its floor was thick with dust. Analysis of the carpet *inside* the sliding doors to

the balcony showed only a slight amount of dust
tracked in from the balcony."

"I don't—" Ditwhiler began.

Selmon cut in, "Conclusion: Myrick didn't use the
balcony. He was not in the habit of going out there at
all. Also, it was eighty-eight degrees and high humid-
ity the night he died, hardly weather to encourage
someone to break with habit and go out on a balcony
not used in more pleasant weather. Dust inside the
locking mechanism on the sliding doors indicated non-
use also. And the railing that we're supposed to think
he accidentally fell over—after going out where he
never ordinarily was—is chest-high on a man of his
height. An accidental fall is practically impossible."

Ditwhiler turned the information over in his mind
while making a dense cloud of acrid smoke. "Then he
was murdered?"

"It begins to look that way."

"Why?"

"You tell me that, and I'll tell you what we have to
do next. But while you're thinking about it, tell me also
where Dr. Hart has vanished to."

"Is the city cop looking into that, too?"

"Yes, and he's worried as hell."

"Surely he doesn't think Hart *also* met with violence."

"He doesn't know. And I don't either. But you
add these things to the arrest of Boyd Reynolds and
the strange behavior we're seeing in the *Adventurer*
crew, plus the Russian disaster and what Dr. K. has
been told about that, and I'm damned worried.
Damned worried."

"Ideas?" Ditwhiler asked.

"Suppose," Selmon said, "there was a plot to
wreck both the Russian and American probes. Suppose it worked on the Russians and has deep roots inside our team. Would they—whoever they are—be

content with one spy or saboteur inside? Or would they have managed somehow to contaminate *several* of our people?"

Ditwhiler did not answer. With sagging eyes he stared at his superior, and his cigar was forgotten and getting cold.

Selmon answered his own rhetorical question. "They would have backups. *If* Dave Myrick was involved as a possible saboteur of some kind, and if they were willing to kill him, then there must be a backup for him."

The two men stared at each other.

"No," Ditwhiler said unbelievingly after a moment. "I can't accept that possibility."

"He's Myrick's backup. If Myrick's role was crucial in some way we can't understand yet, wouldn't he— as Myrick's backup—have to be in their control as well?"

"But Jack Schaeffly has an impeccable record!" Ditwhiler protested.

"So," Selmon replied somberly, "did Dave Myrick."

"If what you say is true, what do we do about it?"

"Pull him. Now."

"But what if we're wrong to suspect him?"

"What," Selmon shot back, betraying the tension, "if we're *right*?"

"Will pulling him be enough, even if we do it? What if there's something fatally wrong with *Adventurer*, with its computers, something we can't detect? What if Buck Colltrap—?"

"We've got to have a worst-case scenario for that," Selmon cut in, "and right now. I've worked something out. Listen carefully and tell me what you think."

Some three hours after the Selmon-Ditwhiler conference back on Earth, aboard *Adventurer*, Christie Hart moved back into the command chair on the flight deck as part of the "daylight" staggered work schedule. She was alone in the forward cabin. A glance at the status boards showed everything normal. She leaned back.

Her headphones came alive: "Adventurer, Houston."

Christie said, "This is *Adventurer*, go ahead."

"Christie," John Selmon's voice said over the abyss of space, *"say status of crew, present disposition in spacecraft, over."*

"Buck is sleeping and H. O. is tending the hydroponics, over."

"Ah, roger that. Read status Ex. Com. panel Main, over."

Frowning, Christie glanced at the bank of light emitting diodes that signaled when someone was plugged into the main communications system anywhere on the ship. They were all dark.

"Nobody plugged in, Houston. Looks like it's just me talking and listening up here."

"Roger that, Christie. . . . Christie, we have some contingency information and planning for your ears only at this time. Do not make notes but listen carefully. Is that a roger?"

"I understand, over."

"Okay, Christie. Now listen carefully."

Christie listened. And as John Selmon's calm, detached voice began to outline unthinkable things, her blood ran cold.

twenty-one

"Move him carefully, now. In his condition, he's helpless to assist."

Hands expertly pulled back the sheet covering Richard Hart on the hospital bed. The squeaky sound of cart wheels sounded again for an instant and he guessed they were moving it closer beside the bed. Keeping his eyes closed and his body limp, Hart allowed himself to be picked up by two pairs of strong hands and moved quickly from the bed onto the gurney. They put straps around legs and shoulders and covered him again.

Without further talk they pushed the cart into motion. Hart heard a door murmur and then the quality of the ambient sound changed, signifying that they had wheeled him into the hallway. He heard distant voices, a telephone, the complaint of the wheels, footsteps.

He was still sickeningly dizzy, confused. But better than he had been before. Clarity seemed to come and go, punctuated by periods of drift, half sleep, disconnected thought. He knew they were moving him now to the other location outside Parkview that he had

heard them discussing . . . when? . . . ages ago . . .
Last night or this morning.

So much time. *One day left . . . maybe less.*

The cart stopped for a minute or two, and then he
heard the sound of elevator doors opening and he was
wheeled in. One of the attendants hummed tunelessly
as the elevator went down. Then the doors opened
again and he was wheeled along for what seemed a
long time. Then he heard electric doors opening and
felt hot, sticky outdoor air. There was a lurch and a
bump and a slide, and a rocking from side to side.

They had put him in a truck or ambulance, he
guessed. After a moment, the slamming of doors and
sound of an engine confirmed his guess. Then he felt
the vehicle moving, stopping, twisting him as it made
a turn, accelerating along a street.

He risked cracking open one eyelid—and stared
into virtual blackness. His drugged mind almost pan-
icked but then he caught himself and opened his eyes
wider, risking it.

Light leaked through the seams of the back doors
of the compartment he was in. As his eyes adjusted,
he saw that his stretcher was fixed to the metal floor of
what seemed to be a carry-all van, one with no windows here in the back. There was nothing else in the
compartment with him, no window to the front, either, so that he couldn't see who was driving him . . .
or how many were up there.

It was hot and stuffy in the dimness. The restraint
straps cut into his thighs and shoulders.

The van stopped again and he could hear other car
engines. Then it accelerated once more. In the next few
minutes the stop-and-go pattern repeated often, and
then he guessed they drove out onto an expressway
because the engine whined through the gears, the tires
thrummed at a higher, continuous speed.

He struggled with a spell of disorientation and

confusion. Then he shocked back to consciousness as the van braked sharply and swerved, and the sound under the tires indicated a rough city street.

There was no way to know how long the trip was going to be, but he knew it might already be almost over.

And if he could not escape now, there might be no other chance.

And there would be no more capsules he might spit out. There would be injections. He knew what the injections could do.

The van was bumping along a rough street, stopping, starting again, making a sharp turn.

The straps were the first problem. But they were designed to keep an unconscious person from being rolled off the stretcher, not to restrain someone by force. Bending his arms back from the elbow, Hart was able to reach the buckles over his chest and work them open.

Then he sat up, and almost keeled over from vertigo.

He fought it. After a minute or two he got better balance. The strap around his thighs went more swiftly.

He tried through the confusion to think of a plan. But he didn't know where he was or what was scheduled to happen next. All he knew was that he had to get out of the van, and as quickly as possible.

Rolling off the stretcher, he went on hands and knees to the back doors. There was an inside handle. He crouched beside it, desperately struggling to be clearheaded. The next time the van stopped—

And it was already braking.

Braked to a full, jouncy stop.

The prospect of opening that door into a totally unknown environment was not attractive. But there were no alternatives. With a sharp wrenching motion, he jerked the handle and shoved the door back.

Sunlight flooded in, blinding him. He saw oil-blackened concrete under the back bumper of the van, some tall buildings vague in the glare, other cars in an adjacent lane, a curb, a trash can.

He jumped out, sprawling painfully to hands and knees in his pajamas. Somebody honked deafeningly. Scrambling dizzily to his bare feet, he darted from the back of the van and onto a gritty sidewalk. There was the mouth of a dirty-looking alley—some kind of warehouses all around, no people on the sidewalk.

He ran into the alley. Behind him, the honking got more insistent and he heard someone shouting, and the slam of a metal door—possibly the door of the van.

The alley ran straight a few yards between stained high brick walls on both sides, and a loading platform covered with trash. Then it dead-ended in another intersecting alley that ran right and left. He reached the corner and cut right, running as hard as he could. There was some broken glass. He ran through it, feeling slivers gash his bare feet.

The new alley was rutted in the center, trashy along brick wall sides, and ahead he saw a high wood fence on one side that bordered high-piled junk cars, a vacant lot on the other, and more aged warehouse-type buildings beyond.

He was already getting out of breath, the cuts on his feet from the broken glass were filling him with bright pain, and he couldn't seem to get his eyes into clear focus. Somewhere behind him he heard a shout. Cutting around another corner to run between the high board fence and a dirty rock wall, he risked a glance backward and saw two men running after him—Silver and the big attendant who had caught him in the computer room.

Two more alleys intersected. Christ, he had no

idea where he was, where he was going. He veered left. Ahead a block or so, a big truck was parked across the pavement, blocking the way. There was a space between two buildings and he took that, and, staggering, his breath filling his lungs with pain now, came to another alley.

He was not going to be able to go much farther. He needed a hiding place. The idea of stopping, and hoping they wouldn't find him, was terror-filled. He wasn't clearheaded enough to sort things out. He had no wind left and cramps stabbed his legs. *Hide!*

On his right, against the wall, was a large municipal trash container, gray steel, a dumpster, with its heavy lid cocked back about a foot or two on one side.

His bloody feet slipped on the metal strut partway up the side of the big steel bin, almost plunging him back to the cobbles. He managed to catch hold of the top rim with one hand, and with a gut-wrenching effort levered himself up, getting his chest on the top edge, toppling himself over.

He tumbled about three feet into soft shredded paper, empty cartons, sacks wet with garbage. He scrambled back into the far corner of the container, furiously pulled some of the wadding and garbage up into the corner over himself, and lay as still as his labored breathing would allow.

He waited.

In the federal building in downtown Houston, the FBI agent-in-charge stood to shake hands with the two men who had just flown in from Washington. He had never met them before. The CIA was not supposed to be involved in domestic counterespionage.

"You have the man you arrested in conjunction with the sale of computer data from the space center?" the taller operative from Washington asked. He was of medium height, perhaps slightly overweight, with a

friendly, open, homely face. His voice had absolutely
no tone, however, and his eyes were cut glass.

"He's in Interrogation B," the FBI agent said. "We
didn't get anything from him—who he was working
for, who his contact might have been, anything. Then
we got the orders saying we should wait for your ar-
rival."

The first Washington agent nodded. "We'll talk to
him now." He shifted the thin attaché case under his
arm.

"My orders are to cooperate with you in every
way," the FBI agent replied. "But this guy is tough. I
don't think we're going to get much out of him."

"We want a name."

"I hope you can get it."

The second Washington agent—beefy, slow-
moving, unremarkable except for eyes even colder
than his companion's—gave the FBI agent a little smile
that chilled him. "We will," he said.

The two Washington operatives were ushered
down the hall. They entered the interrogation room
where the man who had paid Mona Reynolds to pressure her husband, and who had also paid Dr. Boyd
Reynolds for damaging space secrets, was waiting.

They closed the door.

The agent-in-charge returned to his desk. He
knew all too well how vital it was to have some
name—almost any name of a contact or higher-up—
from the spy suspect. Without it, they had no other
lead. A dozen or a hundred other spies and traitors
might stand in the daisy-chain between the local man
and whoever had set things up. The person or power
behind all of it could only be traced one laborious step
at a time . . . one name at a time, the trail leading ever
upward toward the top.

The agent-in-charge did not have much hope that
the Washington boys would accomplish anything. He

had always thought The Company was a little over-rated.

Two hours passed.

The door of the interrogation room opened and the two Washington operatives returned to the agent's office.

"Did you get anything?" he asked.

The tall visitor handed him a slip of memo paper. "Here are three names. We'll be following up also. Good day." The men from Washington, or, more properly, Langley, walked out.

When Christie Hart left the flight deck of *Adventurer*, she drifted down to the sleep bay, assuring herself as instructed that H. O. Townsend was "in the rack." Her fellow astronaut floated in his weblike hammock, one foot floating free, soft snores emanating regularly from his lax, upturned face.

Buck Colltrap was in the pilot's position.

Christie moved out of the sleep bay and onto the next level, going through the tunnellike vestibule leading to the cargo bay. Here the hydroponics nestled vivid green and white in their constantly circulating baths of nutrient fluids under clear plastic retainers.

Christie moved on, worried about discovery but intent on following the frightening contingency plan to the letter. *I can do it if I must,* she told herself. *If it has to be done, it will be done.*

But, oh, dear lord, I hope it doesn't happen.

Opening the EVA equipment storage rack doors, she pulled down her own EVA suit first, and, using the printed checklist, examined it minutely, testing valves, circuits, connectors, and fittings by the book. Sure the suit was fully ready, she then took down the second suit and went through the same procedure. Her hands trembled ever so slightly as she turned an oxygen flow valve, making sure it was free and that the life-supporting gas would circulate freely.

Finished, she restored the second suit to its upright position in the cabinet, closed the doors, and moved back through hydroponics to the other level. Beyond this level, she came to the window with her ham radio antenna taped to the thick plastic and her handi-talkie floating in its tethered holster.

She was supposed to act as normally as possible. In another hour she was scheduled for an optional period of additional volunteer contacts with her fellow radio amateurs. She didn't know if she would be able to bring herself to play right now. Her nerves had never been tighter, and her heart beat sluggishly in her own ears.

Christie decided she would make up her mind a little later. She needed all the rest she could get right now, and if contingencies arose, every bit of freshness and expertise at her command would be required.

She wrapped herself in her sleep harness and willed herself to doze.

In Mission Control, Houston, LeRoy Ditwhiler stood on the observation deck and watched the controllers and technicians monitor their instruments and trade comparative data. *Adventurer*'s flight path was beginning to swing very slightly off course. A tiny midcourse correction maneuver was being calculated by the computers. The flight path deviation, at present only a matter of a few feet, could become tens of thousands of miles in the vastness of space unless corrected fairly quickly and accurately.

Ditwhiler's mind, however, was partly on the scene that must be playing out at this time in John Selmon's office.

Jack Schaeffly had gone sickly white, then fiery pink and furious when quietly told by Selmon that he was being relieved. Now Selmon had the youthful engineer in his office, trying to justify what they were doing without coming right out with the truth: that they feared he might, as Davidson Myrick's second-in-command, carry with him a known or inadvertent instruction or bit of data that could doom the probe.

Ditwhiler knew it was a necessary precaution. But he had felt his stomach lurch with sympathy when he watched Selmon, shadowed by a security man, walk away with Schaeffly.

Ditwhiler looked down at the others on the floor, and at Leonard Murphy, wearing the headphones and boom mike of Mission Control.

What, Ditwhiler thought in agony, *if we've guessed wrong?*

The time display over the major presentation screen scrolled another set of numbers. It read:

PRESENT TIME. . . . . 2131 GMT

ELAPSED TIME

DAYS	HOURS	MINUTES	SECONDS
0006	05	01	13.42

Ditwhiler automatically multiplied. "A hundred and forty-nine hours," he murmured aloud to himself. It seemed more like a lifetime.

twenty-two

Darkness had come, and in the hot stench of the trash container, Hart knew he had to move now or he would be so sick and weak he might never move at all.

Moving across the dark, unstable mountain of trash inside the bin, he made what seemed an unholy lot of noise. He was committed and he couldn't wait any longer, however, so he grabbed the top lip of the container and pulled himself up, poking his head outside into the blessedly cooler, cleaner air of the alley.

A sliver of moon shone overhead, making the alley a pale, clear picture. There was no one in sight. Down a long, narrow shaft of alley between buildings, and past the open webwork of a lumber yard's storage building, he saw headlights moving along a street. The shadows nearby were dense, unmoving.

A gust of renewed dizziness and nausea almost overwhelmed him as he clambered up on the edge of the container, got his legs out, felt for a foothold. His toes slipped off the side strut and he lost his balance and fell heavily to the dirty pavement, sprawling.

There wasn't time for the luxury of thinking about the pain. He scrambled to his feet and started at a trot down the alley toward the distant street's traffic.

He had gone halfway to the moving lights when something moved out of the shadows on his right, and just behind him.

"You!" a hoarse voice called sharply. *"Hennings!"*

Panic rushed through Hart's bloodstream. Nobody but the people from Parkview knew him by that name. So they had been waiting, watching, all these hours. They wanted him that badly.

He should have guessed that. But there was no time to think about it. The bulky shadow was close, terrifyingly so. Hart dodged to the left and ran full-out, and the figure pursued.

By the time he had run two blocks, he had put some space between himself and his pursuer. But he was more dizzy and sick, and he couldn't keep going long.

On the left was the dark maw of the lumber yard storage building, a driveway going in between the two-story, open-timbered warehouses where construction lumber was stored under roof, but with open side walls that allowed air to circulate. The drive-through, for loading trucks, was barred by a tall wire mesh fence. Hart took one look and made his decision, banking everything on his scrambling ability. He hurled himself against the mesh fencing and went up hand-over-hand, digging in with his toes.

Possibly he was lucky, or possibly his fear helped. He went up the fence like a monkey, got a leg over, and dropped sickeningly down on the other side, landing with shocking impact on his feet. Without a glance backward, he scuttled into the deep shade of the nearest tall stack of 2 × 4s, dropped onto one hip, and fought to get air into his lungs.

The other man lurched out of the alley dimness and ran smack into the wire fencing, staggered backward, and filled the air with muffled curses. Hart, seeing him so close, realized that the shadows of the lumber pile added invisibility. Maybe the attacker would go away.

Wrong. With a grunt of anger, the bulky figure attacked the mesh fence, awkwardly clambering up its face just as Hart had done.

Hart bent over the dusty floor of the storage yard and his stomach retched up a thin, acid line of vomit. Shuddering, he got to his feet and moved around the far end of the 2 × 4s, trying to figure out where to go next. There was a rough wood ladder leading up to the top storage deck of the open building. He went up as fast as he could, intent on putting space behind himself and the man making a racket as he climbed the chained fence behind him.

On the second level was a walkway open over a rickety railing to the yard below, and on the other side of the walkway, stacks of planks and lumber. The walkway seemed to encircle the storage area, with storage bins all the way around. At the far end loomed a ground-stacked pile of heavy bags, possibly concrete or plaster materials, reaching almost as high as the catwalk. It blocked a view beyond, into the far interior of the structure. Hart couldn't see any good way out.

Below and behind him, the heavyset pursuer dropped to the ground with an audible grunt, then fell silent. Hart peered down, trying hard to see in the dark. He found the man's shadow; he was standing just inside the fencing, his head cocked to one side, some bricklike object in his hand.

Then Hart heard the soft, guttural voice and realized with thunderclap certainty what was going on. The man had a small radio of some kind and was talking to someone else, probably nearby.

Which meant help—for the bulky pursuer— would be on the way instantaneously.

Another wave of vertigo swung Hart around and he hung on to the rough boards to prevent a noisy fall.

For a second he had a very serious impulse to give in
to the despair and let them have him. But as quickly as
he had that feeling, he felt his anger rise to help. *Don't
be a chickenshit, Hart. Do something.*

He moved along the catwalk toward the interior of
the blackened warehouse. The heavy planks beneath
his feet made no sound. Below him somewhere, his
pursuer was moving, his feet making heavy scuffing
sounds on dirt and gravel.

Hart reached the far end of the walkway. Narrow
aisles led backward between the racks of planks and
sheets of plywood. The heavy smell of wood resins
filled the dusty air. He couldn't see much. Just over
the lip of the catwalk to his left was the stack of big
bags, and he could see now that they were sixty-
pound bags of Sakrete, probably forklift-stacked.

Beyond the stack, silhouetted vaguely in the pale
moonlight entering from the alley and the high, open
side walls, he could make out the big man, moving
more slowly and silently now, groping his way deeper
into the warehouse. He was still talking low into his
little radio and Hart made out some of the words:
"*. . . no sign and I don't know . . . up in the upper
level maybe . . . can hold him here . . . five minutes? Can't
you make it faster?*"

It was the first decent news Hart had heard for a
while. The attacker's help was five minutes away.

Which meant Hart had to do something right
now.

The shadowy figure moved closer, nearing the pile
of heavy bags. "*Ten four. Hurry,*" the voice said. The
figure stopped in the deep shadow cast by the bag-pile
and bent to one side. He was holstering or belting his
radio.

Hart knew instantly what he had to do. He had no
time for calculating odds. All he knew was that he had
a precious five minutes to find a way out and get the

hell away from here—if he could put this one out of commission.

He ducked under the walkway railing and stepped slightly down, precariously balancing on the top layer of concrete mix bags. The stack wobbled sickeningly. Below, the other man made some small sound of surprise. Panic gusting, Hart kicked furiously at the bags on the edge of the pile nearest him. Two or three of them slid off and fell, and then more started in a landslide action, and the whole stack started to go, bags slipping in all directions once the equilibrium was disturbed.

Thousands of pounds of unyielding sacks toppled over onto the man below, with Hart riding the avalanche like a captured skier. He saw a couple of bags hit the man on the head and shoulders, toppling him, and then more raining down on top from all sides. Then Hart tumbled on down with the rest of the pile and hit the ground and felt bags hitting him in a melee of rustling, thumping noises and a cloud of choking concrete powder dust.

Scrambling to free himself from the bags around his legs, he looked for his pursuer. All he could see were the man's legs sticking out from under a three-foot pile of bags that must have weighed a ton. There was no movement through the sifting dust.

Free of the pile, Hart looked deeper into the lower-level warehouse area. He spotted what looked like a doorway with glass in it and a security light beyond. He ran for it.

The door was locked. He put his fist through the glass, feeling nothing, caught the knob on the other side, and let himself through. He was in a dingy office adjunct to the yard, and just ahead of him, across the room, were glass windows looking out onto a street. He hurried across the office, flung open the front door, looked right and left along a dim, deserted sidewalk, and ran for it.

It took only two or three minutes for his breath to be gone, the disorientation to have him in its grip again. The damned drug had been strong and he couldn't maintain straight thinking more than a minute or two at a time. He stopped at a deserted street corner under a feeble streetlight with a newspaper sales box chained to its post. No cars, no pedestrians, no one.

He realized he was standing there bare-footed, in garbage-covered pajamas, and had just broken into a lumber yard. If he had *not* wanted a policeman, the Dallas PD would have been all over him.

No time to think much about that, either.

There was a brick on top of the newspaper rack to help hold it down in wind. Hart took the brick and bashed in the front of the box. Glass tinkled and the lid sprang open, but the money box remained intact. He hit the money box hinges another six times, hurting his already-cut hands. The money box finally broke open, coins tumbling out and rolling all over the pavement. He scooped up a handful, mostly quarters, and ran again.

Two more blocks brought only one pickup truck passing in a hurry, the lone driver giving Hart no attention. There were lights of cars off to the right now, and beyond the lights, downtown buildings filled with illumination. But the nearest traffic was on an expressway, and Hart saw that he couldn't rush into full view when the first car that spotted him might be his heavyset friend's helpers, on the way to grab him.

He ran another block. His feet were killing him and he couldn't get enough oxygen, so he walked, dizzy. More blocks went by, more dark streets and alleys, warehouses and deserted storage lots, a couple of junkyards, devoid of people. He had the dazed thought that he had been left alone on the planet. But an occasional car or pickup rattled past him, the driver not so much as looking his way.

He was moving north. He could see Dallas's

downtown buildings not far ahead, and, closer at hand, the bulk of Reunion Arena where he had seen the Mavericks play once. If he went much farther, he was sure to encounter police and find himself in jail without ID and a bizarre story the precinct cynics would make an after-shift joke of in the wee hours of the morning while he stayed in a cell awaiting more interrogation by the daylight people.

He would have welcomed a black-and-white only minutes ago, but now he saw he couldn't afford that kind of delay. There was no time left. He had to find help on his own, and quickly.

He reached a corner where the only light came from a dingy streetlight on the far side of the street. The nearside lamp had been broken. Beneath it was a pay telephone booth.

He slipped into the booth, bit his tongue as he struggled to compose himself to talk, and punched the first quarter into the telephone.

Kecia almost didn't answer it.

Her telephone kept ringing insistently, however, and she finally wrapped a dense white towel around her wet hair, and padded naked out of the bathroom to the phone beside her bed.

"Yes?"

"Kecia?"

The single word let her recognize his voice, and know there was something wrong: he sounded thick, stressed. "Richard?" she said. "Is that you? What's wrong?"

"Can't find a policeman," he said. His voice was so infinitely weary, so slurred, she had to strain to understand him. "Never around when you need one. Called you . . . had to break a *Dallas Morning News* box for change—"

"*Richard?*" Kecia demanded, alarmed. "What's *wrong*? Where are you?"

"Dallas. I—"

"Dallas!"

"Kecia, listen." It sounded like his voice cleared, trembled with effort. "I tried to call Slagerfeldt. Off duty. Couldn't talk to th' man that answered . . . he though' I was drunk."

"*Are* you drunk?" Kecia blurted.

"No. Drugged."

"Richard, I don't understand!"

"Listen. Listen. Jus' please. Listen. Aw righ'?"

The plea and desperation in his voice halted her. She swallowed to compose herself. "Yes. Go ahead."

"In Dallas. Investigated hospital here. Got name of NASA scientist. Got to get name to Slagerfeldt. Got to get scientist off Mission Control team. Sabotage . . . some kind . . . dunno. Kecia, you've got to find Slagerfeldt. *Now.* Right away. Give him . . . name. Okay?"

"Okay," Kecia murmured, reaching for a pencil and note pad on the nightstand. "Richard, you sound awful. Can I—"

"Slagerfeldt," he repeated thickly. "Fin'. Give name. Got pencil?"

"Yes," Kecia groaned.

Very slowly, and with infinite patience, he gave her the name and spelled it. "Got it?" he asked.

"Yes. I've got it. And I have to find Detective Slagerfeldt and give him this name?"

"An' tell him . . . tell him . . . tell Selmon . . . NASA boss. Get this person out of . . . Mission Control . . . off team. Right away. . . . Now. Emergency."

"All right, Richard," Kecia said. She was crying. "But what about *you*? Are you all right? What can I do to help you?"

"Reunion," Hart's voice muttered softly.

"What did you say? What did you say?"

"Reunion. Reunion Arena. South side. Can stand under . . . roof . . . dark. . . . Watch parking lots,

street. South side. Reunion. Kecia. Can you . . . come
get me?''

"On the south side of Reunion Arena? In Dallas?
Now?''

"Fin' . . . Slagerfeldt first. Must fin' him first . . .
tell. Then . . . me."

"Richard, it will take me hours to get to Dallas!
Don't you know anyone there? Can't the police help?''

"Reunion," his thick voice said, trailing off.
"South. Tell . . . Slagerfeldt first.''

"Richard—!"

The line had gone dead.

For an instant Kecia stood still, the telephone still
to her ear. Then she put it down, anxiously jerking the
table drawer open to find the book.

"Hurry up, hurry up," she moaned in anguish as
the Houston police took several rings to answer.

Detective Slagerfeldt, she was told, was not on
duty tonight. No, she could not reach him at home,
and it was against policy to give out home telephone
numbers. They understood it was an emergency, but
the policy—

Perhaps because she was crying and yelling at
them, they said yes, they knew of the Myrick case, and
yes, they knew about the missing person report on Dr.
Hart. And yes. If she was sure it was a matter of life
and death, they would try to locate Detective Slagerfeldt and have him call her number as soon as possible.

Hanging up, she fled to the closet and started
pulling on some clothes. Her wet body made them
stick and she tore her blouse, but pulled it on anyway.
She was tying on tennies when the telephone rang,
making her jump.

It was Slagerfeldt. She told him about the call. He
sounded stunned. "I'll find my federal pal and tell him
right away," he told her.

"Thank you. Good-bye—"

"Wait a minute! What do you intend to do now?"

"Drive to Dallas. Find Reunion Arena. Find Richard."

"Alone?"

"Yes, alone—"

"My ass," Slagerfeldt told her. "You sit tight. I know how to page my federal buddy and get this message passed. Then—"

"But I'm wasting time, and Richard is sick, he's been drugged—"

"Lady," the detective cut in, his voice brittle, "my car has a special engine and a stick-on red light. It will cruise at one-twenty-five. Any slight delay that waiting for me causes, we'll more than make up for on the road. Now will you please just *sit*?"

"Yes," Kecia said instantly.

Slagerfeldt's exhaled breath was audible. "Good. Now give me your address and make some coffee to put in a thermos, if you can, and wait. I won't be long. I guaran-damn-tee it."

twenty-three

Thursday's dawn light streaked the sky over the salt marshes and prairie country surrounding the Johnson Space Center, but inside Mission Control there was no hint of a change in the perpetual even illumination.

The time counter over the big display board read:

PRESENT TIME. . . . . 1202 GMT

ELAPSED TIME

DAYS	HOURS	MINUTES	SECONDS
0006	19	32	10.07

"In less than five hours, we'll have completed the first full week in space—your seven days," Project Director John Selmon said. "What then?"

"I don't know," Richard Hart said tightly. "I just know the completion of the seventh day is a turning point. After that, we have no time left."

"But *when*, after seven days? And what happens?"

"I don't know," Hart repeated.

He was one of several persons standing on the glass-enclosed deck that looked down over Mission Control. Except for the FBI agent who had come with

Detective Bud Slagerfeldt, they looked like a scroungy crew, Hart thought. And even in his change of clothes after the bullet-swift ride back to Dallas, he felt scroungier than any of them.

He was thinking clearly now, with an occasional momentary relapse that proved the enduring potency of the drugs he had been given at the Dallas hospital. But his head hurt and there was a slight ringing in his ears, and he hadn't been able to eat. And his sense of forboding was unabated.

They hadn't gotten to the bottom of things. He still didn't understand the pattern of everything that had happened. His warning had gotten Leonard Murphy off the work floor and into an adjacent office area where he was still being questioned by the FBI, a NASA security man, and two psychologists. But defusing the threat to *Adventurer* couldn't be quite this simple.

Slagerfeldt, who had driven Hart and Kecia back from Dallas with the intensity of a maniac, was wearing jeans and a blue shirt that looked like they hadn't been off in a week. He needed a shave and his eyes were red-rimmed and sticky-looking. Kecia looked lovely but drawn and pale. LeRoy Ditwhiler's shirttail was out in back and as he glared through the glass at the operation below, he clenched a soggy cigar end in his jaw with the look of a man who had never slept. Selmon, the imperturbable, had a facial tic.

"I wish," he told the FBI man, "your boys would get Leonard Murphy to start talking *now.*"

The FBI agent didn't so much as blink. "They're working on it, sir."

"Yes, but God damn it, we're running out of time!"

"They're working hard on him, doctor."

Selmon turned to Hart. "You're sure he was the man with the trigger?"

Hart hesitated before replying. He wasn't "sure"

about anything. "I can't see how it could be anyone else. His was the only other NASA name I saw in the computer up there. I didn't get through the list. There could be another name later in the alphabet. Or one I didn't recognize."

"Geez," Ditwhiler muttered. "That's encouraging."

"How much longer before your boys are in that hospital with their warrants?" Selmon asked the FBI man.

The agent looked at this Rolex. "They're going in now, sir."

"They know they have to start scanning that computer list first thing?"

"Yes, sir." The agent's face was impassive. "They understand."

Selmon nodded and paced up and down, making eddies in Ditwhiler's cigar smoke.

Kecia moved closer to Hart and took his hand. "You okay?"

"Sure," he said, and grinned at her. "I'm indestructible."

"You're a jerk," she told him. Lovingly.

A voice on the PA speaker said, "We have onboard video on schedule."

Hart, like the others, turned to peer across the big room at the large screen. It filled with snow and then cleared, and the picture was of Col. Buck Colltrap on the flight deck of the spacecraft. H. O. Townsend was beside him in the right-hand chair. Both men were scanning computer displays and comparing figures with charts in one of the operating manuals. Townsend looked up at the camera and made a face at it, then returned to work. Colltrap, haggard and sunkeneyed, gave the lens an angry glance and went back to work at once with the intensity of a man driven by demons.

Below, on the floor of Mission Control, a technician flipped switches and the picture on the screen changed. The next area, the one immediately below the command level, was empty; a microphone floated across the camera's field on the end of a coiled cord, and closed cabinet doors stared from between lightweight wall members.

Other cameras were activated: in the next passageway to the cargo bay interlock area, where the focus was closer, on the bubbling hydroponics; into the bay itself, where the Mars lander crouched in its metal harness like a huge silvery bug with blackwindow eyes that reflected the golden glare of the sun; into the sleep area, where empty hammocks swayed; across the experimental section with its compact scientific gear, and finally into the lower crew section where the camera showed Christie bent over one of her ham radio recorders, changing out cassettes.

In her coveralls, a headband controlling her unruly hair, Christie became aware of the live camera and gave it a bright smile, released the microcassette in her left hand, and let it drift out of the field of view.

Hart's insides lurched. The way he loved her! He could taste his fear.

The screen went to snow, and then blank again, and was replaced after a moment with the computer-generated model of *Adventurer's* flight path across deep space from Earth toward still-distant Mars.

Behind the group assembled on the observation deck, a door flew open. One of John Selmon's assistants, assigned to stay close to the interrogation of Leonard Murphy, rushed in, coat-tail flying. Wide-eyed, he went to Selmon's side and whispered something urgent close to Selmon's ear.

"Jesus Christ," Selmon grunted. He turned, facing Hart. "Murphy just tried to kill himself."

"*How?*" Hart demanded, aghast.

"Jumped out of the chair, took a leap at the office window. If one of the FBI guys hadn't been quick on his feet to tackle him, we'd have a human pancake on the parking lot below."

Bud Slagerfeldt said instantly, "Like Myrick." He too turned to Hart. "Maybe like Myrick went . . . when it was time for him to go."

Something in Slagerfeldt's words and demeanor touched a thought process in Hart's mind, and in a split-second he saw connections that hadn't been apparent before. The chill that went through him was like a gust out of a freezer compartment.

He told Selmon, "I've got to talk to Murphy. *Now.*"

"Why? We've got good people—"

"You don't understand what just happened. Maybe Murphy tried to kill himself *because his job was done.*"

Selmon's face went slack, mirroring the expression of Ditwhiler, staring through a cloud of his cigar smoke. "Impossible," Selmon said.

"We can't assume it's impossible. Look. You said the latest reports from some of our analysts indicate the Russian crew may have screwed up and caused their own mission failure. That ties in with the theory I outlined to you. If the people behind all this could turn people like Myrick and Murphy, they could get to a crew member—program them to make a fatal error, triggered by someone communicating from Earth."

"How could they do all that?" Selmon demanded, incredulous. "How could it *happen*?"

"I don't know. But you said yourself that Colltrap is acting strangely. It's obvious even on television that he's acting strangely."

"That could be unexpected stresses from deep space flight."

"It could be programming, too! Listen. Myrick was in a position to send up faulty information, or in some other way cause confusion or conflict on board *Adventurer*. So was Murphy. Both were in Parkview in

Dallas. Myrick was tortured by feelings that *Adventurer* would meet disaster. Then he died, falling from a balcony. Then we arrested Murphy and he tried to go just the way Myrick died."

"He knows he's caught," Slagerfeldt said. "We have people try to kill themselves in jail—"

"But what," Hart demanded, "if that's not the explanation? What if Dave Myrick didn't die because somebody feared disclosure from him? *What if he killed himself—or was murdered—because his part of the sabotage job was done? —What if Murphy just tried to kill himself for the same reason?"*

Selmon's face twisted. "You mean they were . . . *programmed* to do something, then take their own lives?"

"Exactly."

"Can science *do* that to a person?"

"With the new psychotropics, God knows what they can do. Maybe I would have doubted it too, before I was in Parkview. I got a look at what they can do. If I hadn't known hypnosis, and been lucky, they could have turned me into *anything* in another day or two."

Selmon paced, glaring at the carpeted floor. No one else moved or spoke. "I wish to Christ Dr. K. hadn't been diverted to Huntsville for an aircraft change. I don't know—"

"Consider this," Hart urged, driven by his sense of desperate haste. "What if a crew member on *both* the Russian and American probes could be programmed, somehow, to respond to verbal triggers through post-hypnotic suggestion? What if someone—religious fanatics, Third World crazies, I don't know who—would go to any length to sabotage both trips to Mars?"

Ditwhiler said, "The goddam consortium."

Hart ignored him, concentrating on Selmon, because Selmon was the one he had to convince. "What if a crew member on each spacecraft was psychologically set up to respond with suicidal maneuvers or actions when he heard certain orders—seemingly innocent—from the ground?

"What," he pressed, "if Dave Myrick, when he talked to me in agony about failure of the mission, was not saying he feared failure, but that—unknown to his conscious mind—*he had already done his part to make sure failure would happen*?

"And what if Murphy was the last triggering person, and he tried to kill himself just now *because he already finished his job too*?"

Selmon's eyes bulged. "You mean the fatal signal may already have been sent?"

"Exactly."

Ditwhiler said slowly, "It doesn't hold up. How could Colltrap and the Russian both have been brainwashed? We don't exactly let our crews wander around at loose ends for days at a time, and neither do the Russkies."

Selmon struck his forehead with the palm of his hand. "Belgrade!"

"What?"

"Belgrade! Belgrade! Last year, remember? The goddam space conference. Buck Colltrap was there. So was their man: Zubakov. They had practically a whole weekend of free time. Somebody could have gotten them away from the conference—shot them full of some of these shitty drugs—" Selmon stopped in midsentence.

"Yes," Hart said. "Continued programming—once the initial hypnotic induction had been anchored—could have been done anytime either pilot was off-duty and could be gotten aside for an hour."

"Doctor. If this is true—if Murphy *already* sent some kind of triggering message or something—could you find out from him?"

"Hypnotize him, you mean?"

"Is that what it would take?"

"I don't know," Hart said. "I could try."

Selmon nodded and started for the door. "Come on, then."

Kecia watched Richard Hart, worried and haggard, follow John Selmon through the doorway, which closed behind them. Shock trickled through her bloodstream. She saw LeRoy Ditwhiler staring at her with dark worry.

She asked, "What if it's true?"

Ditwhiler angrily chewed on his cigar. "Can't be. Buck Rogers stuff. Unbelievable."

"So is a beacon on Mars! So is MarsProbe! But it's *real*!"

Ditwhiler continued to stare at her, his eyelids sagging with fatigue and dismay. "We sent up some contingency updates."

"Contingency? What kind of contingency?"

"From the start we had a plan. For a major breakdown in the shuttle configuration itself . . . an onboard fire, computer breakdown, fuel crisis, something off the wall like that. We updated that planning the other day when we started being so worried about Buck."

"You mean there's a way out?" Kecia demanded, desperate for any straw.

"I didn't say that. I just said there's a contingency plan."

"Will it *work*?"

"Who knows?"

Bud Slagerfeldt left Mission Control, intent on making a telephone call he had been trying to complete for two days. He needed a copy of a picture-framer's bill, and a date of delivery.

From an office, he dialed the number he had tried so often that he now had it memorized. Mr. Keenan, the girl said, would definitely be in later today. Could he return the call? Slagerfeldt gave her the number for his pager.

Going back toward Mission Control, he encountered two reporters outside the auxiliary pressroom. One he didn't know. The other was the ever-present Joe Blyleven.

"Hey, Bud!" Blyleven called, stuffing the last of a Mars bar into his mouth. "What are you doing here, man? Has there been another murder? Have you heard anything about Doctor Hart yet? Still missing?"

"Talk to you later, Joe," Slagerfeldt said with irritation.

"Holy moley," he heard the reporter exclaim behind him. "What a crab today!"

Having a bad press was the least of Slagerfeldt's problems. He was close now to the Houston connection. He was so obsessed that he hadn't even talked to his bookie today.

In New York City, seven special agents broke down the door of a Beekman Place luxury apartment. One of the Palestinians in the front room opened fire with an automatic, and was shot to pieces. His brother and two other men—a Greek millionaire and a vice president of the European space consortium—were taken after a scuffle. The man from the consortium, a Swiss, broke down and began telling everything he knew before the special agents had him in a waiting car.

Even the special agents, who thought they had seen and heard everything, were stunned. They had fallen into the mother lode of information about who was behind trouble with MarsProbe, and why.

twenty-four

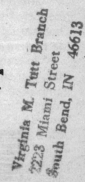

In the dimmed office, Richard Hart sat unmoving in his leather chair, intently watching Leonard Murphy, who was stretched out on the couch close by, his head comfortably propped up with pillows. Across the silent office, the two FBI men stood unmoving, shadowy statues in the dark. It was taking every bit of Hart's professional control to go slowly . . . appear calm.

Except for the whisper of air-conditioning, there was no sound in the room. Daylight was shut out by the vertical blinds at the windows behind the desk on the far end of the room. A telephone on the desk blinked as calls went to and from other offices, but there would be no calls here . . . nothing to interfere with Murphy's hypnotic trance.

The lank scientist's eyes were closed, his legs and arms were perfectly relaxed, his breathing was shallow and regular. No sign of his earlier anxieties marred the soft relaxation of his facial features. He was in deep trance.

Even with John Selmon's angry yelling, it had taken more than a precious hour to convince the security people that they must let Hart try to pry the truth out of Murphy through trance induction. Calls had to be made God-only-knew-where, normal procedures short-circuited. But Hart and Selmon had won, and forty minutes earlier, Hart had finally confronted Murphy in this isolated office with the FBI agents nearby for protection, but under instructions not to move or comment in any way unless Hart signaled them.

Murphy had been on the brink of hysteria, muttering under his breath, sweat-soaked, terrified, disoriented. It had taken all of Hart's experience to start him on the slow drift into relaxation, fixation, and the beginning of trance.

Once the procedure began to take hold, however, Murphy had responded much more swiftly and deeply than most people ever did. It proved he had been hypnotized before—and deeply, Hart thought, although it was not pleasant to imagine those previous circumstances at Parkview.

Now, with Murphy deeply entranced, Hart moved to learn what he had to know.

"Leonard," he said quietly, "you understand that you have nothing to fear from me. You feel very relaxed and very good. You will not be asked to do anything against your will. You will remember everything we have talked about, and you will feel much better because the confusion in your mind will be cleared. Do you understand and agree with me? Please tell me so if you understand and agree."

Murphy lay quiet, as if sleeping. Then, after a long silence, he said softly, "Yes."

"Thank you," Hart said. "Now, Leonard, I want you to remember some things for me. They may seem frightening to you. Remember you will feel better once you talk with me about these things. You are okay and you are not in danger and you will be helping yourself by remembering and telling me about these events. Do you agree?"

"Yes," Murphy said in the same deeply relaxed tone.

"Leonard, some time ago you were a patient at Parkview Limited Hospital in Dallas. Do you remember that?"

"Yes." Murphy's breathing speeded slightly, a sign of distress.

"It's all right to remember . . . all right to talk with me about it, Leonard. Now. Why did you go to Parkview?"

"Smoking."

"I see. You wanted to cut down or quit smoking?"

"Yes."

"I see. Good. How did you hear about Parkview?"

"Myrick."

"Davidson Myrick told you about Parkview?"

"Yes."

"He had been to Parkview and said they were good for him?"

"Yes."

"I see. Good. So you went to Parkview and checked in there for their antismoking program?"

"Yes."

"Leonard, who was your doctor at Parkview?"

"Silver."

Hart's pulse quickened, but he maintained his steady, quiet tone. "I see. And did you undergo hypnotherapy there with Dr. Silver for your smoking?"

"Yes." Again, quickened breathing, the twitch of a hand.

"You feel relaxed, Leonard. Relaxed and calm. Remembering cannot harm you. Talking about it cannot harm you. Now, Leonard, when you left Parkview, were there things besides smoking that you knew you had to do?"

"Yes."

Remembering the words that evidently had triggered Davidson Myrick in his office that day that now seemed an eternity ago, Hart spoke carefully: "Did the plans within your unconscious mind have to do with a *journey*, a *day or two*, or a *short time*, perhaps with *seven days*?"

"Seven days?" Murphy repeated more sharply. "Yes. Seven. Program in. One hundred. Sixty-eight. One hundred. Sixty-eight. All must be in readiness. If emergency comes, the onboard computer must have this program."

Tension clamped its fingers on Hart's midsection and it was a struggle to maintain the calm, even tone. "Were you to send a message to *Adventurer*?"

"Yes."

"When were you to send the message to *Adventurer*?"

"Seven. Seven."

"On the seventh day of the mission?"

"Yes. Yes. Mandatory."

"Leonard, what was the message you were to send to *Adventurer*?"

"All must be in readiness. If emergency comes, the onboard computer must have this program."

Hart was momentarily puzzled: "You sent a computer program?"

"No. Only the message. This message to the commander: All must be in readiness. If emergency comes, the onboard computer must have this program."

This, Hart thought, was it: the message that Buck Colltrap had been programmed to hear and act upon in ways that only his programmers could know. Harmless enough, without meaningful content in itself—except that when Colltrap heard this combination of words, he would be propelled into possibly catastrophic reactions that he had no way of knowing had been planted deep in his drugged mind.

Hart was sweating. "Leonard, do you know what *Adventurer* will do when the message is received?"

"No."

"Are there any other actions or messages you must take?"

"No. Only . . . when finished, I can no longer withstand the pain and I have no honorable course except suicide."

"And is that why you tried to go through a window a little while ago?"

"Yes."

"But you hadn't given the message to *Adventurer*—had you?"

"Yes." Murphy's chest rose and fell spasmodically.

"You already sent the message?" Hart asked, his voice sharpening despite his struggle to control it.

"Yes."

"Leonard. When did you send the message?"

"Seventh day."

"The seventh day of the mission?"

"Yes."

It was worse than he had imagined. Buck Colltrap, out there in the spacecraft, had already been triggered. But why hadn't something catastrophic happened as a result?

He managed to retain his calm, dispassionate tone: "Leonard: Something more is to happen. When?"

"One hundred," Murphy said gently. "Sixty-eight."

"I don't understand. Can you explain what you mean?"

"One hundred. Sixty-eight."

The signs of agitation were becoming sharply prominent. Hart saw he could go no further without risking greater damage to the mind of a man who had already been cruelly manipulated beyond his endurance. Murphy knew no more, he thought. He had been programmed to send a triggering message, and he had already sent it—intervention in the form of getting him off the floor of Mission Control had been too late.

But why hadn't the trigger taken effect?

Murphy was breathing harshly, twitching, going through psychic pain. Hart had to return his full attention to him, talking gently, easing him out of his discomfort, preparing him for the end of the trance state.

It took another thirty minutes or so, a half hour Hart agonized through. As Murphy finally came out from the trance, with shocked remembrance of the things he had recounted, Hart summoned the NASA psychologists, briefly explained what had happened, and signaled one of the FBI men that he wanted to talk outside.

Hart told the agent, "You heard what he said. He was drugged—hypnotized. He wasn't responsible. But now he knows what he did. There's nothing more to get out of him. You have to let the psychologists work with him now. Otherwise his mental health might never come back."

The agent nodded soberly. "I heard it. I think the poor bastard was brainwashed. I'll tell my superior. I agree with your recommendation."

Hart turned away.

"Doc?" the agent said.

Hart turned back. "Yes?"

"Can the spacecraft be saved?"

"It has to be. But we have to figure out *how*."

He went down the corridors and on an elevator, and past Security to reenter the deck over Mission Control. Slagerfeldt was no longer around. Neither was Ditwhiler. John Selmon, Kecia, and a NASA security agent remained on vigil.

"Well?" Selmon demanded anxiously.

"He already sent the trigger," Hart said, putting his arm around Kecia.

"Jesus! Then why hasn't our crew already gone nuts?"

Hart turned slowly to stare across Mission Control, his eyes resting on the big display and the clock. He stared at the numbers.

PRESENT TIME. . . . . 1447 GMT

ELAPSED TIME

DAYS	HOURS	MINUTES	SECONDS
0006	22	17	10.35

As he did so, something clicked in his brain.

"Does anyone have a calculator?" he asked.

"Sure." Selmon took an HP scientific calculator out of a leather holster on his right hip. "What do you need?"

"Take six times twenty-four," Hart said. His voice shook. "Add twenty-two."

Selmon touched keys. "That's an easy one, even for fumble-fingers like me." He squinted at the display. "A hundred and sixty-six."

"A hundred and sixty-six hours, plus seventeen minutes, elapsed time," Hart said through his teeth.

"Want to let us in on what you're talking about," Selmon demanded.

"The keys are numbers," Hart said. "Seven, and then the other numbers. Both Myrick and Murphy repeated them like a litany. One hundred. And sixty-eight. But the last two were not separate numbers; they were a combination."

He stared at Kecia, and then turned to face Selmon. "Don't you see? *Seven* is seven *days*. The number *one-sixty-eight* is the number of hours in seven days. That's the key. That's the time your command pilot up there is programmed to go crazy, once he's been triggered—which he already has been. At the conclusion of Day Seven. *At hour 168*. That's when *Adventurer* is supposed to be wrecked.''

John Selmon stared while the information sank in.

Then he responded characteristically: ''Then that gives us''—he glanced at his watch—''over an hour and a half left.''

''To do what?'' Kecia demanded. ''If Richard is right, the signals have all been sent, and your pilot is set to go off like a bomb at the stroke of hour 168!''

''And right now it's hour 166, plus twenty-two minutes,'' Selmon replied doggedly, ''which means—I repeat—we've got over an hour and a half to do something. —Leroy, get the people we need. Meeting. My office. Now.''

Within thirty minutes, the emergency meeting in John Selmon's office had already reviewed options. The clock was ticking like a time bomb.

Warner Klindeinst had finally arrived, but quickly told Selmon to continue chairing the session. Selmon sat at the head of the conference table, Klindeinst on his left, Ditwhiler on his right. Richard Hart sat next to Klindeinst, with the once-suspect Jack Schaeffly facing him across the table. A NASA psychologist named Best was seated beside Schaeffly, and an engineer named Conrad was on Hart's other side. Charts, tables, and program outlines were thrown all over the work surface, and the air was thick with Ditwhiler's cigar smoke and the fumes from Conrad's chain-smoked cigarettes.

Selmon looked up from scrawled notes. ''All right, then. Let's keep it moving, we don't have all day. We're in agreement with Dr. Hart's view that it's too risky to simply radio up an abort-and-return order?''

The NASA psychologist, Best, nodded. Worry lines washboarded his forehead. He was young, balding, intense. "I agree with Dr. Hart. There's no way to predict what kind of programming contingencies might have been set into Colonel Colltrap's mind. If we send up an abort sequence, it might trigger him into more violent behavior than the other crew members could possibly handle."

"What can we do but abort?" Ditwhiler grated. "We can't just wait for him to go bonkers."

"Could H. O. and Christie overpower him?" Conrad asked. "Give us time to try to figure out how to deprogram him?"

"No, no, no," Klindeinst said, shaking his head angrily. "What are they to do then? Lock him up? In the spacecraft? Go on to Mars with a raving maniac as a prisoner?" He paused, rolling his eyes toward the ceiling. "Or kill him, perhaps? Shove his body out into space? No. It won't do, it won't do. We must abort, return to Earth orbit."

"Then H. O. and Christie still have to get him under control."

"Yes. We have to send them instructions out of Colonel Colltrap's hearing . . . have them take over the ship."

"How?" Selmon asked. "Buck is on the deck right now. He's got the Earth-Comm circuit open to his headset. We've got no way to communicate with Townsend or Christie."

"How much longer is Buck in command and in control of the radio link?" Conrad demanded.

"Two more hours."

A deathly silence fell over the room. Two hours—and they didn't have two hours left.

Schaeffly said into the quiet, "If we had communications, we might retrieve something . . . at least warn the rest of the crew. Christie has the contingency plan and the update. She's checked out the lander herself, unknown to Colltrap, and she's told Townsend by

now that we've updated the lander computers on a frequency Colltrap won't monitor on board *Adventurer*. If
we had a way of letting her and H. O. know what
they're up against, they might have a slim chance."

Everyone looked at Schaeffly. The circles under
his eyes were deep, pain-filled. His complexion was
the color of ashes.

"And incidentally," he added with absolutely no
modulation in his tone, "as soon as this crisis is past,
you'll have my resignation."

Selmon's face fell. "Oh, Jack," he said.

Schaeffly's eyes were ice. "Let's continue the
meeting."

The silence in the room was total. For men like
Schaeffly, Hart thought, feelings of being trusted—
needed and important—were inextricably bound up in
the job. After being pulled off the line on suspicion,
Schaeffly could never feel the same at NASA again.

After more awkward moments of silence, Ditwhiler made a production of angrily relighting his
cigar. "All right. We've got to tell them what's going
on. But Colltrap is on the Comm channel. How do we
tell them what we've learned, and order them to carry
out the contingency program? God damn it, we're
effectively cut off!"

Again no one spoke. Then Hart saw the way.

"No, we're not cut off," he said.

All heads turned to face him.

"Her ham radio rig," Hart said.

Selmon smacked his palm to his forehead. "Yes, of
course!"

Ditwhiler frowned. "Is she on the air right now?
Or is she scheduled today at all?"

Conrad flipped furiously through pages of a thick
operations manual. "The standard day plan gives her
four hours off right now. Second and third hour are,
quote, Ham Radio Operations, Optional, unquote."

"She'll be on," Hart said. He was certain. He
knew his daughter.

"Can we get to a ham radio?" Selmon demanded.

"More important," Conrad said, "can we modify or amplify one to provide sufficient power to override the hundreds or thousands of other people calling her incessantly on a single frequency?"

Ditwhiler shoved his chair back. "We've got hams in this organization. I'll put out a scream on the PA system right now, get them to report here on the double." He hurried out of the room.

Klindeinst also was on his feet. "We will need power. Lots of power. Conrad, consult Communications Engineering. Question: Is any of our high-power radio equipment of the type that can be retuned to the band Christie is operating on? Question: Do we have an antenna tunable to that frequency, or can one be fabricated *quickly*?"

Conrad started for the door. "Some of our amplifiers are broadbanded, and if anybody can get one to amplify a radio amateur frequency signal, I know the guy down there who can." He went out the door.

"Hurry!" Selmon yelled after him.

"Hurrying!" Conrad's voice echoed back from the hallway beyond.

A messenger from Mission Control came in, bringing a thin piece of printout paper with a few words typed across its face. He handed it to Selmon. "This was just transcribed from the *Adventurer* voice circuit, sir."

Selmon grabbed the piece of paper and read it. Frowning, he looked up. "It says Colltrap just said several times, quote, All must be in readiness. If emergency comes, the onboard computer must have this program. Unquote. But he isn't updating a computer, and neither are we. Does anybody know what he's talking about?"

"It's the trigger," Hart said. "He's repeating the trigger sent up by Murphy. He's getting ready to act at hour 168."

Involuntarily, they all turned to stare at the wall clock. They had roughly an hour left.

twenty-five

Drab summer rain pelted Red Square. In a meeting room behind the walls of the Kremlin, a top-level meeting broke up. An observer in the broad stone corridor beyond the meeting room doors would have recognized several of the highest-ranking members of the Politburo, a trio of medal-encrusted generals in the Soviet military, and the dour chieftain of the KGB, along with his top two lieutenants. But there were no observers nearby to record the scene, only soldiers standing stiffly on guard at regular intervals along the enormous corridor.

Heads were going to roll. The best Soviet electronic communications specialists and computer scientists still had not broken the United States's radio encryption system, and the Russian leadership still didn't have any way of knowing everything that was going on aboard *Adventurer*.

But on a related front, vast progress had been made, actions ordered.

One of the most powerful men in attendance at the meeting had to walk a relatively short distance to his own office, accompanied by his private secretary, a young man noted for his efficiency, unquestioned loyalty, and fierce devotion. The high office holder parted from his secretary in the outer office, and went alone into his inner working area.

A visitor was waiting for him.

"Constantine," the high official said with genuine pleasure as he pumped the older man's hand. "It is fine to see you well enough to be out again."

The much older visitor nodded. His heavily lined face was the color of lead, but his rheumy old eyes were quick with intelligence and curiosity. "How did the meeting go?"

"Ah," the high official sighed. "You know of it, and the subject matter, then?"

"Yes. My doctor tells me I cannot attend such meetings, perhaps ever again." The old man touched his chest. "The human heart becomes a fragile instrument when one reaches my age."

"I am sorry, Constantine. Truly. History will remember you."

The old man gestured the compliment away. "Tell me," he ordered simply.

"We have incontrovertible proof," the high official told him.

"Ah. Of who was behind the tragedy to our cosmonauts?"

"The KGB has completed the report on which it was already working when the disaster came. We know now, almost surely, how it was done. More important, we have already arrested six persons within our program."

The old man inclined his leonine head. "And the international implications?"

"The Americans know nothing. For once they are truly innocent. They are as much victims as we."

"But who, then—"

The high official put a fond hand on the old man's

shoulder. "You will know within a day or two, my dear Constantine. The world will know. We have our proof, and everything is already being set in motion for the carrying out of our retaliation."

The old man nodded again, his breath wheezing slightly. "It was a terrible tragedy . . . a terrible national setback and loss."

The younger man's jaw set. "You may be sure, Constantine, that the blows we are about to strike in retaliation will be equally terrible. Of that you should have no doubt—no doubt whatsoever."

"And concerning the beacon on Mars?"

"We will begin again."

"As the Americans will surely do after their cosmonauts die?"

"Yes. With new security, new technology. We shall race again."

In a southern suburb of Houston, Detective Bud Slagerfeldt took the sales and delivery slips from the man he had been seeking for days.

"Is this what you need, sir?" the young picture-framer asked nervously.

Slagerfeldt glanced at the writing on the tickets and felt a surge of satisfaction. "Yes, sir, this is exactly what I needed."

"I hope nothing was wrong with the work."

"No. Nothing like that. Thank you. And remember: we will need to get a sworn statement from you."

The young framer was pale and a little scared. "Yes, sir. I'll be right here. Or at my home number."

"Thanks." Slagerfeldt walked out of the art and frame shop, got back into his car, and headed back toward the highway that led to the space center. He was very pleased with himself.

From the first he had been plagued by the knowledge that the man killed in pursuit of Richard Hart could not have been working alone . . . that there had to be at least a contact man to pass orders here in the Houston area, and probably one or more higher-ups. The FBI's arrests here—the man inside NASA's computers and the one who had been paying him and his wife—did not fill the bill for a local brain. These events had only assured Slagerfeldt that there was a conspiracy of major proportions. His feeling of personal failure for not uncovering leads in Myrick's death, and supervision of the hired gun from New Orleans, had been growing.

Something Hart had told him recently, however, had given him the slim lead he needed. And now it was paying off.

And the man he wanted was at the center today.

Slagerfeldt stuck his red light on top of his car as he hit the expressway, and pushed it up to ninety.

Four junior technicians stood in John Selmon's office: a heavyset man of about forty, a graying but athletic type a few years younger, and two slender youths in their mid-twenties. Two of them had amateur radio handi-talkies on their belts.

Selmon squinted at them. "You're all hams?"

"Yes, sir," the oldest member of the quartet said.

"All right, then. Gentlemen, this is Dr. Richard Hart. Christie Hart, our crew member, is his daughter. You all know, I guess, that she's a ham too?"

The men grinned at one another. The heavy one said, "We've all been trying to get a QSO with Christie, but none of us has made it so far. That frequency is a madhouse. It won't be long now, though. We've got a special freq set up so we can get our contacts with her."

"The whole world is calling her every durn time

she's on the announced frequency," said another. He was younger, with a bulge of snuff in his cheek.

"Well," Selmon growled, "here's the deal. We have to get some special instructions to Christie, for her ears only. This is a life-and-death emergency, gentlemen. We *must* break through that logjam on her ham frequency and talk to her right away."

"Pileup," the gray-haired one said.

"What?" Selmon snapped.

"Pileup. We call them pileups when everybody is calling."

"Whatever. We have to get through and we don't have much time."

The youngest man turned to the senior member of the quartet. "What do you think, Gordon? How the hell can we break that pileup?"

The one called Gordon looked at his feet as he thought about it.

Hart put in, "Your engineers here just reported a few minutes ago that they can retune one of the big linear amplifiers to work on two meters. They're working on it now and it should be ready within thirty minutes, with all the help they've rounded up."

Gordon looked at Hart with new interest, inasmuch as Hart's lingo had shown he knew a little about their hobby. "How much will one of those doozies pump out, do you suppose?"

"Ten kilowatts, give or take a little," Hart told him.

The oldest ham grinned slowly, and the others joined in.

"Holy horse hockey," one of them murmured. "We'll blow in over everybody with *that* kind of power."

"We don't have an antenna," Gordon said.

"Can you retune one of our dishes?" Selmon demanded.

"I don't know . . . I think it would take a few hours—"

"We don't *have* a few hours."

Gordon looked at his gray-haired companion. "Have we still got that scrap aluminum tubing out back?"

"I can do better than that," the youngest said. "I've got a ten-element Yagi in the back of my camper."

"Where," Selmon demanded, "is your camper?"

"Out in the lot."

Gordon rubbed his hands together. "Great. Then all we've got to do is run some coax from one of the dishes over to the Yagi, mount it on the roof, get a bearing on where to point, hook the other end up to the linear—wait a minute, wait a minute—can we feed the linear with one of our hand-helds?"

"Go down to electronics with the radio you're going to use," Selmon said. "They'll cobb up a connector that will run from your radio to the amp."

"What about heading? Oh, hell: Is *Adventurer* on the right side of the Earth right now? These signals are line of sight, and if the wrong side of the planet is pointed toward them—"

"We had video direct less than two hours ago. And I think Christie is supposed to be on your ham band right now. I'll double-check that." He yanked up his telephone and punched a number. "Scott? Is *Adventurer* on our side of the globe right now? Do we have direct data acquisition, or—" He listened. "Good."

Hanging up the telephone, he said, "Our side will be facing them for another eight hours."

"We can get a magnetic heading and elevation?" Gordon asked.

"Whatever you want."

Gordon nodded, thought hard a moment, and

then turned to his friends. "Joe, get over to the lot and drag that antenna in here on the double. Dr. Selmon, we need help getting on the roof, finding a mast and some hardware, locating the right coaxial cable that will run to the amplifier room—"

"You'll have it, you'll have it," Selmon said, reaching again for the telephone.

The one named Joe hurried out of the office.

"Okay, then, fine," Gordon went on. "Billy, get down to the Comm area with your handi-talkie. Are your batteries up?"

The one named Billy nodded. "Just charged."

"Get going, then." Billy departed. "Chaz, when Joe gets back, you'll help him lug the Yagi to the roof and hook it up." Gordon watched Selmon, who was talking on the phone. "As soon as he gets clear, here, we'll find out what the emergency is and what kind of message we've got to get to her up there." He turned to glance at Hart. "She's a dynamite lady, doctor. She's doing a great job up there."

Hart felt sudden heat behind his eyes. *I will not cry*, he thought. And didn't. But he was so tired and upset he was hardly thinking straight.

Selmon slammed the receiver down on the phone. "You've got your hardware, Gordon. —Now, I wonder how many thousand hams will hear us even after you switch to that other frequency."

"Well," Gordon said slowly, "I suppose a few might. But people don't usually scan way up there at the high end of the band, and"—his grin returned—"most hams in the world with two-meter equipment are going to be so busy yelling for a contact lower in the band, they'll never have a chance to listen anyplace else."

Selmon glumly shrugged. "We've got to try it anyway."

Hart listened for a few more minutes, then left the office. Outside, Kecia rose from a chair where she had been waiting tensely. Seeing his eyes, she came to him and put her arms around him. "What *happened*?"

"Nothing," Hart choked. He let the tears go. "She's still fine . . . they're still okay. I'm just so God damned scared—!"

"Oh, Richard," Kecia said softly, holding him in her arms.

"I suppose part of it is aftermath from the drugs, all the rest." He collected himself a little and grinned into her hair. "Just keep on hugging, okay? I need hugs right now."

She hugged tighter, fiercely. "I was so sure I had lost you—!"

"I couldn't tell you what was going on. They might have had a tail on me. You could have been hurt."

She moved to arm's length. "And then when you called from Dallas, I was scared out of my mind. You should have let me *help* you!"

"I told you, Kecia. This was my job. No need for you to get involved."

"Damn that!" she said with unusual force.

He stared, trying to read her expression. All he— the expert—knew at this moment was that she was beautiful. And filled with emotion.

"If we're going to get along for the next thirty or forty years," she told him, "you're going to have to share everything with me. The good and the bad alike. Isn't that what you tell your patients?"

She was smiling nervously now, but he took in only the words and their meaning. They rocked him. "Who said anything about thirty or forty years?" he asked.

"*You* did, damn it. A hundred times."

"Yes, but you always said—"

"When I thought I had lost you, Richard, I saw how dumb I've been. I'm scared. But not as scared as I was when I thought you were gone from my life. Not as scared as when I heard you on the telephone from Dallas. I don't want to lose you. I don't want to be separated from you again. *Ever.* Is . . . is that all right?"

Despite the gnawing fear for Christie, he was astonished and glad. "Does this mean," he asked, smiling, "that, if I was to repeat my oft-given proposal of marriage, the answer might be different?"

"The answer *is* different, doc. The answer is yes."

"Oh, babe." He pulled her close.

"Just a minute, just a minute," she breathed. "Are you going to *ask* me?"

"Ask you?" He felt dazed.

"Ask me!"

"Oh!" He saw. "Kecia: will you—"

"Yes. I love you. Kiss me."

He did.

Tethered near her antenna window aboard *Adventurer*, Christie Hart struggled to act normally, as ordered. Listening to the incredible din of amateur radio stations calling her on her two-meter listening frequency, she jotted three more call signs as she picked them out of the pileup.

"Okay," she said crisply, her voice keying the vox unit of her boom headset. "I roger W5LFK, PJ7NUT and N5IAA. This is KU5B on board the spacecraft *Adventurer*. QRZ?"

As she paused and the vox dropped out, allowing stations to come through the receiver section of her handi-talkie once more, it sounded like many more stations had entered the fray. The rotational orientation of the Earth relative to *Adventurer*'s location was beginning to favor the western United States and the Pacific. She could hear some JA stations—Japan—beginning to come in, and some ZLs and VKs from New Zealand and Australia. She had just logged the first ZL call when the sound of a much more powerful radio carrier hissed in her headset, giving her an instant to wonder before the voice boomed in overriding all the weaker stations:

"KU5B, KU5B, KU5B . . . this is Houston. KU5B, KU5B, KU5B, this is Houston Mission Control. QSY special freq now. Repeat: QSY special freq now. Houston out."

Chilling with surprise and confusion, Christie realized at once that they could only be referring to the special schedule frequency for NASA radio amateurs. What was going on? But without more thought she reached over to her handi-talkie and electronically unlocked the keyboard, quickly entering the frequency of 147.950 MHz. Into the boom mike she said, "This is KU5B listening for Mission Control, over."

There was the slightest pause, and then the voice came back amazingly powerful: "KU5B, this is Mission Control. Christie, this is Jack Schaeffly, and Dr. Selmon is with me. Can you read us clearly? Over."

"I copy five and nine," Christie replied, lapsing into ham jargon. "What's happening? Over."

"Christie, this is an emergency. You have your headset on and nobody else can hear at your end? Over."

"Affirmative, Houston. Over."

"Okay, Christie. We have further information for you. We are activating the contingency plan I gave you earlier. We are declaring an emergency. We have further information for you. Stand by one."

"Standing by."

Almost at once, the voice of John Selmon filled her headphones. "Christie, this is Selmon. Listen carefully. We have very, very little time. I can't risk repeating anything. Listen hard, now."

Christie listened. As the voice crossed the void of space and began telling her what had to be done, and how little time there was for doing it, she began to feel sick at heart. But there was no choice and she listened intently to details, already beginning to brace herself internally for the events that would now follow.

twenty-six

PRESENT TIME. . . . . 1610 GMT

ELAPSED TIME

DAYS	HOURS	MINUTES	SECONDS
0006	23	40	07.31

"Twenty minutes," LeRoy Ditwhiler said, pacing back and forth through the clouds of his cigar smoke.

On the floor of Mission Control, every technician was on position. The maintenance-staffing personnel assignment schedule had been scrubbed and everyone called in, as if *Adventurer* had leaped months ahead, and was in the crucial Mars-orbit phase. Details had not been announced, but every person on board knew that a state of emergency had been declared and what would be attempted.

Word of the unusual activity had already leaked. Reporters from CNN, the Houston *Post*, AP, and ABC-TV News were already in the pressroom, clamoring for answers. The NASA press people were stonewalling temporarily on orders from the White House. In the

media information section, telephones were ringing off
the desks. All three major networks had already had
break-in bulletins about "an undefined emergency on
board spacecraft *Adventurer.*" A telephone call confirmed that congressmen were demanding information, and the president's press secretary had promised
some kind of announcement by three o'clock, EDT,
about four hours from now.

Watching the scene in Mission Control at Ditwhiler's side, Richard Hart tried to convince himself
that so much knowledge and technology could over-
come any crisis. But the one crisis not fully covered in
all the option planning was the one they faced: a crazy
man at the controls of the spacecraft.

John Selmon and Warner Klindeinst stood under
the moving time display, studying the contingency
timetable. It left absolutely no margin for error or delay.

Kecia moved closer to Hart and squeezed his
hand. "How much longer?"

"Until they call him?" Hart said. "Ten minutes."

"And if their orders don't work? If he doesn't
obey?"

Hart hesitated before answering. He felt quite sure
Buck Colltrap would not obey the new orders when
Selmon sent them up. Then the rest of the plan would
have to be activated with all its dangers.

He said, "If it doesn't work, then it's all up to the
other two."

He wished to God he could have answered some
other way.

Outside, Detective Bud Slagerfeldt pulled through
the heavily guarded gates, passing the lines of religious fanatic protesters who seemed more numerous
and vociferous, probably in response to the radio bulletins about MarsProbe trouble.

Slagerfeldt was anxious to get inside and find his man. But he warned himself to proceed cautiously, check with Dallas first, follow procedures.

Slagerfeldt parked near the building and went inside, passed the security desk, and entered the Security Division offices. He got permission to use one of the smaller rooms, currently unoccupied, to make his call.

He used a department telephone credit card number to direct-dial his counterpart in the Dallas Police Department. Waited two minutes. Listened to the pulsing ache of a migraine and stared at a contemporary splotch of color framed on the metal wall, which was not quite in focus due to the visual aurora effects of the headache.

"Captain O'Neal," the heavy voice in Dallas finally answered.

"Chip, this is Slagerfeldt in Houston."

"Yowsa. Missed your earlier call."

"What do you have for me?"

"Silver and Masterson, our two suspects in custody here, haven't cracked an ounce. The feds have Dr. Heath. He's screaming violation of his rights and medical confidentiality, and his lawyers are trying to get a writ or something to spring him. The sons of bitches are scared out of their gourds, but they're still hanging tough."

It wasn't good news. Slagerfeldt was used to that. "Now about the search at the hospital?"

"We've got one name that struck us funny. Also, the federal boys are hot after some deposits in both the hospital accounts and Dr. Heath's personal account. We are talking big goddam money, here, Bud. I mean a million, maybe two. Looks like the checks came from a so-called research organization in Puerto Rico that doesn't exist except on paper. The feds figure it's a money-laundering operation."

"Anything else?"

"They had a bust in New York that blew the lid off at that end. We can't get all the information. But it's big. They've got somebody who tied part of it to the PLO, plus a multinational corporation in Greece, plus an outfit directly linked to the top management of TransOrbital, the European space bunch."

"Jesus Christ," Slagerfeldt muttered.

"So the working theory seems to be that the Europeans didn't want us ahead of their unmanned probe, and sugared the pot to sabotage us. And the PLO and God-knows-who-else came in to form the unholiest alliance you ever heard of."

"I was betting on Libya or somebody like that," Slagerfeldt admitted.

"Hey, hoss, funny you should mention that. I saw on the news a while ago that the CIA made a bust down in Australia last night. Arrested three foreign nationals they said were terrorist-types with links to Libya. Guess where these weirdos were trying to slip in with a handbag full of plastic explosives. Our big space-link radio antennae near Canberra."

"Dynamite," Slagerfeldt muttered.

"No," his literal counterpart in Dallas said promptly. "Plastics."

Slagerfeldt had to smile. "I meant, wow. Shazam. Et cetera. Maybe our very good friends in the Common Market group and the crazies that blow up their airports for them were together on this one."

"Well, maybe," O'Neal grunted. "That's not my department. How about this name we picked up. Guy in your jurisdiction."

"I *need* a man in my jurisdiction," Slagerfeldt said. "I've got a solid lead—"

"Maybe this will help." The Dallas detective paused to consult a card, and read off some dates, and the familiar name.

"Holy shit," Slagerfeldt breathed. "Beautiful."

"Of course he could have really done legitimate work for them."

"I doubt it. This ties in perfectly with information I've developed at this end. I was about to pick him up anyway."

"What charge?"

"Suspicion of conspiracy to commit murder, for one thing."

"Keep me posted."

"Right." Slagerfeldt hung up the telephone and hurried out of the office.

In the aft section of *Adventurer*, Christie Hart and H. O. Townsend finished adjusting one another's gleaming white helmets, and plugged each other into the longest communications umbilicals they had been able to dredge up. They faced each other in silence.

Overhead lights cast golden reflections over the bubble front of Townsend's helmet, making it impossible for Christie to see his face. She knew how worried he looked. She had seen his face as she explained the emergency plan to him, secretly met him down here, helped him suit up.

She felt the same. Their lives were on the line. It was that simple. There just wasn't any time to wring hands about how something this incredible could have happened. It *had*, that was all. And they had no time left for pondering it.

Air moved nicely through the compartments of the bulky white EVA suits, and cooling was operational. They were plugged into both internal and external communications circuits, although they had their microphones turned off for now. They had checked everything they could, and when Christie held up her bulky white wrist to show Townsend the huge chronometer strapped there, it showed they had two minutes before they had to be in the passageway to the flight deck.

Just time enough to make it.

Townsend led the way. Christie drifted after him. They went up one level, then moved forward. They passed her amateur radio rig, and she wondered briefly if they could have even had this chance for safety if it hadn't been for that small, Japanese-manufactured handi. There was no time to think about that, either.

They moved into the passageway linking the lower and upper crew compartments. Townsend floated up toward the handholds and railing that led to the flight deck, where Col. Buck Colltrap was in the commander's chair. Christie stayed close to Townsend's big white boots, following, then both of them holding where they had been instructed, out of Colltrap's sight.

Christie's chronometer showed *time*, and the voice came right on schedule inside her helmet:

"Adventurer, *this is Houston, over.*" That was John Selmon's voice.

From just above Christie's and Townsend's hiding place came the voice of Colltrap, also over the radio and of no different volume or quality than Houston's transmission: "*Houston*, Adventurer *here. Go.*"

"*Buck, this is John Selmon. We have emergency orders which we instruct you to carry out immediately, over.*"

Colltrap's voice sounded sharp with alarm and hardly concealed anger. "*What emergency? What orders? We're right on the flight line up here!*"

"*Buck, this is Houston, Selmon speaking. Here are your orders. Number one. You will relinquish command of the spacecraft at once to Townsend. Number two. You will report to the emergency medical bay where Hart has orders to give you medical assistance. You will take these actions at once.*

Explanations will come later. Do you roger your emergency orders? Over."

Colltrap screamed back, *"Negative! Negative! Are you crazy, Houston? There is no emergency! There is no emergency! All must be in readiness if emergency comes! The onboard computer must have this program!"*

"Adventurer, Houston. Colonel Colltrap, these are your orders. You will surrender command now. You will report to sick bay now. Please roger these orders now. Over."

"No! Negative! No! I have to do things! No one else can save the mission! Negative! Negative! Out!"

The last words, screamed so shrilly they were almost unreadable, preceded a sharp popping sound on the circuit.

Colltrap had cut off communications with the ground.

Townsend looked down at Christie. She could see his face now, and his youthful features were scared. He had the hypodermic syringe in his right gloved fist.

Christie hesitated. If there were *any* other way—

Over her helmet intercom, Colltrap's voice rasped, *"H. O. to the flight deck. Christie to the flight deck."*

Christie and Townsend exchanged alarmed looks. What was this all about?

She recovered first, keying her mike: "What's up, Buck?"

"I have a computer-assisted midcourse correction maneuver. Report to the deck to assist, now."

His voice sounded eerily normal—even quiet. And only seconds before he had been screaming hysterically.

A midcourse correction? It was the last bad news they needed, confirmation of everything Houston had said. There was no burn scheduled, none needed. Any engine burn would only throw *Adventurer* off course.

Townsend was staring at Christie. She swallowed hard and nodded.

Townsend drifted up to flight-deck level, Christie hard on his heels.

A bizarre scene met their eyes. Colltrap, shirtless, streaming sweat, had two panels off computers, wires hanging out, circuit boards suspended. The engine readiness panel was ablaze with lights, signifying a manual-control burn in preparation. Colltrap, his eyes crazier than anything Christie had ever seen, swung around to face them, then recoiled in shock as he saw them in their EVA suits.

"What's this all about?" he yelled. "Get out of those things! Help me! Houston is crazy! If emergency comes, the onboard computer must have this program!"

Townsend moved closer to his commander, the syringe hidden behind his back. "Buck," he said almost tenderly, filled with regret. "You're not quite well, man. Let us help you, aw right?"

"Sit down!" Colltrap yelled. "Strap in! Take orders! If emergency comes—"

Townsend moved swiftly—just as swiftly as the cumbersome EVA suit allowed. The syringe appeared in his outstretched hand and started down toward Colltrap's glistening bare arm.

Colltrap yelled again—sound without meaning— and dodged to the side, reaching for something on the deck beneath his seat. The syringe hit his arm and the needle plunged all the way in. As Townsend depressed the plunger, injecting a massive dose of the fast-acting sedative, Colltrap straightened up and swung his other arm around. He was holding what he had reached beneath the seat to get, and Christie could hardly believe her eyes.

A gun.

"H. O.! Look out!"

Townsend threw himself awkwardly against Colltrap, but in the weightless environment he looked like

the old Pillsbury doughboy trying to wrestle—all soft
curvatures of white spacesuit, with no weight as a base
for force. Townsend's arms tangled with Colltrap, the
gun pinched between them somewhere, and the two
men started to drift out of the command pilot's seat in
slow motion as they struggled.

There was an unbelievably loud, muffled explosion. Colltrap's head shot up, his eyes and mouth
wide with shock. Pink spray wafted out of his back.
He broke from Townsend and his arms went out spasmodically toward the computer console controls.

"*Buck*—!" Christie yelled just as Townsend tried
to stop him.

Too late.

Colltrap's fingers spasmodically jabbed buttons on
the console. There was an instant's barrage of flashing
sequential lights on the panel, a distant thump, and a
shocking jolt of acceleration that knocked Christie
against the bulkhead.

She saw as if in slow motion as Townsend fought
the G forces to close with Colltrap a second time. Colltrap still had the gun and it fired again, the blast mixed
up in the roar and thump of the firing rockets. The
bullet or bullets missed Townsend but shattered instruments and computer components in the ceiling. Angry
little sparks shot all over the place and Christie saw
puffs of the astronauts' nightmare—*smoke.*

Townsend, still in agonizing slow speed, but now
because he was fighting the massive, building G
forces, again closed with Colltrap. But the drug had
suddenly reached Colltrap's brain. He keeled sideways, unconscious.

"*The engine controls!*" Christie screamed. "Shut
them down!"

Townsend turned. But as he did so the vibrations
and roaring stopped.

The programmed engine burn was over. Beyond

the front screen of *Adventurer*, stars and planets whirled in crazy, curving lines. The ship was tumbling wildly off course.

Television monitoring frequencies in Mission Control had been opened, but the large display panel remained grayish, highlighted sporadically by random bursts of electronic snow. Richard Hart, with Kecia at his side, had gone to the floor along with John Selmon and Leroy Ditwhiler.

Jack Schaeffly, in the Comm chair, urgently keyed his microphone. "*Adventurer*, this is Houston, over." He strained to listen to his headphones.

"Put it on the speaker," Selmon ordered.

The man beside Schaeffly flipped a toggle switch, and white noise—hissing static—issued from a small, metal-grilled speaker in the slanted console panel.

"Nothing," Schaeffly said unnecessarily.

Around them, controllers bent over errant displays.

"Control gyro malfunction and dropout," one of them called to Selmon.

"We've lost all data," another called.

"We had an engine burn just at the time of loss of data acquisition," another reported.

"A *big* burn," someone else said with disbelief.

"Try Australia and see if they have signal acquisition," Ditwhiler ordered.

Selmon punched Schaeffly's shoulder. "Try again, try again, man!"

Schaeffly keyed the circuit, speaking into the tiny boom mike: "*Adventurer*, this is Houston EarthComm. Do you copy? Over."

Again, the speaker only hissed and crackled as the technician beside Schaeffly rotated control knobs and flipped switches.

"Still no onboard data acquisition," someone said.

Schaeffly tried again: "*Adventurer*, this is Houston. How copy? Over, over."

Again, nothing. Beside Hart, Kecia squeezed his hand painfully hard with fingers as cold as ice.

John Selmon was ashen. "Just keep trying," he ordered Schaeffly. He turned to Hart. "Doctor, you might want to get out of here right now."

"I'm staying," Hart snapped.

Selmon turned to call across the room, "How about Australia?"

A shirtsleeved man called back, "They've got no signal."

"Voice circuit?"

"Negative."

"Data?"

"Negative."

"Shit," Selmon breathed almost inaudibly. He stared, hands on hips, at the hissing loudspeaker in Schaeffly's console. "Shit, shit, shit." He heaved a heavy sigh and shook himself, then looked up around the room. "Jamison! Bell! Steiner! On the double!"

From different areas of the center, three men detached themselves from frantic groups and hurried over. They faced Selmon.

"All right," Selmon said. "What do we have?"

"We had a burn," said Jamison, a tall, sandy-haired man with the beginnings of a potbelly hanging over the front of his khaki pants. "We definitely had ignition sequencing and a clean burn signal, a hundred and six percent power."

Selmon's face went slack. "A hundred and six percent? Holy hell. *How long*?"

Jamison scratched his bushy head. "No way of knowing. We had data dropout almost simultaneous with the ignition signal."

Selmon composed his face with obvious extreme effort. "What else?"

The one named Bell, shorter, swarthy, with a graying goatee and wildly colored Hawaiian-style shirt, glanced at a clipboard that had nothing on it. "Fire signal, we *think*. It got broken off in the middle of the transmission."

"Where?"

"General. All but the sealed compartments aft."

"The crew compartment?"

"Definitely affirmative."

"Well," Selmon said, "they were wearing their suits. If they followed the plan, they were already in their suits."

"But a *fire*." Ditwhiler winced.

Selmon's chin stuck out with stubborn anger. "H. O. and Christie ought to be okay. They *have to be* okay." Selmon looked at his other consultant, the man named Steiner, the youngest of the trio, thin and strongly resembling a German professional golfer named Langer whom Hart had seen often on TV. "What did you say about gyro control?"

"We had approximately one-point-five seconds of gyro malfunction light," Steiner told him. "We lost data too fast to get a fix on it."

"What do you think?"

"I think the burn—or the combination of the burn and whatever the hell happened—threw the spacecraft off course. I think there has been a major electrical malfunction . . . or worse . . . and nothing out there is operational to restabilize the ship."

Selmon called across the room, "Do we have radar?"

"Radar is not tracking at this time, sir."

"The emergency transponder ought to be working if everything else on board has been . . . deactivated."

Ditwhiler nodded. "It has its own gel cell power. The cells were full-charge on last night's routine status printout, and they were hooked to the solar array." He turned and yelled across the room, "Get radar on the flight path now!"

A youthful technician called from the far side, "Radar is not operating at this time, sir. The work schedule—"

"God damn it!" Ditwhiler yelled, throwing his cigar on the floor. "I want that God damned radar on the God damned air in sixty seconds!"

Blank faces stared for a fraction, then turned away. Men ran in several directions, and a couple grabbed inside phones.

Selmon called out, "I want that radar signal fed directly into the tracking computer and displayed on the big screen."

A young woman hurried in with a notebook in her hands. She was an assistant in the public information office. "Dr. Klindeinst," she said breathlessly, "has told the press that he'll have a press conference starting at noon. He'll need an update five minutes before the hour."

"Fine," Selmon snapped. He raised his voice. "Where is the *radar*?"

At nearby consoles, technicians threw toggles and communicated over their headsets. One by one, they looked up from their panels to the big screen on the far wall. Hart, like everyone else, looked with them.

The screen remained grayish, amorphous. Then it suddenly changed, blinked brilliant red, then green, then yellow, then white. Bars appeared for an instant. Then the familiar planetary orbit presentation appeared, the sun to the left, Earth in its elliptical orbit, Mars in its present location an impossible distance on the far side of the sun, the curved line of *Adventurer*'s flight path showing the small distance already traveled as a solid line, the projected curving intercept course of future months in a broken line.

Almost at the same instant, a winking white blob

appeared where the solid line met the dotted one. There was a sharp, subdued shout of hope in the big room.

"That's it," Selmon said. "The radar is picking up a solid reflection from the onboard emergency transponder." He turned to Hart. "We've got a relatively intact spacecraft out there."

"Sir?" Steiner said, hurrying back to join the group.

"What is it?" Selmon demanded.

"First analysis of the signal from the transponder indicates wobbling circular polarization and a rapidly fluctuating signal strength. Also—"

"Damn!"

"What is it?" Hart demanded.

Selmon glared at him for a moment, then made a decision. "It almost certainly indicates that the spacecraft is unstable, turning rapidly on its pitch or yaw axis, or both."

"Something else, sir," Steiner said.

"What?"

"We won't have enough accumulated data for several minutes, but first analysis puts the exact source of the signal off the predicted flight path."

Selmon put his hands together in a praying posture, touching his fingertips to his lips. No one had to say anything. Even Hart could understand enough. *Adventurer* was spinning off its path, and was probably out of control.

Christie I love you so much—! What's happening to you?

Nearby, Jack Schaeffly spoke doggedly again into his microphone: "*Adventurer*, this is Houston, over."

No reply came.

"It does not necessarily mean the crew has been lost," the gray-faced Selmon said. "The fire could have destroyed vital communications links."

"That's right," Ditwhiler agreed. "They could be going ahead with the plan right now."

"The lander is on its own circuitry," Selmon added. "Once they're in the lander and have it fully powered up, we should hear from them again."

"Would you like to explain?" Hart asked. He was confused and lost.

"Christie and H. O. were ordered to get into their EVA suits and have them fully activated," Selmon said. "You know they were both at the entrance to the flight deck when we ordered Buck to relinquish command. H. O. had a syringe loaded to the hilt with a heavy-duty sedative from the emergency medical supplies. They had to play it by ear. We hoped they would either convince Buck to follow orders, or stick him with the needle."

Ditwhiler winced. "Not very elegant, scientifically. But that was what we hoped."

"But something went wrong," Hart said, stating the obvious. "What?"

"The next step in the contingency plan—if they couldn't seize control of the spacecraft—was to evacuate to the cargo bay and enter the Mars lander. Once there, they could use separate power and radio circuits to report to us."

"What if they *don't* radio back from the lander?" Hart demanded.

"They must."

"How long, if they are doing what you told them, before—"

"Thirty minutes, if all goes well."

"What if things don't go well?"

"It could require hours."

"What do we do in the meantime?"

"Wait."

Movement beyond the double doors to the hall caught Hart's eye. He saw Detective Bud Slagerfeldt out there, arguing heatedly with a NASA security guard. When Slagerfeldt saw Hart's glance, he waved frantically to him.

"Word isn't likely before thirty minutes?" Hart asked.

Selmon shook his head. "Virtually impossible. The antennae have been thrown off-line. Even if they were trying to use *Adventurer's* radios—"

"I see someone outside who wants to talk to me. I'll be right back."

Outside, Slagerfeldt was sweaty and tense. "Doc, I need your help for about five minutes."

"To do *what*?" Hart demanded. "Jesus, Bud! My daughter—"

"I know who our missing man—our Houston connection—is."

"Fine. Great. Get him, then. I've got to get back inside, here. If and when anything more happens, I have to know."

"Tell them you'll be with me. They can page you."

"What the hell do you need *me* for?"

"I need a witness. I need you to help me confront him."

"How can I do *that*?"

"Come with me," Slagerfeldt urged. "It won't take five minutes. I need you. Come on and I'll explain on the way." Then Slagerfeldt said something very uncharacteristic for him. "Doc. *Please*."

Hart was torn. He wanted to tell the detective to go to hell. But the need in the man's whole demeanor was painfully apparent, and he was a good cop. A good man.

"Tell me where we're going," Hart decided, "and I'll tell John Selmon. Then five minutes. Five. That's all."

More than twenty news people were milling around the press auditorium when Slagerfeldt walked in with Hart trailing him. The front lights were on, but Warner Klindeinst had not yet put in his promised appearance at the podium, with its NASA symbol emblazoned on the front. Off to one side, Sam Donaldson, dean of the national TV news core and one of the few survivors of the youth rush of 1991 that had toppled so many of his peers, was talking into a blaze of portable lights and a shoulder-mounted camera. Most of the other press people seemed to be interviewing one another.

Slagerfeldt paused, craning his neck to look for his prey. He spotted the familiar figure and raised a hand, signaling the man to come over. Slow, rotund Joe Blyleven detached himself from a group of three other writers and came up the aisle, notebook flapping open in his big, freckled right hand. His summer suit looked slept in.

"Holy moley." He grinned slowly. "What brings out Houston's finest?" He recognized Hart. "Hey, morning, doc. What's happening with the spacecraft? This is awesome. Are you worried about your daughter?"

Slagerfeldt did not smile. "Joe, remember when you told me you didn't know Dr. Myrick well, and assumed he had never had a sick day in his life?"

Blyleven's small green eyes narrowed behind his bifocals. "Yeah, I guess so."

"You told Dr. Hart, here, that you and Myrick were occasional golf buddies. You knew Myrick had been seeing Dr. Hart before you ever met Dr. Hart. How come you lied to one of us, Joe? And which story was the truth?"

Blyleven's forehead glistened with sudden sweat. "Reporters use lots of gimmicks to extract information. I made an educated guess."

Slagerfeldt turned to Hart. "Doc, please repeat what you told me a few days ago about what Joe, here, said about Myrick's apartment."

Hart said, "He said Dave had a huge framed picture of *Adventurer* on his living-room wall. He said it showed how devoted Dave was to his work."

"What's wrong with that?" Blyleven demanded, his voice rising enough with angry resentment that a few nearby heads turned.

"The problem," Slagerfeldt told him, "is that that big picture was delivered to Myrick's apartment the day he died. I was there a day later when the man from the studio came back, wanting to make sure it had been hung properly, to collect the last half of his payment for it."

"You're mistaken!"

"No, Joe, I'm not. I've got the delivery ticket and sales slip right here. For you to know about that picture, you had to be there the afternoon or night Myrick died. What were you doing there?"

Blyleven's chest rose and fell in a sharp spasm. He wiped a freckled paw over his mouth. "This is bullshit. I don't have to listen to this."

"Oh, I think you're going to have to listen to a lot more," Slagerfeldt told him. "The boys in Dallas found a record of payment to you in the Parkview computer's financial files. —Five thousand dollars is a lot for— quote, public relations consultation, unquote—Joe, wouldn't you say? What did you do for that five thousand? And how many other payments are we going to find when we start going back through the photostat files of your bank transactions?"

All color left Blyleven's face. His splotchy red hair made the pallor of his skin, his darting eyes behind the thick glasses, resemble a cartoon caricature. His thick arms hung limp at his sides. "I didn't know . . . not for a long time. I just thought it was a deal to get a few crummy secrets."

"So you betrayed your goddam country."

"How would *you* like to work for twenty years, and not be making as much money as a head checker in a Safeway store? How would *you* like it, always having to kiss the ass of some arrogant scientist around here to get a story? I'm a good person. I deserve better. Nothing has ever been fair for me. All I've ever had is bad luck—" Blyleven suddenly stopped, realizing that he had admitted everything. His eyes widened with shock and pain.

"Thanks, doc," Slagerfeldt said quietly. "I thought you might want to help, and be among the first to know who coordinated a lot of this shit here. —Joe, maybe it's better you don't say anything. You're under arrest. You have the right to remain silent. You have a right to be—"

With a hoarse animal cry, Blyleven threw his spiral notebook in Slagerfeldt's face. With virtually the same movement he lurched against Hart, crashing past him on the way to the back exit door. Slagerfeldt lunged at him but missed. Hart caught the back of Blyleven's coat and hauled back with all his strength, throwing the much heavier man off balance. Blyleven staggered and fell with a crash into the chairs beside the aisle. With quickness that gave Hart a primitive chill, Slagerfeldt pounced on the reporter, straddled him, whipped his wrists behind his back, and slammed handcuffs around them.

Two NASA security types hurried in.

"It's okay, guys," Slagerfeldt said, breathing heavily. "It's all taken care of." He looked up at Hart. "Hey. Thanks again. I'll want another statement later . . . when things are smoother with everything else."

"Thank you for letting me be here," Hart said.

"I know it doesn't really help your kid out there or anything like that—"

"No, it doesn't. And it doesn't bring anybody back to life, either. But it feels good to know you've got a local ringleader. Maybe he'll lead to others."

Slagerfeldt's jaw set. "He will, doc. He will."

A reporter from CNN hurried up in a blaze of portable lights. Thrusting a microphone in Slagerfeldt's face, she gushed, "What's this all about, detective? Please tell us what's happened here!"

Hart fled the room, hurrying back to Mission Control.

twenty-seven

In the rolling, wooded countryside of West Germany not far from Stuttgart, evening was near. It had been a cool, overcast day, and now a fine mist was falling, making the sky a gloomy gray. On the distant autobahn, cars' headlights burned. The TransOrbital Works plant on the edge of the forest had sent its day shift home at 5 P.M.

Out of the woods on the sheltered south side of the TransOrbital grounds, five men in black nylon jumpsuits appeared and moved swiftly to the high wire security fencing. Black hoods covered their heads. Each carried a machine-pistol and two had small packs slung on their backs.

No one saw their approach.

Two of the men knelt at the base of the four-meter fence and quickly opened a hole with heavy cutters. All five moved inside, skirting a tan metal storage building, slipping between a pair of hulking electrical transformers, then trotting down a narrow alley separating two of the major assembly-test buildings for Ariane Plus, Europe's hope for victory in the race to Mars.

The men broke open a steel door on the building where the totally automated Ariane lander-searcher vehicle, heart of the Ariane Plus system and the only one of its kind in the world, had been taking shape for months. A plant guard looked up from his glassed-in office inside the building, saw the intruders, and started to reach for the alarm. A silenced automatic weapon made an ugly burping sound and the hand which fell short of the alarm switch was already dead.

The team moved deeper into the building, following detailed architectural plans all had committed to memory. They reached the main lab. There, suspended in its work cradle, the enormously complex machine that was the Mars lander gleamed in the dull illumination of security lights.

The team required less than five minutes to do its work. The men went back the way they had come, exited unseen through the hole in the fencing, and vanished into the forest.

Eight minutes later, TransOrbital's assembly building blew sky high, leaving the heart of Ariane Plus—and Europe's hope for Mars—a pile of smoking rubble.

Only minutes after the devastation near Stuttgart, sixteen Soviet attack bombers screamed out of Afghanistan at an altitude of less than five hundred feet. Hugging the harsh, barren terrain to avoid radar detection, they split into three groups of five, five, and six.

With incredible speed they approached their targets undetected, and made their runs. Three of the Arab League's queen cities were raked by rockets and cluster bombs, with special attention centering on presidential palaces and irreplaceable industrial centers. Then, as swiftly as they had come, the attacking aircraft were gone, swallowed up once more by the desert vastness.

*   *   *

It was not yet 2 P.M. in Washington when word arrived. The director of the Central Intelligence Agency pieced together the first fragmentary reports and called the White House.

The president came on the line. The CIA chief explained.

"What do you make of it?" the president asked, puzzled. "Are the incidents related? If so, how?"

"Mr. President, all our information so far points the same direction. You have our reports on the events in New York City, Texas, and Australia. Industrial interests in western Europe had everything to gain and nothing to lose by setting Russia's and our Mars probes back as badly as possible. You know what many of the nations in the Middle East think about infidels being the first to solve the riddle of the beacon. We've been steadily gathering more and more and more proof that we had some strange bedfellows in this one, who banded together to sabotage both the superpowers for their own reasons."

There was a long silence on the other end of the line. Finally the president said, "You think the Soviets reached the same conclusion . . . and retaliated?"

"Yes, Mr. President, I do."

"How long will it be before we have better information on the explosion at the TransOrbital site?"

"It's coming in now, sir."

"And?"

"They're out of business. Period."

"And the attacks on Tripoli, and so forth?"

"The Russians have some of their people under arrest, and of course so do we, now. The raids today weren't completely sanitary—many civilians died. But so did many high-ranking leaders in those countries. It was a very serious blow."

After another briefer pause, the president said, "I

think our position on this will be that we don't know anything about anything, Fred."

"Yes, sir. Will State condemn the Soviet attack? Without our data, I don't see how we can prove—"

"No, no. Not this time. We'll not be hanging any rap on our friends in the Kremlin this time, Fred. I hate to think the sons of bitches knew some of this and could have warned us. But their cosmonauts are dead. Our crew's status right now is unknown; I have someone on another line to Houston at this moment. I think I sort of like the Russians' style on this response, and they'll have no static from us about it."

In the office near Mission Control, Richard Hart put an arm around Don Dillingham, Christie's husband. It had been more than two hours now since all communication had been lost with *Adventurer*, and Dillingham could only stare with the eyes of a dead man.

"You heard what they said, Don," Hart told him. "The transponder signal indicates that the spacecraft is still in one piece. Christie and H. O. were in their EVA suits, so the decompression shouldn't have harmed them."

"But why aren't they in contact, then?" Dillingham demanded hoarsely.

"Nobody knows. There could have been major damage to the transmitters—"

"They were up there with a madman, from what you've explained to me! He could have killed them!"

Hart glanced at Kecia, who stood nearby, pale, a Styrofoam cup of coffee in her hand but forgotten. *Help!* his look said.

Kecia came over. "Don, let's not borrow any trouble, okay? Richard is right. Christie and H. O. could be getting into the lander, powering it up. All that takes time. There's nothing to do but wait and see, and keep hoping."

"She should never have gone. I didn't want her to go. It's insane. Who the hell cares if there's some stupid radio beacon out there on another planet anyhow? She should have stayed home!"

Hart patted his back. "Hey. We've talked about this. You know how Christie felt. Some time, a long time ago, there were beings out there. Maybe like us . . . maybe profoundly different. They left that beacon for us to discover one day, and follow. We're *humankind*, Don. We have to go out there and discover. It's what we've always done. It's the way we are, the thing that makes us have value. We can no more ignore that signal, beckoning to us, than we can go back to living in the trees."

Dillingham's eyes filled. "I'm scared shitless," he choked.

"So am I."

Jack Schaeffly walked into the office. All of them turned with a shock, and Hart felt like his whole nervous system jolted to a halt.

"There's nothing new," the pale, drawn scientist told them. "The boys in Communications think the spacecraft might have tumbled off its axis of slow rotation when they had the burn. If that's the case, then all the antennae may just be pointed away from Earth. The theory is that Christie and Townsend may be working to try to reorient the antennae. That would take some onboard computing and a little bit of guesswork. Or the radios themselves could have been damaged. Either eventuality would take considerable time."

"When will we *know* something?" Dillingham rasped.

"They think it could be a few more hours—"

"*Hours!*"

"I thought," Schaeffly said with stiff control of his features, "I might brief you, Mr. Dillingham, and members of the Townsend family, who are down the hall in another office, on events that have taken place as we understand them. I'll try to answer all your questions. Would that be okay?"

Don Dillingham nodded with the air of a man who didn't care about details. Schaeffly took him by the arm and guided him toward the door. Over his shoulder he said too casually, "Dr. Selmon would like to talk to you in Mission Control, Dr. Hart."

After they had gone, Kecia asked, "What was that all about?"

"I don't know," Hart said. "Let's find Selmon and hear what he has to say."

In Mission Control the scene was much as it had been for hours now: every available man at his station, the clock rolling on, the status boards blank, the screen showing only the wink of the transponder light aboard the spacecraft. John Selmon saw Hart and Kecia enter, and walked over to meet them in the aisle at the back of the room not far from the No. 1 Comm console, where LeRoy Ditwhiler himself now hunched at the panel, a cigar clenched in his teeth.

Selmon looked like death warmed over. "Doctor, we don't know a damned thing more than we did before."

"Jack Schaeffly said it might be hours."

"It might be." Selmon was avoiding his eyes, uncomfortable. "We should have heard something by this time, however. The consensus is that we still have hope. But every passing hour, realistically, diminishes it somewhat. We may have to start facing the serious possibility that the outcome is not going to be favorable, here."

He looked at Hart as he spoke the last words, as if he couldn't avoid seeing Hart's reaction. Hart was struck by a sharp pain, accompanied by the absurd thought that this was how people dealt with catastrophe—with euphemisms.

He said slowly, "'Not a favorable outcome' meaning the crew has been lost?"

"We haven't given up hope yet."

"Yes. I see."

The enormity of potential loss rose up and threatened to overwhelm him. He looked around the big room. *So much science. They should be able to do anything.* He turned to Kecia.

With a little mewing sound of pain, she put her arms around him.

He stood still, letting her hold him. He felt numb around the core of the agony. In his memory was the happy, excited sound of Christie's voice on the telephone, from the Cape. And their last evening together, how close they had been.

They had been close since she was a little girl. The prospect of her loss was so great that his mind and feelings could not fully comprehend it. It couldn't be. It couldn't be.

A burst of static from a nearby loudspeaker startled the silence. There was a racketing sound on the speaker, a split-second more of noise, and then a clear, strong voice: *"Houston, this is Lander, how copy?"*

Hart's insides crumbled even as he saw heads turn, Kecia begin to beam with renewed hope, LeRoy Ditwhiler grab for his microphone. The voice had been Christie's.

Ditwhiler bawled into the mike, "Lander, this is Houston. Go ahead!"

Men around the room were slamming each other on the back and gesturing for quiet so all could hear every precious word.

Christie's voice came back, crisp, well, alive: *"Houston, this is Lander. Townsend and I are aboard the lander in the cargo bay. Signal acquisition from the lander antennae has been blocked by the spacecraft. Spacecraft is rotating out of control. We estimate ten minutes before our antennae are again blocked and we lose signal. Over."*

Hart turned to Kecia. His eyes were blurred by tears. She hugged him. He felt some of the agony begin to break loose after being held in so long.

But it was far from over. He forced himself to pay attention to everything.

Selmon took the microphone from Ditwhiler. "Christie, this is Selmon. What is the status of *Adventurer*? What is the condition of Colonel Colltrap? What are your intentions? Over."

"John, Adventurer is tumbling slowly out of control. Comm circuits are out, electrical system is wrecked. It's finished. Buck refused orders to relinquish command. He had a gun—"

"Jesus!" Ditwhiler exploded.

"—and when H. O. tried to take it from him, it went off, and Buck was shot in the chest. He had an engine burn sequenced. He managed to start that. We went out of control and off course. By the time we started to get things sorted out, Buck was dead from the gunshot wound. We left his body in the cabin. Over."

Selmon rolled his eyes to heaven for a moment and took a deep breath, composing himself. "Okay, Christie. I see we're getting data readouts now. We believe you should detach from *Adventurer* and conduct the contingency plan course correction burn as soon as possible. Over."

"Roger that, Houston. We're ready for computer readout and update, over."

Selmon shook his head. "What a woman," he breathed. Then, keying the microphone: "Roger, Lander. Stand by for computer updates. The burn will be manual, is that a roger?"

"Roger, manual burn control."

"Christie, are you and H. O. unhurt? Are you both okay?"

There was a slight pause, then: *"H. O. says there are no candy bars in the lander pantry, over."*

"Roger! Stand by for computer update."

Hart looked across the room where he could see the stream of digital data presented on a screen as it flooded out through space to the Mars lander's flight computers. It was being sent much too fast for the human eye to read, and he could not have read it anyway because his eyes were filled with tears.

"We're not going to have signal long," Selmon told the group hastily assembled around him. "We'll get the computer data up, check it, and get a general status readout. That's probably all we'll have time to do before the spacecraft turns and gets itself between the lander and us again. Anybody disagree with that assessment?"

No one spoke.

Selmon turned back to the mike. "Lander, this is Houston. Are there any vital questions you need to talk about before we lose voice communications, over?"

Christie's voice came back, cool as could be: *"We can't think of any, Houston. Over."*

"Roger that. You'll detach from *Adventurer*, drift free, align yourself, and do a manual course-correction maneuver burn. Roger?"

"Roger, Houston. No problem we can see, over."

"She says 'no problem'!" Selmon groaned, throwing up his hands. "It's just something we've never done before . . . complicated and dangerous as hell. *God*, I love these people!"

Christie's voice came again: *"Houston, we estimate four minutes until loss of communication."*

"Roger, Lander. Stand by for status transmission."

"Roger."

"What do we do when they lose contact again?" Kecia asked no one in particular.

LeRoy Ditwhiler shifted his cigar from one side of his face to the other. "Wait again. What else?"

The signal from space vanished five minutes later.

twenty-eight

Strapped inside the tight steel cocoon of the Mars lander, Christie Hart and H. O. Townsend brushed elbows of their pressure suits as they rushed to conclude preparations for disconnecting from the crippled shuttle. The rotating mothership had turned its belly Earthward an hour ago now, blocking signals to and from the antennae of the lander, still locked in the cargo bay.

Computers were updated and functioning, and the status of all systems looked normal. One oxygen tank's pressure was slightly high but within acceptable limits. Status lights for the main lander engine were all green. Beyond the deep shadow of the cargo bay's opened doors, the unblinking light of the stars shone against the background radiation of the sun.

Adventurer continued to rotate on both its pitch and yaw axes, off course, fatally damaged, doomed. Its movement enormously complicated the undocking and separation maneuver that Christie and Townsend now had to perform if they were to escape alive.

After exiting *Adventurer*'s airlock and entering the cargo bay, they had laboriously detached the major structural components holding the lander in place, doing a job designed for two three-hour shifts in something less than an hour. The lander was now held fast to the floor of the cargo bay by three explosive bolts that could be triggered from inside the cabin.

The tiny craft was already detached from the *Adventurer* umbilical and operating on its own battery power. Gauges showed the power cells holding up well. But specifications said only minutes remained to get free of the shuttle and deploy the lander's solar panels before the batteries would begin to slump.

"Main power still okay?" Christie, in the left seat, asked.

"Point-eight," Townsend said, speaking as she had through the plug-in intercom system connecting their suits.

"Computer final setting?"

"Affirmative."

"Okay, H. O., I've got fuel okay, electrical okay, status panel clear, lights up."

"Rog," Townsend said.

They fell silent for an instant. Both of them knew the peril that faced them.

The first crisis lay with blowing the explosive bolts. All three had to blow.

After that, the lander would be free. It had to float clear of the cargo bay and well away from the shuttle before they could risk a main engine burn designed to drive them a hundred miles off into space and on the start of the long looping trajectory that would reverse their course and head them back toward Earth. Christie knew she could use the maneuvering jets with extreme caution to assist in moving out of the bay. But with the shuttle's erratic motion, the smallest error could bump the two craft into one another; *Adventurer*'s much larger mass could damage the lander in a twinkling, or even crush it.

If they got the bolts to blow and managed to drift free of the shuttle, they had to time and execute the main engine burn manually, using computer data but depending on their own skills to start and stop ignition for the right trajectory. A mis-timed burn might send them careening back into the parent spacecraft, or off on a course into space with such a velocity that they could never make enough later correction to hope for a return home.

If they managed these maneuvers, they faced many days in space, cramped, existing on the most marginal rations and water, probably facing other course corrections—and at the far end, if everything went well, attempting an Earth-orbit rendezvous with the space station which no one had anticipated or rehearsed.

Buck Colltrap's death and the other shocks of the last few hours had left Christie numb, but not so numb that she was not keenly aware of the odds. She knew Townsend was as aware as she.

"Point-seven on the number two cell," Townsend said now.

They had to get into free space and deploy the solar panel.

"What do you think, H. O.?" Christie asked, scanning the readouts in front of her and across the ceiling panel.

"Well," Townsend said, and the drawl was back in his voice, "I think we better light this somebish and start home."

Christie checked her restraints and put her gloved hands lightly on the control jet levers. "Ready to fire the retainer bolts?"

"Roger. Ready."

"Fire."

Townsend pulled a switch. The little craft rocked to the echo of three near-simultaneous explosions, the bolts going. The lander popped free and started to rise out of the cargo bay like a cork floating out of a bottle. The enormity of deep space swam up around the side windows, and the brilliant silver of the stricken *Adventurer*'s fuselage filled the front canopy, then began to slide beneath them. Christie gingerly touched a control jet and the gap between *Adventurer* and its baby began to widen.

"So long, Buck," Townsend said softly beside her.

In Mission Control, every eye was on the big screen which would show if and when data again began to flow in from space. Richard Hart, along with Kecia, Don Dillingham, and the parents and wife of H. O. Townsend, stood in the observation room to the rear, watching with everyone else.

Without warning of any kind, the display came to life. All around the floor of the control room, status indicators lighted up. On the screen, the bright white line that indicated the flight path of *Adventurer* suddenly became a double line, one continuing on as before, the second and new one curving downward on a different course.

The voice of Jack Schaeffly came over the ceiling loudspeakers: *"We have lander separation and full acquisition of lander data. Course correction engine ignition appears nominal. Thrust is nominal. Time of burn nominal. The lander is now approaching eighty statute miles separation from the shuttle. Preliminary trajectory analysis indicates nominal return-to-Earth tracking."*

The people in Mission Control were applauding and slapping one another on the back, and in the observation area Townsend's wife hugged his parents and all three were weeping. Hart hugged Kecia, shook Don Dillingham's hand, then hugged him too.

"I love those 'nominals'!" Hart exclaimed.

"They did it!" Dillingham said, his grin ear-to-ear. "I knew they would!"

"Once they're back," Kecia said, "I hope we never, ever, try anything like this again."

Hart looked at her in astonishment. "But you know we will. We must. That radio beacon is still out there, hollering at us."

"I love you, do you know that?" she said. "But I think you're a little crazy."

He hugged her again, lifting her entirely off her feet and swinging her in a circle. "Crazy with relief right now. Yes. And I love you, too. Have I said that?"

She struggled to be let down. "Do you really think they'll make it now? Are they really going to be all right?"

"Of course they'll make it now," Hart told her with a grin. "They have to."